THE STEAMIE

Also by Tony Roper

THE REV. I.M. JOLLY – BOOK 1
HOW I FOUND GOD AND WHY HE WAS HIDING FROM ME

THE REV. I.M. JOLLY – BOOK 2
ONE DEITY AT A TIME, SWEET JESUS

THE STEAMIE

A NOVEL

TONY ROPER

BLACK & WHITE PUBLISHING

First published 2004
by Black & White Publishing Ltd

This paperback edition
first published 2005
by Black & White Publishing Ltd
99 Giles Street, Edinburgh EH6 6BZ

ISBN 1 84502 065 0

**FT
Pbk**

British Library Cataloguing in Publication Data:
A catalogue record for this book is available from
the British Library

Cover design: www.henrysteadman.com

Printed and bound by Nørhaven Paperback A/S

*All characters in this book are fictitious and
any resemblance to real persons, living or dead,
is entirely coincidental.*

My thanks to the editorial team at
Black & White Publishing for their
expertise, patience and understanding in
helping me finally finish this novel.

T.R.

THE STEAMIE

ONE

It was the kind of day that made you feel good to be part of the human race. To be alive and able to bask in the warmth of the afternoon sun hanging brazenly on a translucent blue sky, seemed like a privilege that was only bestowed on a deserving few.

The noise of women laughing and exchanging comments as they hung out their washing to dry on the expanse of the Glasgow Green, that had newly been allocated by the City Fathers for that purpose, drifted upwards and mixed with the seagulls that were floating aimlessly on the up-currents created by the nearby tributary working its way towards the River Clyde. It somehow added a sense of well-being and set the scene that all was well with the world.

It was the eighteen eighties and there was an eager anticipation in the population that they were on the brink of a new and vibrant world, a world that promised advancement beyond everyone's imagination. Travel was soon going to be possible by means of the newfangled automobile and unbelievably they had heard that men were even trying to take to the air and fly just like the seagulls above their heads. Also, it seemed as if they had now begun to conquer illnesses that had plagued mankind since its very beginnings.

Glasgow City Fathers had launched an ambitious scheme to root out disease by installing public washhouses so that clothes could be properly boiled and cleaned to a standard that was befitting this new age. Already there was a marked decrease in the instances of infectious agues that had cut short the lives of many in the city. The women also found that there was an added bonus of attending these new washhouses. They had given them a central meeting place where larger numbers of them could congregate. Events and news could be updated and friendships could be renewed while their natural thirst for the latest gossip was being slaked.

The men had the shipbuilding to keep their bodies and souls together and, in so doing, fulfil their tribal needs by congregating en masse as they strove to float mighty vessels down the slipways and into the lifeblood of the city, the River Clyde.

With the advent of these new washhouses, the women had found a modus operandi that now matched that of their menfolk. The women had swiftly dubbed these wash places by the generic term The Steamies. This was due to the steam that was produced when the wash places were full and boiling water was hissing magically out of the faucets and into great steel sinks that held swathes of their weekly wash.

All this was of no consequence to a group of boys who were playing among the sea of washing that was hung out to dry on lines that stretched for hundreds of yards. Sheets and blankets were dancing lazily in the soft breeze while the lads were playing at the new game of football that had gripped the men of the city in a fever of exuberance that was a complete mystery to their women. The boys had tied a bunch of old rags together to form a poor approximation of the ball that was used in the large stadiums that had sprung up all over the city. There were shouts of 'To me!', etc. coming from them. There were also shouts of 'Watch what you're doin' wi' that ball!' from the women, which, of course, were totally ignored by the lads who were fully engrossed in the monumentally difficult task of trying to score a goal.

Inevitably the inevitable happened. The ball was smacked by a wayward clearance from the foot of nine-year-old Andrew Caven and found its way to the centre of a pristine white linen sheet that had just been hung on the line by Agnes Tait.

The instant the dull thud of the ball made contact with her sheet, Agnes spun round to observe the culprit and also take in the extent of the damage to her once-clean sheet. A large dirty brown imprint was now on the sheet and the evidence was lying directly beneath it. Andrew looked on in horror as he vainly tried to think of a way out of his obvious guilt. His eyes darted up to where Agnes was standing with her hands on her hips surveying the damage. As their gazes locked in on each other Andrew was frantically thinking of an excuse he could use to explain why such a catastrophe had happened and thus avoid a skelping if his mother found out about it.

Agnes's eyes softened and with a good-natured grin she said, 'It's all right, Andrew. Come and get your ball.'

Andrew knew that all-out contrition was his best bet as far as pleading innocence was concerned.

'I didn't mean to hit it into your washin', Mrs Tait,' he said in a voice that was reeking with penitence.

Agnes shook her head ruefully. 'I know that, son – here.' She picked up the bundle and held it out to him.

'Thanks, Mrs Tait,' he said as he moved in to retrieve the ball.

'You're gettin' good at the football, eh, son?'

Andrew nodded as he reached out to get the ball and then felt his ears ring as Agnes's other hand had seemingly come from nowhere to land on the side of his head.

'You keep that ball away. D'you hear me? I'll no' tell you again.'

3

Andrew felt the beginnings of tears well up inside him at the injustice that he had suffered from Agnes Tait as he ran towards his mother and blubbered out, 'Mammy, Mrs Tait hit me.'

Andrew's mother's reply was not what he wanted to hear. Without looking round from hanging her own washing, she said, matter-of-factly, 'Well, you must have deserved it.'

'I get the blame o' everything,' was Andrew's only line of defence.

'That's because you're always to blame, son. It's the only talent I've seen in you so far. Noo stop your greetin' and help me tae fold these sheets.'

Andrew's ears could not believe what he was hearing. 'My pals will laugh at me if they see me giein' you a hand wi' the washin', Mammy.'

'Well, we'll no' let them see you then, will we?' was her unhelpful reply. 'Here, grab the end of this sheet and don't let it trail on the ground or you'll greet on the other side o' your face.'

As Andrew tried not to cry, ignore the pain coming from his ear and hide from his pals all at the one time, a group of girls, who were a similar age, ran past squealing with the excitement that was being generated in their game of hide-and-seek. They were hell-bent on finding whoever was 'het' which was their word for the one who was being chased and had to hide to avoid capture and the inevitable punishment of accepting a dare as a consequence of being found.

In this instance, the prey was Mary Culfeathers. She was a lively six years old and had bright blue eyes that shone above a small nose that perched above a pair of lips that seemed to be forever smiling. She was, her mother and father thought, as close to an angel as you could get and today she was playing with her pals and having more fun than it seemed she could contain without passing out from the sheer pleasure of it all. She dived behind a man's shirt that was almost a punctuation mark in a row of bed sheets. Then, realising that her legs could be seen, she moved behind a large still-wet blanket that was almost, but not quite, touching the ground. As she stood there trying not to breathe in case her pursuers heard her, the owner of the washing parted the blanket and stood beside her. 'I hope your no' goin' to get my blanket all dirty, Mary Culfeathers?'

Mary looked up at her pleadingly. 'Gonnae no' give me away please, Mrs Black?'

At that moment the sound of the chasing posse arrived on the other side of the blanket. Anne Black looked over the top of the blanket and addressed the posse. 'Who are you all looking for? Is it Mary Culfeathers?'

'Aye, Mrs Black,' they chorused. 'She's het, so she is. And we've to find her,' said the leader of the bunch, breathlessly.

'Have you seen her?' another of them chipped in.

Mary's hand flew up to her mouth and sucked her thumb. She didn't know why she did this in moments of high drama – she only knew it usually helped. She stood on one leg as she figured that there was less chance of discovery with just one leg sticking out from below the blanket than two.

Then her heart raced as she heard Anne Black say, 'Yes, I know where she is.'

Mary's face, glowing with the thrill of the chase, turned upward, her eyes pleading with Mrs Black not to give her away.

'I'll tell you exactly where she is.' She turned her gaze away from Mary's. 'She's over there – behind the washhouse building.'

The chasing pack turned away, their voices clamouring and squealing in that way that is peculiar to young girls the world over.

'Mary Culfeathers! Here we come – ready or not. Mary Culfeathers! Here we come – ready or not.' Their voices receded as they raced away. Mary wrapped the blanket around her. Her spirit soared as she realised that she had triumphed in this battle of wits with her adversaries.

She could still hear them. 'Mary. Mary.'

Maybe it was her imagination but the tone of their voices seemed to change in their desire to contact her. 'Mary. Mary.'

There was a desperation that was taking over the previous note of fun. Mary felt ill at ease with this new turn of events. Her grip tightened on the blanket.

TWO

'Mary, for God's sake, waken up, Mary.' Mary heard her husband Harry's voice rasp as it struggled with the effort of trying to breathe.

As the fog of sleep drained from her and consciousness began to invade, she called out, 'Harry, is that you?'

'It's no' Clark Bloody Gable! Help me over to the window – I can hardly draw breath.'

Harry Culfeathers was now in his late seventies and sweat was oozing from his body with the effort of trying to breathe. As he swung his legs out of the bed, Mary could see steam rising from his head, even though it was December and the room was so cold that ice had formed on the inside of the windows. They had known each other for over fifty years and Mary could still remember their first meeting as if it was yesterday.

Harry had been her only beau and, although he was a few years older than Mary, every one of their friends had said they were made for each other, not least because they were both called Culfeathers. It seemed only right that they should join together and both sets of parents had given approval right away. But Harry would not tie the knot until they had saved up enough money to set them up in their first home. In time, though, they were married and their two boys were born. But the joy of being parents was cut short by the human blight that was the First World War. It darkened every doorstep in the land and Harry, being the man he was, volunteered to serve his king and country. Thankfully he came back to her safe and sound – if not in mind, at least in body. He never spoke very much about his experiences of that hell on earth and she got a sense that he did not really want her to know what he had endured.

He did, however, waken in cold sweats during sleep when his dreams dredged up the night that he was onboard a ship taking a segment of his regiment to a new field of conflict up the French coastline. She never found out the whys or where-fores (she suspected that there was a fire) but, whatever the cause, the vessel got into difficulties and everyone was forced to abandon ship and take their chances in the freezing cold water.

Like most of the men who had suffered the horrendous sights of that terrible time, Harry had determined that, if he ever got back home, then he would make the most of life and do as well by his wife and family as his talents would allow. One night, after he had been labouring in a blacksmith shop all day, he had broached the subject with Mary of starting a business of some kind. 'I'm just no' sure what kind of business to go for, though.'

Mary had said, 'Harry, I had a sense that you were unhappy inside yourself. I thought maybe you had got fed up wi' me – after the excitement of bein' away in foreign parts during the war.'

He had smiled, in the lopsided way that had first attracted her, shaken his head and whispered, 'Not on your Nelly.'

Her heart could have burst with happiness but she confined herself to saying, 'In that case, I'm with you – whatever you want. I'll back you on it.'

Harry had thought for a while before looking at her

earnestly. 'I know that, Mary, and it's no more than I would expect of you. However, I've come to the conclusion that it's not just me that is in this wee family so I would like your suggestions as to what you would feel comfortable with. Have you a wee notion of what might be suitable?' He searched her face for encouragement. He sensed she was struggling with herself. 'Go on, say what you feel, hen.'

She shook her head. 'Och, no – it's silly. I would feel stupid even suggesting it,' she explained.

His gaze was fixed firmly on her and she knew she was going to have to come out with it. She was, however, loath to share her secret ambition, in case it did not meet with his approval, so she stared in a non-committal way into the fire.

He stood up and crossed over to stoke the fire. Kneeling down, he grasped the poker and thrust it into the glowing embers. As they burst into small flames, he said, with his back to her, 'Our lives are like this fire, Mary. If you don't disturb the flames every so often and start to rekindle them, then eventually it'll just fade out and die. Say what's in your mind, hen.' Mary bit on her bottom lip – a sure sign that she was perplexed. 'The fire'll no' go on indefinitely, you know,' Harry said gently.

'I've always wanted to own a haberdasher's that sold buttons and threads and bows and dressmaking material but that's out of the question.'

'Why?' he asked, continuing to prod at the fire.

'Well, what would *you* do in a place like that? It doesn't bear thinking aboot.'

Harry poked at bit of coal that sparked and fizzed as he disturbed it. 'Hmm! Aye – I see your point,' was his unenthusiastic response.

'I told you it was silly,' Mary said, feeling annoyed that her secret dream was no longer a secret.

'Why a haberdasher's?' he continued, with an expression that signalled neither interest nor disinterest.

'I don't know. It's just something I got into my head as a wee lassie. I've always sewed and I just like the different colours of the materials and . . . well, I just do and that's that. I cannae help it. It doesn't matter.'

Harry stared into the fire. 'You know, if you stare into a fire long enough, you can always see a face in the coals. Have you noticed that?'

Mary did not answer.

'I've just seen your face in the fire, Mary, and it's surrounded wi' bright red thread and scarlet ribbons so I think that is, as they say in the Bible, a portent of things to come.' He stood up, stretched his arms and then announced, 'That's what we'll do – a haberdasher's it is.'

'But what are you gonnae do? You're no' going to work in a woman's shop surely?'

'You're no' wrong in that assumption, hen. But I've seen a place in Partick that could be split into two different shops. The blacksmith I work for is always complainin' that he cannae get enough nails and shovels and the like because they have to come from the other side o' the river. Well, if I was to open up an ironmonger's alongside of your haberdasher's, one o' them might just do the trick. What do you think? Will we give it a go?'

And they did. Mary's haberdasher's became what's called a wee gold mine. Harry's ironmonger's did not do so well but he swapped over to selling paint and eventually his shop was successful enough to bring up their two boys. Indeed, as all their neighbours said, 'They want for nothin', they two boys.'

They gave them the best education they could afford and brought them up as good law-abiding young men. Life was indeed good and, eventually, the boys did what boys do and got married, giving Harry and Mary the great gift of grand-children. Except that they had both gone abroad when all this happened and had never managed to make it back and visit their parents.

This was a silent heartache that both Harry and Mary carried with them, always making excuses that their boys were just so busy that they could not get away – after all they were thousands of miles away.

They had even contemplated saving up and going to visit them but the sad truth was that Harry's health was failing badly. Years of working with paint had taken their toll and the fumes had gone for his lungs. However, their spirits took an upsurge when first one then the other son wrote to say that they were coming back from Canada and were going to be living in London. Alas, London may as well have been Canada as they still did not visit. Harry had, by this time, given up his shop – mounting debts caused by ill health had not allowed him to tend to his business properly. Mary had sold her haberdashery years before, as soon as Harry's business was established, in order to be at home for the boys while they were at school. Now times were tough and they were struggling. A life that had seemed full of promise was replaced by a void that held none.

Mary had taken to doing the washing of well-off customers and looking after Harry. She suspected that Harry was beginning, as her mother used to say, to go a bit addled. Little signs, such as the natural forgetfulness of growing older, became more marked. He would wander into a room, look about him, shake his head, sigh and then walk back out. He had stopped reading the newspapers, saying there was nothing in them that he wanted to read, but Mary suspected that his brain just could not concentrate for any length of time. Indeed, the same thing was happening to her. People outside were continually talking about things that she could not identify with in the modern Glasgow of the nineteen fifties.

That night was Hogmanay and the following day would signal the start of nineteen fifty-four. But, to Mary and Harry, it mattered not a jot – life, as they had once known it, had passed them by and was now merely an existence.

As Mary surveyed Harry and listened to his efforts at trying to draw a decent breath, she felt a sadness come over her that was becoming a familiar part of her day. Every so often, a large sigh would escape from her and she would feel embarrassed and look round to check that no one had heard her. She felt there was no need to burden others with her problems. That was the way all her age group thought and she and her husband were typical of their generation.

She put her arm around Harry for support as she helped him to his feet. 'If I can just get to the window and open it, I'll feel better. I just need some fresh air, Mary,' he said, wheezing as they made their way to the window.

Mary nodded. 'Of course, you will. That always helps, sure it does.'

'Aye, it seems to, right enough,' Harry nodded back in agreement.

The window was positioned above the kitchen sink. They had taken to living in the kitchen as it saved on coal money if they just lit the one fire. The bed was set in a recess and, all in all, it was a handy arrangement.

'Rest yourself on the edge o' the sink, Harry, and I'll get the window open a bit and let some fresh air in.'

'Thanks. I'll be fine in a minute.'

Mary brought over a cardigan and wrapped it round Harry's shoulders. She saw how scrawny he had become. She thought of how those same shoulders used to give her a thrill when he took off his jacket after a day's work at the blacksmith's and how the muscles in his shoulders would jut out from the braces that he used to hold his trousers up. She edged up the bottom of the window and immediately felt the blast of cold winter howling through the small gap that was created.

'Oh! That's better.' Harry wiped sweat from his brow and sagged with the effort of being alive.

'I'll get you a cup o' tea. Watch you don't catch a draught.'

Harry nodded and gasped at the air hissing in through the gap in the window. 'It's startin' tae get cold, isn't it?'

'Aye. I'll get a fire goin' as soon as I've put the kettle on.'

Harry stared bleakly out the window, nodded in assent and sighed.

As Mary turned the tap on to fill the kettle, she shivered a bit. 'Will I shut the window now?'

'Aye. It's bloody freezin' in here. What time is it? I've no' got my glasses.' Harry waited for an answer but, as one didn't come, he carried on with his next bit of news, 'It's bloody cold, isn't it?'

'I'll get a fire lit before I go to the washhouse.'

'Is this the day you go to the washhouse?'

Mary's thoughts were somewhere else and she didn't really take in what Harry was saying. A flash came into her brain and reminded her that she'd been dreaming. 'I must have been havin' a dream when you wakened me.'

She glanced at the clock on the mantel and saw it was ten past seven. Harry was still staring at the blackness outside the window. She picked up a box of matches from the table and crossed to the cooker. 'I can remember it as clear as anything.' She turned on a gas ring, struck a match and then lit the ring with it. 'Aye – very vivid.' Mary had always told Harry about her dreams but Harry had never been in the slightest bit interested. As she picked up the kettle, she continued with the vivid recollection of her dream, 'I was in this forest and I was being chased by this pack of . . . they looked like midgets but maybe they were wolves.' She put the matchbox on the mantelpiece and tapped it as if trying to tidy up her memory of the dream. Picking up the kettle, she was still trying to separate the midgets from the wolves as she put the kettle on the gas – unfortunately it was not the ring she had just lit.

Harry shivered. 'There's a draught comin' from somewhere.' He scanned the room trying to pinpoint where the draught was getting in.

Mary had started to set out the fire for lighting. She lifted the ashes from below the fire bowl and, selecting some of the cinders that had not become total ash, she wrapped them in a sheet of old newspaper and placed them on top of some kindling she had laid along the bottom of the grate. 'Maybe it wasn't wolves. It might have been just dogs.' She pondered this hypothesis for a moment. 'Mind you, if it was dogs, they were awful big yins.'

'I've found the draught. It's comin' from the window. I'll shut it.' Harry got up on his feet, leant on the bottom of the window and then gave it a shove which successfully closed the window. 'I've fixed that draught. It should be OK noo.' He stood, surveying the room in his cotton long johns and cardigan. 'It's bloody cold, i'n't it? Have you seen my fags? Where did I put my fags?' His gaze settled on the table. 'Ah! There they are.'

Mary was screwing more old newspapers into spills for the fire. 'Have you found your fags? Good.'

'No, I haven't found the fags but I've found my specs.' Harry picked up the wire-rimmed National Health specs that cut into the bridge of his nose, leaving two permanent red notches at each side, and slotted them on to the respective red welts. He could feel in his bones the pain of the effort he had to make to walk over to the fireplace. Reaching the fireplace, he scrutinised the top of it. His gaze fell on the cigarettes on the mantelpiece. Lifting them and the matches, he took a deep breath before walking to his easy chair.

Mary was now on the final stage of lighting the fire. She was placing small bits of coal on the primed kindling. 'Where did I see them noo? Are they no' on the mantelpiece?'

Harry had settled in to his chair and was drawing the cardigan round him for warmth.

'They might have fell down the side of the armchair. Have you looked down the side o' the armchair?'

There was no reply from Harry.

'Well, if they're no' there, I don't know where they are.'

Mary also felt her bones protest as she stood up. 'Aye, auld age doesn't come by itself,' she muttered as she looked in vain on the mantelpiece for the matches. 'Where did I put they matches?' She patted the pocket on her dressing gown. 'I could have sworn I had them here a minute ago.'

Harry looked up from his freshly lit cigarette and shook the matchbox. 'Use these. Is that tea nearly ready? It's bloody cold wi' no fire on, i'n't it?'

Mary crossed to the fireplace with the matches and said, as she tested her bones again by bending down, 'No' be long.' She lit a match and began to coax the fire to light. She watched it for a sign that she had been successful. It was not promising. 'I'll maybe need to block it with a newspaper and get the up-draught goin',' she thought to herself. 'But it might smoke the place oot and that's the last thing Harry needs wi' his chest. I'll give it a minute or two yet.' She continued to stare at the fire in hope.

'Did I tell you I had a terrible dream last night?'

Harry continued to stare out the window, noticing a milk-cart horse clopping along the cobbles in the yellow glow of the lamplit street below.

THREE

Wullie Patterson had been delivering milk, man and boy, for twenty-three years. He'd started as a delivery boy while he was still at school. His family had never been financially solvent due to the fact that his father had been afflicted with a chronic thirst, which was only slightly alleviated by alcohol consumed in large quantities. Wullie had helped his mother feed the family by going on the milk. When his boss died suddenly of a heart attack due to overwork, he was promoted from milk boy to milkman. He took over his boss's run and milk cart, which he loaded each morning at 5 a.m. and then pushed all the way round to each of his customers.

It was back-breaking work and, not wanting to wind up like his erstwhile boss, Wullie had decided to chuck it in and go for something a bit less strenuous. But, when his employers informed him they were upgrading and would provide him with his very own horse, he decided to give it a month to see how it panned out. That was twelve years ago and Wullie and his horse had been partners ever since. His horse was also his best friend. Due to the unsociable hours of his calling, he had never found any woman to share his life with and, if the truth were to be told, he wasn't all that interested in women anyway. He was an avid follower of politics and a prominent member of the Glasgow Humanists' Society – which was a bit of an anomaly, seeing as his best friend was a horse. Wullie's boast was that he did not like to go with the herd and always liked to do things his own way.

He had renamed the horse Thornton as a tribute to the Rangers footballer Willie Thornton. Wullie was actually a Celtic fan but he had decided to honour the Rangers centre forward when the said player returned from the war having won the Military Medal. Of course the post-war shortages had put paid to Wullie's milk round for a few years, but Wullie had taken odd jobs and managed to keep Thornton in oats. Now the bad times were over and Wullie was back in the old routine.

He even had his own squad of lads to run up and down the stairs. There were three of them but Wullie did not know their actual names as sometimes one boy would leave and another would swiftly take his place and Wullie found it very difficult to remember who was who. To save him the effort of trying to recall any new boy's name, he developed the strategy of always referring to them as Larry, Curly and Moe after the Hollywood comedy team known as The Three Stooges. This worked out well as the boys were not really interested in furthering their acquaintanceship with Wullie outside of the twilight hours anyway.

As the cart turned the corner into Melton Street, the three stooges jumped off and grabbed the appropriate number of milk bottles for delivery to the various tenement closes and the houses that were on their lists. Larry and Curly were due to deliver to number 3 and number 6. Moe loaded up his crate with milk and headed for number 9. As he lurched across the street he felt the milk crate dig into the creases of his fingers making them sting in the cold early morning air. The bottom of the crate dug into his thighs and he was thinking to himself that he would pack in this way of enhancing his pocket money when Wullie's voice cut through the gloom and frost.

'MOE!' he shouted to him. 'Make sure you get the money aff Magrit McGuire. Two weeks she owes – eleven and six-pence. Tell her nae money, nae milk.'

Moe nodded and continued on his way. He was whistling the Guy Mitchell tune 'She Wears Red Feathers and a Hooly-Hooly Skirt'. Guy Mitchell was Moe's favourite singer and he knew all of his songs off by heart. As he delivered the milk, he collected the week's money and, now and again, got a 'wee mindin" – which was Glaswegian for a tip. The McGuires' door was on the top landing and, unlike the other main doors which had all been modernised by sticking a large piece of plywood on top of the original panelling and then painting it (usually cream), theirs was still in its original state. The practice of overlaying plywood was known as flushing the front door and was very fashionable at the time. However the only thing that was flushed in the McGuires' was the toilet. Peter and Margaret McGuire and their two boys and a girl lived on the edge and life was what is known as a struggle. Peter was a strongly-built red-headed descendant of Irish immigrants and had a job as a 'hauder-oan' in the yards. This consisted of holding on (haudin-oan) to a sledgehammer on one side of the bulkhead of a ship, while a riveter rattled through a white-hot rivet on the other side. The action of holding the sledgehammer against the hot rivet caused the tail of the rivet to flatten against the bulkhead, thus joining up the various panels of metal that constituted the bulkhead. It was hard, deafening work and most of the men who worked in this environment were prone to conditions such as arthritis or white finger, due to the staccato pressure from the riveting gun, and also to deafness, due to the din created in the shell of the ship that was being built, like a thousand ball bearings being rattled in an enormous tin can.

Peter was still in his thirties and had all that to look forward to. It was, therefore, no small wonder that, come the weekend, if they were not working overtime, he liked to forget all about the week that had gone before and the weeks that were still to come. Like a significant number of the workmen, he found that a few wee haufs and a hauf pint chaser helped him to relax. It helped him so much that he would be as relaxed as a newt by closing time.

He'd then sing or get in a fight, depending on whether or not his singing or his point of view was agreed on by his peers. Eventually, he would wind up falling in the front door and collapsing in the hallway, where his wife and family would ignore his existence except for rifling through his pockets for any loose change. This traditional practice had the effect of leaving the man of the house skint and in need of a moneylender by the Sunday. This was, however, never a huge problem as the moneylenders were always waiting outside the shipyard gates, to help out, so to speak.

When Moe came for the milk money, Peter was doing what he did best when he wasn't holding on to rivets – sleeping.

Moe had reached the McGuires' door and, clutching the two pints of milk that were destined for the McGuires, providing they coughed up the money owed, he knocked firmly on the door. As he waited for a reply, he changed from Guy Mitchell's 'Hooly-Hooly Skirt' to his next favourite singer Dickie Valentine's hit 'All the Time and Everywhere'. Moe decided that an early-morning drag at a fag was in order. He gave the door another knock and extracted a half a Woodbine from a five packet in his trouser pocket. The five-Woodbine packet was known as the flat fifty due to its diminutive status and was usually smoked near the end of the week when money was too tight to buy Senior Service or Player's cigarettes. He gave the door another knock and then started to sing quietly, in the style of Dickie Valentine and to the tune of 'Who Were You With Last Night?':

Woodbine's a rare wee smoke
(gie's a light, gie's a light, gie's a light)
Woodbine's a rare wee smoke.
If it wasnae for Woodbine
We wouldnae be here
Woodbine's a rare wee smoke.

Moe prided himself on his Dickie Valentine impression and was not quite happy with his rendition that time – something about the vowel pronunciations were not quite right. He placed the dog end in his mouth and fished around in his pocket for a match, eventually finding one, but unfortunately it was a match without a box around it. He searched for a surface to strike the match on. Normally the stairs would have done but they were damp. His eyes finally spied a metal air vent high on the wall between the opposing houses on the stairhead landing. He realised he could reach it by standing on the upended milk crate. Laying the milk on the landing he turned the crate on its side, stood on it and struck the match. As the match head ignited, sparked and finally flared into flame, he instantly cupped it with his hands so it would not be extinguished by a stray draught. Sucking deliciously on the Woodbine, he stepped down from the crate and bent down to pick up the milk – only to discover that it had vanished into thin air. It did not take Sherlock Holmes to guess where it had gone. He had lowered his guard for only a few seconds but that was enough for the opportunists behind the McGuires' door to seize the moment – and the milk.

Moe battered on the door frantically but, it has to be said, also futilely.

'Mrs McGuire, the driver says I've to get the money for the last two weeks – Mrs McGuire – Wullie'll kill me if I don't get the money. Gonnae gie us the money, please?' he shouted through the letterbox. 'At least gie us the empties.' He continued in this vein, chasing what's known as a lost cause. However, the unflushed door was not forthcoming and, finally, conceding defeat was all that was left to him and Moe trudged down the stairs with a heavy heart.

From the McGuires' front window that looked down and on to Melton Street, ten-year-old Tim McGuire, dressed in a semmit and underpants, surveyed the milk cart as he sat on top of the kitchen sink. This grandstand seat provided him with an excellent view of Moe running to the cart and explaining to Wullie what had happened to his milk and the two weeks' money that was owed. Wullie looked up at the window and shook his head. Moe looked up and shook his fist. Tim gave them both a look at his middle finger which he used as a microphone while miming crooning into it in the fashion that Dickie Valentine used when singing the latest hit tune of the day.

FOUR

'That's him away, Ma,' Tim informed his mother.

Margaret McGuire or, to pronounce her name the way that Glaswegians did, 'Magrit' was busy getting herself ready for battle with the forthcoming day.

'Did you give him the milk money?'

'Aye, I gave him it, Ma,' said Tim, jumping down off the sink and crossing over to the bed that contained his nine-year-old brother Frankie and their father. Pulling back the bed clothes, he got in beside them. Both Peter and Frankie were still sleeping so this afforded Tim the opportunity to count the money that should have been in the milkman's hands but was now in his. Pulling the bedclothes over his head, he surveyed the loot and, in a shaft of light that shone through a gap in the sheet, he swiftly counted his haul.

'Jeez! Eleven and six.' A silent gasp of delight escaped from his lips as he realised he was now in possession of a small fortune. He lay there, warmth coming back into his body and eyes shining with excitement as he tried to come to terms with his new-found wealth. At that moment, the sheet was yanked from his grasp and he found himself hauled out of bed.

'Right, ya thievin' wee swine, where is it?' Magrit's hand was round the back of his neck in a grip that her husband would have found hard to surpass in his capacity of hauder-oan.

'I gave him it, Ma – honest.'

'Do you think I'm deaf – eh? Do you think I didnae hear him shoutin' through the letter box?'

Tim was desperately trying to think of an out. 'Ah . . . but . . . Ah . . . but . . .'

Magrit's grip tightened. 'Ah, but – Ah, but – Abbot and Costello.' She released her grip so she could whack him round the ear. 'Where is it?'

His head ringing and his ears burning, Tim handed over the money.

'That's better.' She gave him another clout for good measure. 'If I ever catch you at that again, I'll knock you into the middle of next week.'

Tim could have been forgiven for thinking he was already there.

As he fought back the tears, his father's voice worked its way into the ear that was not ringing. 'What the fuck's happenin'? What's all the shoutin' aboot?' Peter emerged from the depth of the bedclothes. His face was that of a man who had never willingly under-indulged in his life. His mouth felt like sandpaper and tasted like the proverbial camel's crotch.

Magrit spun round to answer him. 'Pig.'

Peter stared at her bemusedly. 'Eh?'

'You heard,' Magrit explained.

'What the fuck's happenin'?' Peter persisted, trying to come to terms with whatever was happening.

'Oh, aye, that's your answer for everything – eh!' she replied in a whining voice, mimicking his tone. 'What's happenin' – what's goin' on? You make me sick, the whole bloody lot of youse.'

Peter looked askance, then looked at the clock. 'It's no' half seven yet and you're moanin' already.'

'I'll moan whenever I like,' Magrit threw back at him as she stormed out of the kitchen and into the bedroom.

'Ach! Away and shite,' Peter shouted after her.

'You're an animal – that's what you are – you're just a fuckin' animal,' screeched Magrit through the dividing wall. 'God forgive me for swearin' but you drag it oot of me.'

The sound of furniture being thrown around the room and a door slamming signified that all further questioning was now at an end.

Peter scratched his head ruefully, vainly tried to swallow, gave up and surveyed Tim who was trying to fix his face into what he hoped was a look of innocence. 'What's up wi' her noo?' he asked him.

'Tim tried to nick the milk money,' yawned Frankie, as he sat up in bed and picked his nose.

'Dear Christ. Is that all?' Peter sighed. 'Did she get it back?'

'Aye,' nodded Tim.

Peter knew instinctively that he should do what any proper father would do if he caught his son stealing but it was just too early in the morning to figure out what it was he should do.

'Did you get the milk?' was the best he could come up with.

'Aye.'

'Good. Away and make your da a cup o' tea, son.'

'Och, Da, it's freezin',' Tim wheedled, heading back towards the bed and settling under the sheets beside Frankie who was now in repose again having dislodged whatever was offending his left nostril.

Peter sucked at the roof of his mouth. Still no moisture. 'I've got a right dry mooth on me – be a good boy, son.'

Peter crawled back into bed between Frankie and Tim. 'Go on, son – eh?'

Tim now felt warmth and security envelop him as his eyes closed. He heard his father murmur sleepily, 'Tim, son.' But he ignored it as the peace and quiet of the moment took hold of him. The moment was only disturbed by his father's voice barking, 'Tea!' followed by his father's leg propelling him out the bed and on to the cold linoleum.

'Big shite,' he muttered under his breath as he made towards the sink.

He trudged across the cold lino feeling a deep injustice that it was he who had to make the tea and not Frankie. It seemed to Tim that, just because he was a wee bit older than Frankie, he was put upon. As he reached for the teapot and filled it with water this sense of injustice welled within him. Lighting the gas as high as it would go, he placed the teapot on the gas ring and waited for it to boil. He could hear his mother still banging drawers open and then shut behind the closed door of the bedroom.

This was to let everybody in the house know that she was still raging mad. Tim thought it a waste of time as his mother was always mad at something – usually him. He decided to try and get on her good side and avoid any further retribution over the milk incident. Crossing to the bedroom door, he knocked on it gently and said, 'I'm making you a cup o' tea, Ma.' He waited for her to reply, 'Thanks, son.' He waited in vain. 'If it was Frankie that had made her a cup o' tea, she would have been all over him,' he thought as he turned away. He could hear the water begin to boil in the teapot. As he looked for cups that were clean, he saw that there was only the one which had not been washed from the night before. There were still the dregs and tealeaves in it and a fag end jutted out from them, at the bottom of the cup. Tim picked it up, smelled it and grrhoo-ed in disgust at the stench.

He was still screwing up his face as he placed a teaspoon of tea into the teapot and then stirred it around the now boiling water. Turning off the gas, he got clean cups out and put milk and sugar into them, then filled them with the tea. He went back to the dirty cup, reached down with his finger, dislodged the fag end and, lifting it out, removed the paper from the wet shag. He distributed the loose tobacco back into the cup and filled it with tea.

'Frankie's.' He smiled, putting in an extra spoonful of sugar to disguise the taste.

As he stirred the cup he heard his mother shout through to his father, 'Are you gettin' up for your work or will we just dae withoot money for the New Year as well as the old one?'

Peter rose from his bed and surveyed Tim standing over the teacups. 'Thanks, son – did you make one for your wee brother as well?'

Tim nodded. 'Aye, Da.'

Peter ruffled his son's head. 'You're no' the worst – eh?'

FIVE

Wullie stared at Thornton's enormous muscular rear end. There was something comforting to Wullie in the easy way it swayed left and right as it strode unflinchingly, despite the weight of the cart loaded with milk, along the milk round. The black wiry tail contrasting perfectly with the dark brown of its coat rested easy on Wullie's eye. In the summer, there was always a shimmer of sweat that gave Thornton's vast bum a slick sheen that made Wullie think his equine pal was perhaps a descendent of some sleek Arab stallion. They had been on this round so long that Wullie had no real need to use the reins to guide the horse – it now knew where to go off its own back.

Wullie wondered, not for the first time, what thoughts were going through his big pal's head. After all, the horse knew nothing about politics, sport, religion, all the things that kept humans in contact with each other. It never met any other horses to exchange ideas with. It never was short of money and needed a tap till pay day. It never really communicated in any way whatsoever with Wullie – in fact, logically, Wullie reflected, he should have found the horse boring and uninspiring. Yet this was not the case. Whatever it was that made him love his big pal would remain a mystery and maybe it was better that way.

As Wullie sat lost in his thoughts, Thornton turned into

Granton Street and headed for Wilson's grocer's and news-agent's, where the empties would be offloaded and he would receive a well-earned bag of oats. Shaking his head and blowing the cold through his nostrils, Thornton reached his journey's end and automatically stopped – his whole persona was one of a job done and dusted. He stood, quietly majestic, thinking of . . . who knows what?

Wullie noticed Dolly Johnson hurrying towards him.

Dolly was in her early sixties and was the type of woman who knew everything about everybody. Her husband called her Pathé after the cinema newsreel *The Pathé News*, whose motto was 'The Eyes and Ears of the World'. She had the proverbial heart of gold and would have rather done you a good turn than a bad one. She also had 'the bow' or 'bowly legs' that a lot of people of her generation had because they had suffered from rickets in childhood. This was caused by either a lack of vitamins or making your baby walk too quickly – Glaswegians could never agree on which was the accurate diagnosis. Whatever the reason, it had the unfortunate effect of causing the bones in the leg to bend outwards and this gave the sufferer a tendency to walk with a side-to-side motion or shauchle as the locals called it. In fact Dolly's brother was called Shauchley – not to his face of course. Dolly's hobby was talking. It didn't really matter where, when or to whom – as long as she could have a blether, Dolly was happy. It took Dolly four times as long to go for the daily groceries as most other women due to the fact that she would meet someone every couple of yards and swap the gossip. She gave Wullie the customary greeting, 'You all right, Wullie?'

As Wullie jumped down from the cart, he acknowledged her. 'Mornin', Dolly. You all set for the bells thenight?'

Dolly's wee red round weather-beaten face creased into a smile. 'Oh, aye. Lookin' forward to it. It's awful cold, isn't it?'

Wullie nodded as he blew into his cupped hands for warmth. 'Get a wee goldie into you. That'll warm you up.'

'I'll wait tae thenight – I've too much work to get through. Hullo, Thornton – that you finished for the day? He's a big darlin', isn't he?' She nodded to the horse.

'We're nearly finished – just get the empties unloaded, the big yin brushed doon and fed and that'll be me for this year. As the surgeon said to Vincent Van Gogh, just before he operated, "Happy New Ear when it comes," Dolly!'

'Oh! He's had an operation, has he? I don't know the man personally but, if you see him, tell him fae me I hope his operation's a success,' Dolly replied, earnestly. 'Happy New Year when it comes, Wullie. You as well, Thornton.'

Dolly waved goodbye as she pushed open the door of the shop. Mamie Wilson came through from the back on hearing the sound of the bell that warned her there were customers in. She and her husband had been on the go since four o'clock getting everything ready for the Hogmanay rush. It was always a strain as they had to get through four days' work in the one. But they were no different from everyone else who ran their own business so they just made up their minds to enjoy it and get on with the job in hand.

''S awful cold, i'n't, it Mamie?' Dolly said, plonking two message bags on the counter.

'Bloody freezin', Dolly. Wait a minute – I've got they loaves you ordered.' She bent down under the counter and came up with four unwrapped plain loaves. 'Well-fired crusts. That right, Dolly?'

Dolly placed the loaves in one of the message bags. 'Thanks, Mamie. You'd better gie me two dozen rolls as well – a dozen ordinary and a dozen well-fired. Oh and my paper.'

Mamie nodded. 'Did you hear Cissie Gilchrist's man's died?'

'Aye. I read aboot it in the *Evenin' Times*. Cissie'll be

heartbroken. He wis younger than her, wis he no'?'

Mamie handed Dolly the rolls, which she'd packed into four large paper bags. 'Watch you don't get them crushed. I think he was younger, right enough – fine big woman though, Cissie.'

'Oh, she is, Mamie – very striking.'

Mamie helped Dolly to pack the rolls into her bag. 'I don't know what she ever saw in him.'

'Oh, naw! He was a shelpit wee nyaff,' agreed Dolly. 'I'll take six of your Paris buns as well. He thought he was above everybody else. You know how he sold insurance and that?'

Mamie nodded. 'Aye, that's right, so he did.'

'He came up tae my hoose wan time. I wasn't gonnae open the door 'cause he rang the bell and I usually only open the door if somebody knocks on it or rattles the letterbox, you know. I always think, if it's the doorbell, that it's somebody wantin' money.'

'Aye, right enough, Dolly,' Mamie agreed.

'Anyway, for whatever reason, I don't know, but I answered the door and he's standin' there wi' this form. And he says, in yon pan-loaf voice o' his, "Good evening, Mrs Joansin. Eh was wondering if the master of the house was in?" "You're lookin' at her," I says to him. "Well," he says, "Eh was wondering if you would consider cheynging your poalicy?"'

'And what did you say, Dolly?'

'"Naw!" I says, "It is my poalicy never to change a poalicy." 'Cause my mother told me always to haud on to your poalicies or you'll lose money on them.'

'You're no' wrong there, Dolly' Mamie agreed again, nodding sagely.

'Are your fern cakes fresh, Mamie?'

'Naw, Dolly – they're yesterday's.'

'Oh.' Dolly's face registered disappointment.

Mamie thought for a second or two before replying, 'I'll gie you them for half price.'

'Gie us six then.' Dolly had a mental check up if there was anything else she needed. There wasn't. 'So that's the end o' wee Gilchrist,' she sighed.

Mamie picked out six of the best of yesterday's fern cakes and put them in another bag. 'Aye,' she sighed, echoing Dolly. 'Sad, right enough. You feel sorry for Cissie, though, eh?'

Dolly had another mental check up. 'Aye. Gie me a bereavement card and a dozen drop scones.'

The shop doorbell rang to announce the arrival of Sadie McCue.

'Aye, Sadie. This you getting ready for thenight?' Dolly beamed.

Sadie was a few years younger than Dolly and had a face that always seemed to be dissatisfied with something. She shook her head in an instantly recognisable sign that she was fed up to the back teeth. 'Aye, Dolly. I hate this time o' the year. You feel as if there's no' enough hours in the day, don't ye? 'S bloody freezin' as well, i'n't it?' Her gaze swept over Dolly and landed on Mamie. 'Aye, Mamie. Have you a couple o' hot rolls?'

Mamie nodded and pulled two from a large batch that rested behind her on a tall rack. 'These are only a couple o' minutes oot the oven. But I wouldnae eat them tae later on. It can gie you an awful sore stomach when the dough's too fresh.'

Sadie took the rolls from her and said with a sniffle, 'I'm no' wantin' them for to eat – I want to get a bit heat in me.' She opened her coat, lifted her thick woollen pullover and shoved the two rolls inside her bra. 'Oh that's lovely, so it is,' she said with a shudder as the heat transferred through her body.

Dolly chortled heartily at Mamie and said, 'Have you got

a couple of crumpets for her airse while you're at it?'

Mamie replied, 'If she asks for a doughnut, she's gettin' barred.'

Dolly and Sadie hee-hawed to cries of, 'You're a helluva woman, Mamie, so you are.'

Sadie adjusted her bosoms and gave her nose a wipe with a hankie she kept permanently up her pullover sleeve for that sole purpose. She looked round the shop. 'Noo, what did I come in for?'

'To heat up your chist,' said Mamie.

'Apart fae that, though,' Sadie chewed her bottom lip in concentration. 'I'm gettin' awful forgetful these days.'

'Don't forget you've a couple of rolls shoved up your jersey or you'll get the soap all dough when you have a wash later on,' Dolly reminded her.

Sadie smiled. 'Aye, right enough.' She continued to ponder. 'I need milk – four pints – and gie me four loaves as well, Mamie. A half a dozen eggs and . . .'

As she tried to recall whatever it was she had to recall, Mamie piled Sadie's order on to the counter.

'Raisins – that was it – raisins. Have you any more o' they big blue ones I got aff you the last time?'

Mamie nodded, 'Aye, I have them. They're lovely, so they are.'

Dolly nodded in agreement. 'Are you makin' a dumplin', Sadie?'

Sadie sucked in some more warm air and nodded back at Dolly. 'I'd get thrown oot the hoose if I didnae make a clootie dumplin' at the New Year. I'll put it on when I get back.'

'Have you got spice?' Mamie enquired as she poured the large blue raisins on to the weighing machine.

'Hell, naw. That's another thing I nearly forgot,' Sadie groaned.

'Do you want a pound o' these?' asked Mamie, glancing at the raisins.

'Aye, that should dae. They're lovely and juicy, Dolly.'

'Aye, they are, right enough, Sadie,' Dolly signalled agreement by nodding whole-heartedly. 'They'll keep your dumplin' juicy, stop it fae drying oot – unlike the rolls, eh?'

Sadie stuck her hand up her jumper again and fiddled about. 'They're startin' tae itch a wee bit. I think I'll take them oot.'

Dolly watched as Sadie fished out what were now two very flat rolls from her bosoms. 'What are you gonnae dae wi' them?' she asked as Sadie placed them in her message bag.

'I'll gie them to him wi' a sausage for his breakfast,' she said, referring to her husband. 'Mamie, I'll take two flat sausages as well.'

'A couple o' Lorne sausages – right, you are.'

'Speakin' o' dumplin's', Sadie – did you hear that Cissie Gilchrist's man's died?'

Sadie was in the last throes of adjusting her brassiere. 'Wee pan-loaf Gilchrist? When did that happen?'

'I think it was a couple o' nights ago,' said Dolly earnestly. 'It's a terrible time of the year this. A lot o' deaths at this time of the year – my mother used to say that.'

Mamie and Sadie murmured their agreement of this indisputable fact.

'My Uncle Harry died on a New Year's Day,' Dolly informed them.

Sadie gave her a sympathetic look. 'Was he ill for long?'

'Naw, he was drunk and fell doon the stairs,' Dolly replied, then added, philosophically, 'What's for you'll no' go by you, eh?'

Both of her companions nodded in concordance at this example of Dolly's wisdom.

'Poor Cissie. That's all you need at this time o' the year, eh?' Sadie's face reflected on Cissie's grief. 'Mind you, he wasn't liked hisself, though.'

'Naw,' Dolly concurred, 'He was a wee nyaff – good tae her, mind you! Funny tae think you'll never see his wee pinched face again, eh?' Dolly said, shaking her head.

There was a moment of silent reflection, only broken by Sadie. 'I never thought his face was pinched.'

Mamie finished packing Sadie's bag. 'Me neither,' she said, earnestly.

'Aye, it was,' Dolly said back, convinced that right was on her side.

'Naw, it was definitely no' pinched, Dolly,' Sadie insisted, forcefully.

'You're right, his face was not pinched, Sadie,' said Mamie, emphatically.

'How was it no'?' Dolly was beginning to get worried that she was being ganged up on.

'Well, because, if he was gonnae pinch a face, he would have pinched a better one than the one he had,' said Sadie.

'Oh! You'se are hell of a funny!' Dolly smiled. 'I'll need tae get oot o' here before I die laughin' at youse. You goin' oot after the bells tonight, Sadie?'

Sadie's face registered resignation. 'Aye, we'll first-foot my mother and then we're all goin' roond to my sister's after that. But that's a long way away yet – I've still got a dumplin' tae cook, a pot o' soup tae get ready and the hoose tae clean. I've got to go to the steamie at two o'clock this afternoon . . . then the ironing. I could see it far enough, so I could.'

Dolly adjusted her scarf against leaving the warmth of the shop and, as she paid Mamie for her shopping, gave out her itinerary, 'I'm goin' thenight tae the steamie. I've got a stall booked for seven o'clock. That was the earliest they had left so it'll be tight gettin' everything ready before the family comes up. Mind you, I've told them they better no' show up till efter the bells – 'cause I'll just no' let them in.'

Mamie placed the cash from Dolly and Sadie in the register and, as the till kerching'd out its happy note (well, happy for Mamie, at any rate), she wished them the season's greetings. 'Have a good New Year when it comes and don't get too drunk.'

'Same to yourself, Mamie,' chorused Dolly and Sadie as they left the shop still chatting about the trying time ahead for them.

SIX

Peter McGuire emerged from the gloom of his tenement close-mouth into the darkness of the last day of the year. He surveyed the dim and the dampness that was an all too familiar sight in the city and felt his spirits drop even further than when he had wakened that morning to Magrit's voice strafing his ear with what seemed to him like a never-ending torrent of complaining. A grunt of utter discontent escaped involuntarily from his still-parched throat as he saw the bus he had to catch approach the bus stop. It was cruelly just within catching distance – providing he ran. Considering how he felt, this would not have been Peter's ideal way of starting the day but there was no alternative. With another grunt and an oath to confirm his dissatisfaction with the world, he set off. His boots clattered on the pavement. One of the nails, that formed the horse-shoe pattern which held the sole of his left boot on, emerged slightly and dug into him, forcing him to limp and then hop as the nail freed itself and burrowed deeper into the pad of his big toe. He had about ten yards to go when he heard the bell on the bus clang, signalling that it was about to move off. Peter bellowed at the back of the bus and ignored the pain that was shooting up his big toe as he strained, through gritted teeth, to catch it. With a leap that would not have disgraced an Olympic long jumper (admittedly an unfit one), he grabbed the handrail at the back of the bus and swung himself on to the platform.

His breath, what remained of it, came in all too short waves from what the Capstan Full Strength cigarettes had left of his lungs. As he gasped and fought for the air that seared the top of his chest, he inwardly cursed. Cursing was a thing the men of the Clyde did without thinking. It was used more as an adjective or a punctuation mark than an actual vehicle for blasphemy. They rarely used the curse words to describe what they actually meant. For example, if you were described as a 'clever bastard'. It only meant that you were highly intelligent and not that you were highly intelligent and illegitimate. The word 'bastard' meant absolutely nothing – it was merely a way of finishing a statement while keeping the rhythm of the sentence.

Peter was excelling himself at rhythm-keeping as he stood coughing his lungs up on the platform. When he had regained enough of his breath to move, he headed upstairs to where you could smoke.

As his head gained altitude to the top deck, the smoke hung in the air like something that was living. It wafted around the heads of the puffers engulfing them in a grey haze that resembled a travelling Turkish steam room. Peter surveyed the familiar scene and greedily sucked in the second-hand smoke as he searched for his own fags so he could add to the pleasure of his fellow travellers. As he did this, he spotted the only spare seat that was on the top deck.

Lurching along the passageway, he grabbed the rail and sank into the vacant seat, which was covered in brown moquette suffering from alopecia. The occupant of the seat next to him lifted his head from the back pages of the morning paper and gave him a nod of recognition.

'How you doin', Peter?'

'How does it bloody look?' Peter growled at John Hood.

John was younger than Peter and had recently got married to Doreen. They were what's known as a nice young couple.

John had a fresh face that was fashionably topped off with a Tony Curtis haircut. He was a time-served carpenter – or shipwright, as it's called in the shipbuilding industry – and earned good money which, unlike Peter, he shared with his wife and partner in life. Along with the majority of the bus, he worked in the same shipyard as Peter did.

'You sufferin'?' John asked, unnecessarily – as a blind man could have seen that Peter was not tickety-boo, as they say in the south of Britain.

'I got right fuckin' blootered last night.' Peter smiled through the pain. 'I had a wee three-cross treble aff the bookie in the efternoon – threw me a few quid – so I went in for a small celebration . . . All's I can remember is wakenin' up wi' face-ache poundin' my eardrums fae the startin' flag aboot milk money or some fuckin' thing. My head's loupin'. You've no' got a bottle o' beer on you, have you?'

John shrugged and shook his head sympathetically.

Peter sucked at his cigarette, coughed with the effort and continued, 'I'll need a swally o' some kind – I'm skint as well. I think she might have hoovered my pockets last night.' He blew out the smoke. 'Havnae a bean tae I get the wages at dinner time. You want a fag?' Peter offered John the packet.

John felt a minikin of pity for Peter. As he took hold of the packet, he could tell by the rattle coming from inside the carton that there were, at most, only two cigarettes inside.

As he handed the packet back, he said, 'Naw, you're all right, Peter, I just put one oot.'

Peter nodded and put the packet back into his pocket.

John gave him a nudge and, drawing his hand out of his own pocket, he slipped a pound note into Peter's hand. 'There's a quid till dinner time.'

Peter took the pound and squeezed John's knee. 'If you were no' a Prodestant, they'd have to canonise you for that, pal. I'll pay you back at dinner time – that's a promise.'

Peter sank back into his seat, closed his eyes and, thanks to John's benevolence, blew out a sigh that spoke volumes for his new-found ability to get rid of his pounding head and his raging thirst.

As he relaxed in this state of plenty, the conductor wended his way along the top deck until he stopped at Peter. 'Fares? Any mer fares, there?' He stared at Peter. 'Any mer fares?'

Peter opened his eyes and passed him the pound note. 'Thruppence.'

As he took the pound, the conductor surveyed him sadistically and proceeded to hunt around his cash bag for halfpennies and other small change to dish out to Peter.

Noticing the glint in the conductor's eye Peter said pointedly, 'I'm no' wantin' to be carryin' a pocket full o' pennies.'

The conductor was coming to the end of his shift and it would suit him nicely to ditch all of his small change. 'Well, that's all I've got – so that's what you're getting.'

Peter felt the good feeling that he had, a second or two ago, ebb away. His voice sounded exactly like he was feeling, 'Is it a necessary part o' your job to be a total prick – or have you just had a sudden notion for a sore face? 'Cause I am just dyin' tae whack the first obnoxious bastard that gets on my tits this mornin'.'

Peter didn't rise – even his voice didn't rise – but, wisely, the conductor could tell that this was not an empty threat. 'Aye! Well . . . I'll let you aff this time, OK?' He sniffed, handing Peter the pound note and making his way back along the top deck and down the stairs to safety.

John went back to reading his paper and Peter sank further down in his seat and concentrated on his fag. He was delighted that John had supplied him with the wherewithal to buy a new packet of fags or he would have had to rely on scrounging roll-up cigarettes till his pay came through. The way his hands were shaking, he doubted if he could have managed to control the delicate task of keeping the loose tobacco in the Rizla cigarette paper.

He glanced at John who was engrossed in an article of the newspaper. Sucking in a lungful of smoke, he dragged it right down to the bottom of his very being, held on to it for a few seconds and sucked it even further down. He then released it, at last, as a mist of grey smoke and it merged with the other man-made clouds on the top deck of the bus.

His brain was starting to emerge from the confusion of the early morning. He stared at the end of his cigarette and noticed, not for the first time, that, when the smoke curled up from the fag end, it twisted and wrapped round itself in a blue wisp-like strand that had a subtle form and grace. However, once he inhaled it and then blew it out, it lost its shape and turned to a powdery grey. He stared abstractly at the other blue wisps winding their way through the grey and thought, 'What a load of crap.'

Turning to look out the window, he noticed an expression of consternation had formed on John's face. 'You're helluva concerned aboot somethin' in that paper. Have the Rangers signed a Catholic or somethin'?'

Without looking up John nodded. 'Aye.'

'What?' Peter replied, incredulously, his body snapping bolt upright in the seat. 'Have they?'

John nodded again and continued, reading aloud from the newspaper, 'It also says that . . . hell has frozen over and loads o' pigs have joined the RAF.'

'Bastard,' was Peter's only reply.

John continued, 'What it really says is that the corporation have plans tae build a big housing scheme called Drumchapel.'

He quoted from the paper, '"All brand new houses with bathrooms and inside toilets in them. Each house will have its own front garden."' He shook his head in wonderment. 'Goin' to be some place, eh? Doreen wants us tae move somewhere like that.'

Peter's face echoed John's in its stupefaction. 'Bathrooms and lavvies? In all the hooses?'

'That's what it says.'

'How many hooses are they buildin'?'

John scanned the paper and then announced, 'Eh, it says here . . . "to accommodate upwards of twenty thousand people".'

'Twenty thousand? And there's a lavvy in each hoose? That's a lot o' lavvies!'

'Certainly is.' John nodded in agreement. 'Some fuckin' smell aff it, eh?'

'They'll need all their baths,' Peter replied. 'You and Doreen goin' oot for the bells thenight?'

John nodded resignedly. 'Just the usual. Her family, then my family. I could see it far enough. Lookin' forward to a couple o' days off, though. She's goin' tae get her hair done, then she's goin' tae the steamie. She's aw excited aboot it.'

'She's excited aboot goin' tae the steamie? You should take her oot mair.'

'No. She's excited aboot gettin' her hair done. She left me a note sayin' she was gettin' it done in a bubble cut and she hoped I'd like it. I'll need tae remember and tell her it looks great or her face'll be trippin' her. Does Magrit carry on like that?'

Peter thought for a moment. 'Don't know. I don't ever remember her gettin' her hair done.'

41

Doreen Hood hummed along to the wireless. It was playing Dean Martin's rendition of 'That's Amore'. Doreen danced as she hummed and tried to remember all the words in case she was asked to sing at one of the parties she and John would be going to after the bells. She always sang 'My Yiddishe Mamma' and everyone invariably said she sang it beautifully but, as she wasn't Jewish and neither was her mother, she had decided, this year, she would sing something different. She danced over to the mirror above the fireplace and tried to sort her hair into a shape that she would not find too awful. She screwed it up at the back but that made her look too old-fashioned. Then she tried the front in an approximation of a bang. 'More like an explosion,' she thought. No, it was an impossible task – it needed cut and that was that. Once she had it cut into the new fashionable bubble cut, all her troubles would be over. With that consoling thought, she put a headscarf on and made her mind up to go out and get it done.

After Dean had stopped singing.

SEVEN

With their father having gone off to his work, Tim and Frankie McGuire were sitting on the edge of their bed still in their underpants and vests, eating breakfast – two large doorsteps of plain bread with jam. Frankie had intimated that he felt a bit sick in his stomach. Magrit, who was busy doing the hundred and odd things she had to attend to before she could leave the house for the morning, had said it was maybe something he ate.

'Or somethin' that you drank?' Tim enquired innocently. 'My tea tasted funny, so it did,' he added, hoping to turn suspicion away from him and his machinations with the soggy fag.

Frankie's face screwed itself into an expression of distaste mixed with discomfort. 'So did mine.' He rubbed his stomach with both hands and groaned.

Tim patted his brother sympathetically on the back and then deftly deflected any suspicion away from him by looking as if he was thinking hard before coming up with, 'It might have been the milk, so it might. That milk boy might have poisoned it, Frankie.'

Frankie groaned and lay back on the bed.

Tim placed his hand tenderly on his brother's forehead and said, 'Mammy, I think Frankie's got a temperature. Will I go for a *Dandy* and a *Beano* so he can take his mind aff no' bein' well? Maybe even get him a Mars bar and me a Wagon Wheel? OK?'

43

Magrit hurried over and felt his forehead. 'He's fine. Youse are gettin' hee-haw.'

Tim groaned along with Frankie at this and sank back among the crumpled bedclothes in despair that his machinations had come to nothing. As he writhed in unhappiness, his sister Theresa appeared from the bedroom that she shared with her mother.

She had just recently turned thirteen and was lost in the perpetual angst of being a teenager – and a female teenager at that. No one understood the tribulations that Theresa had to endure – well, no one, that is, except her best friend Rena Reilly. Rena was nearly six months older than Theresa and, with that wealth of extra experience of life, was the only one Theresa felt that she could turn to for advice. There was no point turning to her parents as they just did not know anything about anything. Ignoring her younger brothers, she said, in a voice that was heavy with anguish, 'Mammy, can I change in here in front o' the fire? It's freezin' in the other room.' She held her arms around her bare shoulders and hugged herself, conscious that she was in her vest and knickers and that her brothers should not be privy to viewing her in that state.

'Dae what you want. I'm too busy,' was Magrit's reply as she swept the lobby and banged the edge of the brush against the skirting board. As Theresa started to lift her vest off, she turned round quickly, in time to catch her brothers chewing on their jam and bread and staring at her. 'Mammy, will you tell they two to take their pieces into the other room? I want to get dressed and they're staring at me.'

Her mother shouted back, above the clacking of the brush and skirting board, 'I'm cleanin' that room in a minute – anyway you said yourself it's too cold.'

Her voice went up a level as she shouted to the boys, 'You two, turn your backs and don't look at your big sister.'

Tim had risen from among the swirl of the bed sheets so he could get a better look at his big sister. 'We're no' lookin' at her, sure we're no', Frankie?'

Frankie, now miraculously recovered, peeked from beneath a blanket, threw the blanket aside and stood beside his brother. His face leering and his hands cupped suggestively, he shouted, 'Naw!' to his mother.

'Turn your backs when you're told, then,' Theresa scolded in her best big sister voice.

They gave a gesture of wronged innocence and, shrugging their shoulders, turned and faced the other way. Theresa slid out of her vest and put on a clean one that her mother had left over the big chair that was in front of the fire along with clean knickers. She thrilled to the warmth of where her vest had been heated by the fire and started to remove her knickers. She had thrown her knickers on top of her vest when she heard suppressed sniggering coming from behind her. Whirling round she saw that, although the boys' backs were turned, their faces were tilted upwards, staring into the mirror that was hanging on the opposite wall. They were beside themselves with mirth and Frankie was almost choking with the effort of not guffawing out loud.

Theresa howled with embarrassment. 'They pigs are watchin' me,' she screamed at them and her mother. 'I hate youse,' she raged at Frankie and Tim who were now hanging on to each other and making pouting faces as their hands simulated the female form with figure-of-eight curvy gestures.

'I hate everybody in this hoose.' She ran into her room and passed her mother who had run out of the room and into the kitchen to see what all the commotion was.

Magrit sized up the situation immediately. 'Ya dirty little perverts.' She made a dive at them but they adopted the tactic of splitting up and, for a moment, threw her. That moment, however, was enough to see them dart into the lobby, through the door and into the room where Theresa had gone in her anguish. Theresa screamed again, ran out of the room and into her mother who had recovered remarkably quickly and was in hot pursuit of the Brothers Grim. As Theresa and Magrit collided just outside of the room, they heard the door slam shut and the sound of a chair being wedged against it.

Magrit pushed fruitlessly against the door. 'Open this door. Do you hear me? Open this door till I batter youse!'

Tim and Frankie's streetwise sense of self-preservation made them decide against this option. 'It wasnae us – it was her, Ma,' Tim pleaded in mitigation, from behind the door.

'Tim's right, Ma,' Frankie added, as the chief witness for the defence.

Magrit had neither the time nor the patience to continue this childish argument so, with a cursory kick at the door to shut them up, she issued her judgement on the case in question. 'Right, I'm goin' tae ma work. See when I get back, you two are getting sore airses and then straight into bed – that's the pair o' youse for the night! I mean it.'

With cries of 'But, Ma . . . honest . . . we did nothin'' ringing in her ears, Magrit left the lobby and entered the kitchen where Theresa was kneeling in front of the fire, sniffling and feeling sorry for herself, as she wiped tears away with the back of her hands.

Theresa looked up at her with eyes that registered the deep unhappiness she was going through and stifled a sob. Magrit consoled her as best as she knew how. 'Right, get dressed and stop snivelling.'

Theresa shuddered and gave a tiny gasp that she hoped would convey the dreadful hopelessness of her plight. 'I feel as if I've nae privacy in this hoose,' she snuffled. 'Everybody just loves tae stare at me.'

Magrit put her coat on and buttoned it up as protection against the coming cold blast of winter. 'Well, you're wrong there,' she intoned as she looked for her message bag. 'I'm sick lookin' at you.' She spied the bag behind a chair. 'I'm away tae my work. I'll be back up aboot eleven o'clock. You can put the kettle on for me – I'll need a cup o' tea.' As she left the kitchen, she also left Theresa with the comforting words, 'Never mind they two. It's no' their fault – they're trainin' tae be men.'

EIGHT

Harry Culfeathers sat half upright in his bed. His pyjama jacket was opened and he was sweating with the effort of a recent coughing fit. His arms lay spreadeagled by his sides where they had collapsed, all strength having left them, Only an involuntary twitch of his left pinkie gave any sign of energy.

Mary looked on helplessly as she sat at the side of the bed. 'Maybe you should take more o' that bottle the doctor gave you?' was the best she could offer in the way of aid.

'Aye, maybe,' was the best Harry could muster as an acknowledgement of her effort.

'Will I get it for you?' Mary persisted.

'Naw, it's bloody useless. I'm all right.' Harry's whole being gave lie to his statement as he lay there, mouth open and chest heaving up and down at double the speed it should be.

Mary nodded in resignation that there was little she could do to alleviate her husband's plight. 'OK. Drink your tea then.'

Harry snatched for a deep breath, then looked round his surroundings. 'What tea?'

Mary surveyed the same surroundings. 'Did I no' bring in your tea? See my memory, it's gettin' worse,' she said, despairingly, and made to rise from the bedside.

Harry's voice stopped her. 'It doesnae matter. What time is it?'

Mary looked over to the mantelpiece where the clock that

48

they had been given as a wedding present still ticked accurately in testament to the Swiss craftsmen who had made it. 'It's nearly ten.'

Harry gave no sign that he had heard and Mary knew that he didn't really care what the time was – it was merely a question to bridge a moment.

They both sat in silence.

'Nae letters or cards, I take it?' Harry intoned without any real expectation of a reply in the affirmative.

'The lassie McCartney handed in a Christmas card. She said she forgot to give us it at Christmas.'

'Oh. Did we gie her one?'

'Aye.'

'She's a nice lassie.'

'Aye, she is.'

'Nothin' from . . . the boys, though?'

Mary tried to sound casual. 'No. They've probably just been too busy – I think it gets very busy in London . . . at this time o' the year.'

Mary could hear the sound of Harry's teeth grinding. 'Oh. They're obviously busy – too busy tae send a bloody Christmas card tae their mother and faither – ungrateful bastards.'

Mary fought back the feeling of helplessness that made her want to find relief by bursting into tears. She took a deep breath and laid her hand on Harry's arm. 'Harry . . . don't . . . don't get angry . . . please.'

'I just don't understand it. We did everything for them boys. Then they grow up . . . leave home . . . and just . . . drop you! That's it, isn't it? You've served your bloody purpose . . . noo, don't annoy us . . . we've got better things tae dae than . . . than be bothered . . . wi' . . .'

Mary was losing the battle. She turned her face away from him. 'Harry . . . please . . . stop.'

49

Harry stared into space, his anger having given way to perplexity.

Mary patted his arm, as she would a child. 'I'll get you another cup o' tea.' She looked round. 'Where's your cup? Where did you put your cup, Harry?'

Harry continued staring into space. 'Maybe they'll turn up . . . unexpected . . . as a . . . kind o' . . . surprise.'

Mary continued to look for the cup.

NINE

Doreen Hood entered Mario Francini's, the acknowledged best hairdresser in the district. In fact, Francini's was so far ahead of the other hairdressers in the vicinity that it was called a salon – SALON FRANCINI, read the sign above the door. This was *the* place to be seen if you were below thirty. It was as near to Hollywood glamour as Glasgow got. Indeed, on the walls were actual photographs of Mario alongside stars like Rita Hayworth, Betty Grable, etc. With a bit of luck, you might even get Mario himself to do your hair and then he would regale you with stories of what the stars had confided in him as he coiffed their coiffures. Of course, what they did not know was that Mario had simply joined a long list of people who had paid to get their photographs taken with a film star. Doreen paused a little before she entered, ostensibly to check the contents of her handbag but, in reality, to let people see that she got her hair done in Francini's. She turned round just as Mario himself opened the door and ushered her in. She loved the fact that Mario said, loud enough for people to hear, 'Mrs Hood, a pleasure to welcome you again. May I take your coat?'

Doreen preened for a second or two at the entrance in the hope that she would be noticed by a few more passers-by before entering. As Mario helped her to remove her coat, she explained perhaps a little too eagerly for one who was trying to exude sophistication, 'I'd like a bubble cut, Mario.' As she handed Mario her coat, her eyes shone with the hope and expectation of someone who knows they have successfully followed the tramlines laid down by her parents as the way to live your life – tramlines that guarantee you will end up at the terminus of the good life.

Meanwhile, Magrit was outside the shop front of Wallis's Fashions. Another place that was only for those and such as those, it had been named after the American fashion icon Mrs Wallis Simpson who had caused Edward VIII to abdicate (although he was never crowned king due to the fact that Mrs Simpson was divorced). Magrit also paused at the entrance. Like Doreen, the owner of the shop came to the front door to meet her. Unlike Doreen, she was greeted curtly and then given the keys to the back shop where she could collect a bucket and mop to clean the floors with. As Magrit took the keys, her eyes did not shine – but they had . . . once upon a time.

Theresa McGuire was with her best friend Rena, standing at the corner of Dander Street and Dyke Mains Cross. Dander Street was about half a mile long and eventually led down to the dockside. This corner was the gathering place for all the pubescent pretenders to adulthood. Theresa and Rena were relishing the fact that they were on holiday and there was no school to go to. This meant that they did not have to wear their school stuff. They were, of course, not at a school that demanded a uniform but they did have clothes that definitely said 'THIS GIRL IS STILL AT SCHOOL' and today they did not have to wear those. Both girls were bedecked with white ankle socks and white sandals and flared skirts, topped off with mandarin collared blouses. They stood chatting, their feet freezing and their faces blue with the cold, but that was a small price to pay for the opportunity to show off to the boys who were also standing around in their baseball boots, fourteen-inch drainpipe denim trousers and open-neck shirts. Like the girls they were also freezing but the banter and jousting as they showed off to the girls, who stood to the side and pretended they were not interested, made it well worthwhile. Also it did not cost any money and, as none of the participants had any, this made it the best game in town. Rena imagined that one of the lads, who the girls all gave the ultimate accolade of the name 'Fine Boy' to, was giving her the eye. When it turned out that the reason for his constant winking was a nasty sty, she got peeved and suggested to Theresa that they go up to her house and listen to Johnnie Ray instead of, as she put it, 'Hanging about with that lot.'

Dolly Johnson had still not made it back to her house and was talking to her eleventh crony-come-confidant since leaving Wilson's the grocer. The conversations were all about the same subjects and were liberally peppered with phrases such as 'Is that right?', 'So I heard', 'You never know the minute', 'As true as I am staunin' here', 'Och well', 'I'll need tae go', 'Me as well', 'Before you go', 'Did you hear', 'Is that right?', etc, etc.

TEN

While this was going on Peter McGuire was having his ears assaulted by noises of another sort, namely the ear-splitting rattling of riveting guns on countless rivets, that pinged and rang as they were thrown from one side to the other of the ship's slowly-forming bulkhead. Welders' rods were fizzing, their blinding arc lights sparking with a blue brilliance and then dying in a shower of dead embers that mimicked stars in the firmament as they worked their way along the seams of the embryonic vessel. The acrid smell of burners, gas guns, heating and bending metal hung in the cold air as the tradesmen of the boilermakers union did their stuff and forged flesh on to the skeleton of the emerging ship. Peter could not have been in a worse place with a hangover. His head felt as if it had a hundred wee motor cars, without drivers, all running about and banging into each other. He had to escape before the top of his head blew off. He signalled to his gaffer that he needed a crap and was going to the outside toilet that was situated behind the enormous shed that fed the materials to the ship in waiting. The gaffer nodded and gave him the thumbs up, accompanied by his index finger pointing to his watch to signify that he would be timing Peter's crap. Grasping hold of a rung, he climbed the ladder that led to the top of the particular hold that he was about to desert from. After about sixty-odd feet, he reached the top at last and felt his head clear slightly for the first time that day. It wasn't much of an improvement but it was a definite one. As he shook his head, vainly trying to clear it further, Archie Watson, another gaffer who was affectionately nicknamed 'Batchy' (meaning nutter), was walking along the top gantry. Before Batchy could question what he was up to Peter explained he was going for a crap. Batchy just sniffed and pointed at his watch. 'Must be a sale on of crap watches,' Peter thought to himself as he made towards the vicinity of the toilet. When the toilet hove into view, Peter saw there was no one around and it entered his head that, if he skipped behind the building, there was a large wall. This wall was the only thing that separated him from the outside world and, if he climbed over this wall, he could swap the horrendous noise of work for the happy noise of a pub. There was no contest.

Entering the Bay Horse was like entering the gates of heaven. He checked to see what spondulix were available and was relieved to find the pound note that John Hood had given him still nestling cosily in his trouser pocket. As he settled at a corner of the large polished mahogany horseshoe-shaped bar, the barman approached wiping a pint glass dry. 'What would you like?' he asked, smiling at Peter.

'If you can swally it, I'll like it,' Peter replied. 'Half o' Bell's and a chaser and ten Capstan. That should do the trick.'

'Comin' up,' the barman replied. He passed Peter the cigarettes from a display cabinet behind the counter and then selected a whisky glass and placed it below the optic that contained the golden elixir that was about to find its spiritual home at the back of Peter McGuire's parched throat. 'That you finished for the day?' he enquired, handing over the whisky.

Peter took a loving look at the wee goldie and nodded. 'Eh! Probably – in fact, aye it is.'

'I thought it might be your tea break,' the barman ventured as he poured a beer from the pump into a small glass as a chaser.

'If it is, it's fuckin' great tea your servin'.' He sank the whisky in one and felt its fiery glow send warmth all over his aching head and body. Rot gave way to rapture as the world started to swing his way again. He smiled. 'Gie's another cup.'

Magrit collected her wages from Simpson's. The manageress had put an extra five shillings in as a New Year bonus, which went down very well with Magrit. She took the offering with a nod of thanks, placed it into her purse and, wishing all in the shop a happy New Year, she put her coat on and hurried off to her next assignment.

Peter had been joined by more sufferers of upset-stomach syndrome in the pub and was indulging in a New Year bonus of his own. They were regaling the tale of how a squad of them had been sent off to the shipyard's vast store about a mile away. This enormous space held most of the iron that had rusted or proved faulty in some way and was to be sold on by the company for scrap at a suitable date. There had been a lean spell in the industry and Peter and a dozen others had been sent to fill in their time by organising this metal into some form of order and also to make a list of all the scrap that was available for selling on.

Of course, when they got there and surveyed the vast quantity of scrap lying around, it did not take too long before someone came up with the idea that a lorry load of it would not be missed. This was such an obvious statement of fact that, in due course, a truck was waved down and a deal done with the driver on an equal split, thirteen ways.

There is a theory that you will work far harder for yourself than for an employer due to the fact that you reap the rewards for your own efforts. Indeed, Karl Marx founded his philosophy of communism on this very premise.

None of the squad had ever read *Das Kapital* but Karl would have been proud of Peter and his twelve apostles as they manhandled rusting hulks of varying shapes from anchors, anchor chains, bulkhead plates, etc., weighing a ton and over, up and on to the back of the truck. When the driver was despatched with a trusted member of the squad to the nearest scrappy, it became obvious to the remainder looking around that the lorry load had made no significant difference to the naked eye that anything was missing. So, they reasoned, why not another lorry-load?

A roar of laughter went up as Peter relived the moment with a few of his fellow communists. While they were sharing the experience with their audience, one of them announced, 'My round. What are youse wantin'?' to cries of 'OK – but my shout next time!' and 'What happened then?'. They gave their order and then settled for part two of Peter's party piece.

Magrit wiped a bead of sweat from above her eye and plunged a scrubbing brush into the bucket of hot water she was using to scrub down the stairs of Collins, Young and Hunter, Solicitors at Law, who shared three flights with a similar bunch of barristers, all of whom employed the services of Magrit McGuire, Cleaner at Large, to ensure that at least one part of their business was not stained. She adjusted the mat she was kneeling on and wondered what the time was.

'Anyway, wan thing led to another and, before we knew it, we had emptied the place.' Peter guffawed into a fresh pint which had just been placed at his disposal (and Peter was the very man to dispose of it). Another of the partners in pilfering chipped in with his own memory of the event. 'No' so much as would have made the wife a wee bangle left. Mind you we were aw loaded so we could, at a pinch, have bought her wan – as it happened none o' us did.'

'Fuck me, we put away some drink though, eh!' remembered another.

'Anyway,' continued Peter, 'this was on the Thursday night and we'd tae go in for oor wages the next day. We were shittin' oorselves because we knew that the gaffer was comin' doon that night tae see how we had got on wi' squarin' the place up. And he couldnae help but notice that the place was emptier than Partick Thistle's trophy room.'

'We'll win somethin' this year,' said a Thistle fan, which made the collective collapse with laughter at the absurdity of the statement. 'You just wait,' said the Jags supporter, trying to ignore the peals of laughter that were erupting all around him.

'What happened when they found oot? Did youse get done?'

'Well! I'll tell youse but first let me get some bevvy in – 'cause it's my shout.' Peter stood up and rummled about in his pocket, alas to no effect. 'I'll need tae chuck it 'cause I'm boracic and I'm no' poncin' drink if I cannae stand my round.'

He turned to leave but was halted by shouts of 'You're awright.' 'Here's five bob.' 'Get oan wi' the story', etc.

Peter nodded and accepted the taps. 'I'll pay youse back when I get my wages at dinner time. I might be a lot o' things but I'm no' a ponce, ye know?' As they slapped his back he sank back into his seat and called the barman over to place his order.

Magrit collected her money from Mr Hunter, of Collins, Young and Hunter, and noted there was no New Year bonus. 'Miserable shower,' was her thought as she returned his wishes for a happy New Year. She noted from the clock in the office that it was leaving half past eleven. 'Where does the time go?' She complained to herself as she hurried down the stairs and out of the entrance into the rain.

Peter glanced up at the wag-on-the-wall clock which as well as telling you the time also managed to advertise the message that Guinness was good for you, without reference to the perhaps more truthful message that you were even more good for Guinness. 'Is that all the time it is? We've another hour yet before we need tae get back and pick up the wages.' He finished off one pint just as the barman set down another. 'So, as I was sayin', we were all crappin' oorselves 'cause they were gonnae inspect the place later on.' He paused while he took a long pull at the fresh pint, then, in a sure sign that he was not yet drunk, wiped the froth from his top lip. 'See when I sobered up and went hame I couldnae sleep the whole night.' There was a murmur of understanding from the rest. 'The next mornin', we were all up the back keepin' oot the road and wonderin' what was gonnae happen. About quarter o' an hour had passed and then we see Harry Carr – he was the gaffer oan the job – makin' his way towards us. He comes up and staunds in front o' us. "Youse are no' goin oot this mornin," he says. "The polis want tae talk tae youse," he says. We never says nothing. "Youse made a right airse o' that yesterday – upstairs are goin' mental. I got earache fae them oan the phone there. So who was responsible?" We still never says a word. "The place has been gutted – there's nothin' left. The polis know who done it so youse might as well own up. Which o' youse was supposed tae lock up?" he says.

It was Tommy Wearston, God rest his soul, that eventually says, "What do you mean lock up, Harry?" Harry looks at big Tommy as if he was stupid.

"I mean fuckin' lock up – shut the fuckin' gate – close the

fuckin' door. It's a concept even your fuckin' brain should be able to figure oot. Youse never shut the fuckin' gate when youse left, did youse? The place was open aw night and somebody ransacked it, stole the whole fuckin' kit and caboodle, di'n't they? Fortunately the polis have caught them, otherwise you lot were for the high fuckin' jump."'

'I don't understand . . . What happened?' piped up the Thistle fan.

'Well,' Peter continued, 'We were so oot o' oor skulls that the last thing any o' us thought aboot was lockin' the place up. We'd just left it open – which turned oot to be a shrewd oversight on oor part. What happened was that, after we left, a rag and bone man and his son were passin' by the place oan their wee cart which was bein' pulled by a horse. They saw the place open, swung the horse and cart inside and flung oan the odd wee bit o' metal that we had left. As they were leavin', a polis motor happened tae be passin' by, doin' their rounds, and stopped them. They've been caught bang tae rights, haven't they?'

'Did they get done for the lot?' asked someone in disbelief.

'Aye. No' only did they cop it for the total blag, they also got done for cruelty tae the horse.' Howls of laughter greeted this statement of injustice. 'When your luck's oot, it's fuckin' oot all right!' was the general consensus of the moral of the story. Such was the warmth of the mood in the pub that the barman wiped the tears from his eyes and then announced that the next round was on him.

Magrit weaved her way through the wind and rain towards her house. She was conscious that the two boys would be needing something to eat before she set off for her next cleaning job. The cold wetness of the day was beginning to get into her bones. Her only consolation was that Peter would be suffering more than she would because of his hangover. 'Serves him right,' she thought as she waited for a tramcar to pass before crossing to the other side of the street. 'I'll get them some rolls oot o' Wilson's,' she decided. 'Maybe put some cheese in them. That should dae them.'

Peters' eyes were starting to go out of focus as he sat staring at Wullie McPhee, one of his pals, who was explaining his philosophy of . . . Peter was not quite sure of what. Neither were any of the others but they were all agreeing with the theory being put to them by Wullie – whatever it was.

Wullie waved a hand in front of them as if trying to capture an imaginary fly as he pressed home his theory. 'Because . . . that's . . . that's . . .' He struggled for the exact word or phrase that would sum up whatever he thought he was talking about. 'That's . . .' He searched through the alcoholic fog that was surrounding his thoughts and his hands were now mimicking washing an imaginary window. 'That's . . . that's . . .' Then the word that he had been searching for jumped into his brain. 'That's . . . RIGHT . . . right? Am I right? . . . Am I wrong? . . . Right.'

'You're right . . . right enough . . .' agreed another student of life.

'You're are dead right,' was Peter's verdict.

'Fuckin' right – I'm right. You better believe it,' Wullie stated, resting the case for the defence.

A hand was placed on his shoulder and then it patted him on the back. 'That needed sayin', by the way,' was the verdict of the owner of the hand.

'Fuckin' right it did,' Peter said in a slurring-his-speech sort of way.

Then, changing the subject, he informed the company, 'I'm gonnae tell youse somethin', right – see my wife, she doesnae know what I'm aboot. She just . . . doesnae understand me . . . or what I'm tryin' tae achieve in my life.'

'Mine's neither.'

'They're aw the fuckin' same,' agreed the gathering.

Magrit hauled herself up the last flight of stairs before reaching her landing. She searched in her bag for the keys. The largest of them, known as the big key for obvious reasons, was under her purse, which was buried at the bottom of the bag under a mountain of other domestic detritus for safety reasons. However, try as she might, she could not lay her hands on it. 'Where the hell is it?' Magrit muttered to herself. Recently, she had noticed that she frequently talked to herself – it didn't worry her as she reasoned she was the only one she ever got any sense out of. With a sigh of satisfaction, she found the key and fitted it into the lock. She always locked the door – not so much to keep burglars out as to keep Tim and Frankie in. As she shut the door behind her she noticed with no small degree of relief that there was no noise of fighting from the kitchen.

'Is that you, Ma?' Frankie's high-pitched boyish voice found its way round the door to her ears.

'Naw, it's Ava Gardner. Your ma asked me to look in and see if youse were a'right.'

Magrit saw at a glance as she entered the kitchen that both of them were still in their vests and pants and socks, sitting up in the bed. Tim was reading about Jeff Arnold and the 'Riders of the Range' in the Christmas edition of the *Eagle* comic while Frankie was lost in the exploits of Dixon Hawke and the Black Slink in the *Adventure*.

'Dear God, are youse no' up yet? Get up and get dressed,' she commanded as she took the rolls and cheese from her message bag.

'Gonnae gie us somethin' to eat? We're starvin'.' Tim replied without taking his eyes off the page.

'What d'youse want, well?' she asked as she took her coat off and filled the kettle from the cold water tap. There wasn't a hot water tap and this was a thing that Magrit desired with all her heart. It would have been heaven to have hot water on tap. She was saving up for a gadget that you had connected up to the gas and it gave you hot water whenever you needed it. 'Luxury,' thought Magrit. There was no reply to her question from the poor and hungry who were still engrossed in their comics. 'I asked you what do youse want tae eat?'

'Anything at all,' said Frankie. Tim's head nodded up and down in acquiescence – it saved him having to talk.

'Do youse want a cheese roll?'

'Naw,' said Frankie. Tim just shook his head negatively.

'D'you want some o' that soup, well?'

'Naw,' Frankie informed her, as Tim's head continued shaking.

'A piece in Spam? . . . A roll in jam?'

'Naw.'

'Well, what *do* youse want?' Magrit shouted in exasperation.

'Anything at all,' they said.

Magrit lit the gas and planked the kettle on it.

'Get thae dirty things aff and get your clothes on. Put them on that pile in the tin bath. I'm goin' to the steamie thenight and I'll no' have time tae play hunt the sweaty socks – do youse hear me?' she roared at them.

'Aye,' Tim nodded, still deep in the dangers that Jeff and the Riders of the Range were facing – which were not nearly so dangerous as those he was facing if he did not put the comic down. When the comic was suddenly swept from his hands and propelled across the room, he looked at his mother in genuine shock.

'What have I done noo?' he asked, his face registering mystification as Magrit stormed out of the kitchen and into the bedroom where the tin bath lay in wait.

Frankie shrugged his shoulders and tapped the side of his head with his index finger to signal that his mother was losing her mind.

'Gie's a page o' your comic, eh?' pleaded Tim, now at a loss as to what to do with the remainder of his life.

'Naw,' was Frankie's sympathetic response. Tim grabbed for the comic and Frankie shouted frantically at the woman who was losing her mind. 'Ma, he's tryin' tae steal my comic.'

'Wee clipe,' hissed Tim, pulling at Frankie's comic with one hand and at the same time nipping him on the leg with the other.

'He nipped me, Ma,' Frankie shouted through to the mad woman.

'Naw, I never,' Tim shouted at Frankie.

'Aye, you did,' screamed Frankie at Tim.

'Shut it or I'll belt you,' threatened Tim to his brother.

'I'd be as well talking to myself,' muttered Magrit – to herself.

ELEVEN

Theresa and Rena were in Rena's bedroom. Theresa thought that Rena was the height of sophistication because she had her own room and someday, Theresa vowed, she would have her own room as well. However, that was in the future. At the moment she and Rena sat on Rena's bed, both of them weeping their hearts out. The reason for their outpouring of grief was that they were listening to Johnnie Ray singing his hit song 'Cry'. As Johnnie sobbed his way through the heartache of his life, it was as if he were singing to each of the girls personally. His words of woe rang incredibly true and cut deep into their psyche, uniting them in their grief. Theresa clutched a magazine that had a photograph of Johnnie on its front tightly to her chest. Rena dabbed at her eyes with a hankie and both of them sniffled and gulped greedily at their grief as if it was food.

> If your heartaches seem to hang around too long
> And your blues keep getting bluer with each song

Johnnie wailed rhythmically, each word building towards his final absolute anguish as the swell of the orchestra dug further into their private selves with the expertise and precision of a surgeon's scalpel.

Remember sunshine can be found behind cloudy sky

His voice sang softly, before pausing dramatically while a solitary violin pierced their hearts with a soulful minor chord. Pushing them to the limit with this, he then sent them into the depths of despair as he finished his plea to the sufferers of the teenage world by imploring them to 'Let your hair down . . . and go on and cry-y-y-y-y-y-y-y'. Theresa and Rena did not let him down.

Through her tears Rena pronounced, 'Oh, Johnnie – I love you.'

Theresa wallowing in the moment confessed, 'I love you too, Johnnie.'

'Will I play it again?' Rena asked.

Theresa smiled tragically, 'Please . . . aye.'

Rena got off the bed and crossed to the Dansette record player that sat on top of her sideboard and reset the record. The record player was another thing for Theresa to covet about Rena's lifestyle.

Rena settled herself beside her friend on the bed and they both listened with tense expectation as the dry hissing sound from the Dansette announced that the record was spinning and soon Johnnie would be massaging their tear ducts with his music.

If your sweetheart sends a letter of goodbye,
It's no secret you'll feel better if you cry

He crooned as he continued down Lamentation Lane.

Rena's mother Betty Reilly's voice cut through their sobbing.

'Rena – turn that off – I'm sick listenin' to it.'

'In a minute,' Rena shouted back.

Johnnie continued relentlessly in his quest to have the girls on their knees with distress.

If your heartaches seem to hang around too long

Betty flung the door of her daughter's room open.

'For God's sake – can you no' play somethin' else? My ears are bleedin' listening to it. What the hell are youse bubblin' aboot?' she asked, her face a study of incomprehension.

Rena, her voice echoing her feeling of being alone in the world, replied, 'It doesn't matter – you wouldnae understand.'

Betty surveyed the scene. 'I understand – of course I understand – I was young once as well. I know you'll no' believe it but I was – and I understand how music can get to a young lassie . . . it's just . . . it's just that . . . well . . . he's rotten.'

Rena's mother's heresy rang in the girls' ears as she left the room. Rushing over to the door, Rena wedged her shoulder against it in a poignant gesture she had seen Barbara Stanwyck apply in almost every film she had ever done. With one hand on the door handle and the other clutching at the frame, she pressed her back against the door and wailed, 'See what I've got to put up wi'!'

'It's the same in oor hoose,' Theresa consoled. Then, after a pause, she added in a voice that was heavy with innuendo, 'Do they . . . stare at you all the time as well?'

Not to be outdone in the paranoia of being picked upon, Rena nodded her head. ' Aye . . . constantly,' she lied. Theresa gave a sigh of relief that she was not the only one to be constantly under scrutiny for the crime of being a teenage girl. Rena sighed back in what she hoped sounded like the sympathetic tone of a fellow soul in torment. She crossed over and sat next to her pal. They sat in silence, each of them bound up in a maze of doubt and confusion. Theresa placed her hand over her friend's and, in a gesture of companionship, gave it a squeeze.

'At least you've got a room tae yourself – somewhere to get away from them all,' she offered, not realising that this was placing the onus on her friend to come up with something that suggested she was just as unjustly treated as Theresa was.

'I know . . . but . . .' She tried to think of something that would put her on an even keel with Theresa. 'But . . .'

Theresa stared at her waiting to be updated on the next injustice visited on Rena by her family. She could not imagine what Rena was going to come out with. Not wanting to put pressure on her pal by asking outright, she just continued to stare at her. Rena could not for the life of her think what to come up with as a new complaint in the litany of imagined shabby treatment by her parents. 'They . . . they . . . they . . . listen to me,' she gasped, grasping at a passing straw in her brain.

'They do not, do they?' Theresa gasped in horror.

'Aye, through the door. I've caught them at it.' Rena's head was nodding intently as she tried to say this with such conviction that she would convince herself that it was true and, in a split second, she had.

Both girls lapsed into silence again. Theresa gazed into Johnnie Ray's blue eyes on the front of the movie magazine while Rena stared at a photograph she had been sent by the Johnnie Ray fan club.

'Do you think if we wrote tae Johnnie Ray and explained what we had to put up wi', he would take us oot tae America with him?' Theresa asked, her eyes full of hope at the prospect.

'He might,' Rena responded quickly. Then, reason triumphing over optimism, she flung herself back on the bed and lay staring at the ceiling as she dismissed the suggestion.

'Naw – that's stupid. He probably gets thousands o' lassies writing to him – he couldnae take them all oot tae America.'

'It's worth a try,' Theresa said in defence of her idea as she drew her knees up to her chin and, folding her arms around her legs, rested her head on her knees. 'Mebbe.'

Rena shrugged her shoulders in a sign that she was no longer enthusiastic.

They both drifted back to their secret thoughts and stared at the ceiling and the wall respectively.

Suddenly Rena jumped up from her prone position and announced excitedly, 'Wait till you see what I got.' She rushed over to a set of drawers and opened one. After a brief rummage around, she finally withdrew what she had been searching for and held it aloft. It was a postcard. She danced over the floor to the bed and deposited it at Theresa's feet. 'Look,' she said, her eyes alive with the thrill of the moment.

Theresa picked up the postcard and looked at the front of it. It was a night-time scene. There was a depiction of the Statue of Liberty with a ship passing beneath it and an aeroplane flying just above it.

'It's New York, so it is,' Rena announced.

'So it is.' Theresa gazed rapturously at the depiction of all her girlish fantasies. 'Is it real? I mean is it actually fae New York? Who sent you it?' The questions tumbled from her lips like rain in a thunder burst.

'Aye, it's genuine. My cousin sent me it – she works on a big ship – a liner it's called.'

'Is that it on the postcard?'

'Naw, that's just some ship they've stuck on tae let you see how big the Statue o' Liberty is.'

Theresa could not believe she was actually holding a postcard that had, at one time, actually been held by someone in New York. It somehow drew her nearer to her dream and

69

seemed to offer hope that, one day, she would actually get to the land where film stars and famous singers walked about the streets.

'What does your cousin do on the ship?' she asked.

'She's a stewardess,' Rena informed her.

'What's that?'

'I think it's like a waitress – like in a restaurant, except more important. Know what I mean?'

Theresa nodded her head in understanding.

Rena continued with the lesson, 'And, because it's more important than a waitress, you have to be called a stewardess – you know?' Theresa nodded again. Rena took the postcard from Theresa's grasp and held it up to the light. 'I've put wee holes in the side o' the ship wi' a pin. If you hold the card up to the light like this and look through it, it's as if there was lights shining through the portholes. See?'

She passed the card over to Theresa so she could study this example of Rena's ingenuity. Theresa studied the postcard and imagined herself sailing on the high seas in a similar ship. The lights coming through the pinholes seemed to draw her inside the ship and she could almost hear the sound of laughter and music coming from the dance floor.

'That's what I'm gonnae do – travel the world,' she announced. Her mouth set in resolution.

'Me as well,' Rena avowed. 'My cousin says she's gonnae speak for me to her boss, like, you know?'

Theresa fixed Rena with a look that spoke volumes about her intent to escape from the drudgery of Glasgow. 'Would she speak for me as well?'

This took Rena aback somewhat. She was not sure that she wanted Theresa to be on the same level of glamour as she would be if they both went stewardessing. 'I don't know – naw,' she announced defensively.

'How no'?' Theresa said, injured by the unexpectedly terse reply from her dearest and only real friend.

Rena was at a complete loss to answer this. How could she say to her dearest and only real friend in the whole world that she really did not, in her heart of hearts, want her to be as glamorous or as important as her? She struggled again for an explanation as to how she could not plead Theresa's case to her cousin. The answer came at last. ''Cause I'll no' see her to ask her, will I? She's on a boat, isn't she?' She noticed that Theresa was close to tears with the frustration of not being allowed to be a stewardess. 'But,' she continued with more assurance now that she had the upper hand in the relationship, 'when I get started – once I'm established, like – I'll speak for you.'

Theresa buried her face in a pillow. ' That'll be years away. I'll be an auld woman by then.'

Rena touched her friend's hair gently and said sadly, in full Barbara Stanwyck mode, 'I'm sorry. It's the best I can do.'

Theresa sat up and, resting on an elbow, turned her face eagerly towards her friend. 'Could I no' write to the ship personally?'

This blew Rena from Barbara Stanwyck mode to somewhere between Bette Davis and Joan Crawford. 'Naw,' she said, not very helpfully. 'It goes all over the world, you see. Your letter could be years tryin' tae catch up wi' it. Anyway, they'd probably ask if you had experience of stewardessing . . . and . . . you havnae . . . so they wouldnae give you a job.'

'You havnae got experience either,' was Theresa's logical thrust back.

'But I've got a cousin, haven't I?' Rena countered.

'Well, how am I going to get experience?' Theresa threw her hands in the air and bit the side of her lip in exasperation.

Rena nodded her head sagely at the immensity of the problem, secretly glad that she was not Theresa. She was now heading for Barbara Stanwyck again. She wished she could smoke as she could just imagine Barbara wrestling with this problem, striding over to the bar that all Americans had inside their house, pouring herself a drink and then lighting a cigarette and blowing out the smoke as she said, 'I don't know, honey – maybe you'll just have to start on wee boats and work your way up. There's boats doon at the dockside – we could go doon there and ask . . . perhaps.'

'You called me "honey",' said Theresa suspiciously.

Rena shook her head. 'Look, do you want to go doon to the docks or no'?'

'To find oot who tae write tae like?' Theresa said, hope starting to loom in her brain again.

'I suppose so,' Rena shrugged.

'Would you come doon wi' me?'

Rena started to get worried. Theresa was obviously getting serious about this.

'I don't like the docks – they're dead smelly,' Rena said.

Theresa's look, showed that she felt totally betrayed by her only friend.

Barbara Stanwyck took a deep breath and then said, 'Awright.'

'Brilliant. Come on, we'll go the noo,' exploded Theresa, jumping from the bed and racing across the room to put her coat on. 'They'll maybe be startin' waitresses – I mean stewardesses – for the New Year.'

Rena couldn't believe her ears. 'What are you talkin' aboot? You're still at school. You're too young tae be a stewardess.'

'I'm nearly fourteen.'

'Naw, you're no'. You've just turned thirteen. It'll be two years before you can start stewardessing – on wee boats – and at least another two years before they would let you near a liner.'

Theresa sank to the floor with despair. 'I cannae stay in that hoose another two years. I'll kill at least one o' my wee brothers.'

Rena sat down by her best friend and put her arms around her. 'Well you'll just have to. You're too young.'

Theresa started to sob into her sleeve. 'I hate being young. I just hate it.'

TWELVE

Mary Culfeathers sat at the dining room table. The table was oak and had been given to her by Harry's parents, along with six chairs, as a wedding present. It was polished once a week and had a dark red chenille table cover over it to keep it from spills. These days it was very seldom used but Mary polished it anyway. On top of the tablecloth was a Christmas card and two envelopes. Mary brushed back a strand of hair that had fallen over the lens of her spectacles as she read over a second Christmas card. It said, in a hastily written scrawl:

Dear Mum and Dad Hope this card reaches you in time. I've been very busy. Helen and the children are fine and we're hoping to get up to see you soon.
Merry Christmas
Your loving son.

Mary took up the pen that was lying on the table and wrote 'Alan' at the bottom of the card.

She put the card in one of the envelopes, licked the gum and sealed it. She picked up the other card, reread it for mistakes and then placed it in the other envelope and sealed it as well. With a sigh of satisfaction, she rose up from the table and crossed the room. At the door to the hall she took her shoes off and padded silently to the front door. Lifting the flap of the letterbox, she let it clang shut and then dropped the two envelopes on to the linoleum that covered the hall floor. As quickly as she could she padded back into the dining room. Just as she reached the door she heard Harry shout, 'That's the front door, Mary. Will I get it?'

'It's alright – I'll get it,' she shouted back as she slipped on her shoes. She returned to the front door and picked up the two envelopes. Trying her best not to sound suspicious she called out, 'It's the postman – a couple o' letters or cards maybe.'

She paused as she collected her thoughts on how to respond when Harry shouted back, 'Maybe they're from the boys?'

She gathered herself and tried to look and sound non-committal as she entered the kitchen and crossed to the bed where Harry was raising himself into a sitting position. 'You open them up. I'm tidyin' up in the dining room,' she said, leaving the envelopes on top of the bedspread. Harry nodded and looked around him.

'Where's my glasses? Have you seen them?'

Mary turned back and shrugged her shoulders. 'I don't know where they are. You're always losing them. I've told you, you should tie them on a string round your neck, then you'll aye know where they are.'

Harry snorted back, 'I'd look like an auld man – it's alright, I've found them,' he called out to her as she left the kitchen and made her way across the hall. She stopped just inside the dining room and listened for a reaction from Harry.

Harry's voice rumbled disgruntledly as he tried to open the envelopes, 'Bloody stuck wi' cement these things.' She heard him mutter, 'It's a couple o' cards. Christmas cards.'

'Oh. Who from?' Mary did her best at feigning innocence, as she answered back. She was not used to deception and knew she could easily blow the whole charade.

She let out a silent sigh of relief as Harry called out, 'Aye.

They're from Alan and Duncan.'

She could hear him reading the cards. Lately he had taken to reading in a semi-whisper that she found irritating, as it stopped her concentrating on whatever she was doing, but this time she did not mind as it served as a pointer of how her plan was progressing. 'They're from the boys, right enough. Can you hear me?' he called out.

'Aye, I'm just getting ready tae go to the steamie but I'm listening,' she called back, smiling at the success of her duplicity and putting her coat on.

While she got her bag out and loaded it with bars of soap, a scrubbing brush, a black rubber apron and other tools of the washhouse, Harry continued to enlighten her as to the contents of the cards. 'They were busy right enough – they're gonnae try and come up and visit us soon, though.' He was still scanning the cards when Mary entered the kitchen.

He held out the cards for her to read. 'I'll read them when I get back,' she said. 'Will you be OK?'

Harry nodded, 'Aye, of course I will. How would I no' be? Bloody cards are hell of a late gettin' here – it's bloody New Year's Eve.'

Mary tutted at him, 'Your language is gettin' worse.'

'Well, nae wonder – that's a hell of a time tae take. Oor other cards got here on time.' His eyes narrowed as he scrutinised the cards and then the envelopes. He looked at Mary from beneath his brows and Mary shivered in anticipation of being found out. His voice was undercharged with disappointment as he shook his head forlornly and informed her, 'I know why they're so late – the silly buggers never put stamps on the envelopes.'

Mary allowed herself a small, if somewhat self-satisfied, grin. 'I'll be back aboot half nine – if you're sleepin', will I wake you for the bells?'

Harry was still studying the cards and envelopes. 'Naw – what?'

'I said, will I wake you for the bells?' she reiterated.

'Whit bells is that?'

'It's Hogmanay. We always bring in the New Year wi' a wee whisky at the bells.'

'Oh, aye, and listen for the horns,' Harry replied, searching for something in the bed.'

'What horns? What are you talkin' aboot?'

'The ships' horns. We always open the windows and listen for the ships' horns doon on the river,' he said a bit tetchily.

Mary wondered what he was looking for and was about to ask him when she realised that she had forgotten about the horns. This realisation had the effect of making her forget to ask Harry what he was looking for. 'Of course, the ships' horns – I'd forgot aboot them.' She shook her head from side to side in a gesture of exasperation. 'See my memory, it's getting worse.' She walked back into the dining room. 'There's somethin' I've forgot and I don't know what it was.' She surveyed the dining room for a clue. No luck, she turned back towards the kitchen and studied Harry lying in the set in bed. 'Was it something to do wi' you? Aye, that's it, somethin' I had to ask you aboot.' Harry was still studying the cards. She gazed at him. 'There was somethin' I meant to ask you and it's gone right oot my head. My mother always said my head gives my feet a lot o' work. I didnae know what she meant at the time but I know noo.'

She turned and headed for the outside door. 'Right that's me away – I'll see you when I get back.'

Harry's only response was to growl in irritation, 'You'd think they'd have brains enough to put a bloody stamp on an envelope.'

As the front door slammed shut, he made a mental note to

speak to Alan and Duncan and tell them about their oversight when they arrived. He lifted up the sheets and searched around before yawning. 'They'll turn up sooner or later, I suppose.' He lay back on the raised pillows and shut his eyes. His breath came in short sharp uneasy bursts. His brows furrowed in concentration, then his eyes sprung open and darted about the room. 'I wonder,' he thought to himself. Raising his right hand towards his nose, he felt gingerly with his index finger from the tip up to the bridge, where its progress was halted by his spectacles. 'I thought that's where they would be,' he said smugly – to no one.

THIRTEEN

Magrit had left Tim and Frankie bickering. The shops would all be shut for almost a week over the holiday period. Time was running out and she had to get the groceries in now or she would not get them in at all. Turning into Wilson's, her spirits sank even lower when she saw there was a queue. She would have gone somewhere else but Wilson's allowed her to buy stuff without immediate payment (or 'tick', as it was known), to be settled at the end of the week – and this was the day to settle up. In better-off sections of Glasgow society, this form of shopping was termed 'on account' – however, in the lower orders, it was called 'tick'.

Magrit had not only the previous week's groceries to settle, she would also have to placate Wullie Patterson over the morning milk episode. At this precise moment, she was not in the mood for placating anyone and it was perhaps just as well for Wullie that he had finished his day's graft and gone home.

Doreen Hood paused at the door of Francini's and checked if it was raining. She looked up and noted happily that there was no immediate sign of rain in the unbroken blanket of dull grey overcast Glasgow sky. Although with the help of Mario and a hand held mirror, she had studied her new hairdo from every conceivable angle, she again glanced at herself in the reflection of Francini's side window to check that it still looked as good as it had done two minutes ago. It did indeed still look all that Doreen had hoped it would. She smiled to herself and, despite the chill in the air, she felt a rush of warmth surge through her with the realisation that she was young, married to the best man in the world and looked a million dollars. Buttoning up her coat, she set off for home.

Theresa McGuire stood at the window of Thomas Cook's and stared at the posters advertising the vacations that were on offer. She was searching for anything about cruises. She searched in vain. As she stood there forlornly, she heard a snatch of the conversation Dolly Johnson was having with Agnes Malloch as they passed her by – something about somebody called Gilchrist whose husband had apparently died was all she heard as they sauntered by her.

Mary Culfeathers walked resignedly to the steamie. She had been obliged to take in washing for people in the district as a way of supplementing her income. Harry knew nothing about it of course. She had decided not to tell him as it would only have upset him to think that his wife had been forced to do other folks' washing. Harry was under the impression that she went to the steamie only to do their own washing. He was also under the impression they were still living on their savings. Harry had always insisted that they watched their money and put by a proportion of it for a rainy day. She could of course have applied for what was called 'social security money' but that was not her or Harry's way. They had pride and would never consent to be 'on the parish' as it was called. Mary had no false sense that it was demeaning to take in washing – as far as she was concerned, no work was demeaning. She just felt that Harry need not know about it as it would upset him if he felt that he had failed in some way to provide for her. Beside which, she enjoyed getting out and being among other women – although she did notice, with a tinge of regret, that a lot of the conversation bypassed her and she did not always get the gist of what they were talking about. However, that was a part of being old and there was nothing she could do about that.

The one o'clock hooter bawled out, signalling that the yard had finished for the last time that year. The gates were flung open and the workers poured out of them like a dam that had burst and spilled its contents on to the roadway, turning it almost instantly into a river of human fish. They resembled some kind of rag-tag army because, although it was not planned, they had somehow created a uniform that was endemic to each and every one of them.

Each of them wore flat caps that had become so imbued with oil they were now waterproof. All of their shirts, despite the cold wind, were open necked and encased by equally oil-saturated jackets and broad leather belts that held up their dirty oil-soaked trousers which fell tightly round the top of their steel toe-capped boots. There was a great deal of back slapping and mock punching that led to someone being chased. This led to deft dodging in and out of the throngs that had now swamped the road. Money that had been loaned was being repaid with phrases such as 'Thanks – you saved a life there', and replies of 'Nae bother. You goin' for a bevvy?', 'Aye – bloody right I am', 'I'll stand you a pint', and so on.

If indeed it had been a river, the swell of sound and un-mistakable lust for living would have deemed it an extremely healthy one.

Magrit left Wilson's, her message bags straining with the weight and bulk of groceries that were to last the family for the next week. Her face was fixed in a state of concern, which was due to the fact that, although her message bags were now full, sadly her purse was almost empty. Her face relaxed slightly as she headed for home with the knowledge that Peter would be in with his wages when she got back.

Mary Culfeathers handed over the money for three sessions in the wash house and made her way to stall number fifty-seven. It would be after nine o'clock before she would see the street again.

Doreen heard the doorbell and checked herself out in the mirror. She patted her hair for the umpteenth time before rushing to open the door, eager for John's opinion on her new hairdo. She swung the door open. John stood on the threshold surveyed her hair and said, 'Nice. I like that. It suits you.'

Magrit had just finished putting the groceries away when she heard the door being knocked. 'He's forgot his keys again – thank God that's him back,' she thought, not because she missed him – more because she was glad that she would have some money to see her through the week. She opened the door and Peter fell past her and landed face down on the lobby carpet. Two of his pals, who had helped him up the stairs and were almost as blootered as he was, opened their mouth to say something that would make Magrit laugh with their sparkling wit. They were stopped in their tracks, however, as the crash of the door slamming in their faces drowned out their opening line.

Dolly Johnson was battering her husband's ears with every-thing she had heard that day about Cissie Gilchrist's man, wee pan-loaf Gilchrist, having died as she swept the living room floor. Her husband Boab sat in an armchair, not listening, reading the morning paper and grunting in annoyance when Dolly told him to lift his feet as she swept underneath him.

Mary Culfeathers undid the rope that was tied round her rubber apron as she trudged out to the front door of the wash house. She had finished the first wash that had been left for her attention and was in need of a breather. Mary decided not to go outside and risk catching a chill but just to stand inside at the entrance. As she paused at the front door, she welcomed the change from the humid atmosphere of the steamie to the cold of the late afternoon air that wafted in each time the door was opened to admit a new customer. Also there was the wee bonus that everyone who came in stopped for a chat. No matter that it was always a brief encounter, Mary welcomed it just the same. After about five minutes, the guilt and the cold got the better of her and she decided to head back in again and start on the second wash.

Doreen headed home, her shopping bag full with last-minute items. She had told John to go and have a drink with his pals because he worked hard and deserved it. This was their first Christmas and New Year as husband and wife and she had loved every minute of it. However, she was looking forward to the end of the old year and the beginning of another exciting one in the life and times of Mr and Mrs John Hood. While she hurried home, she smiled a smile of self-praise and why not? She had it all mapped out. John would get promotion because he was popular and good at his job. They would have children (at least one of each) and would not stint in their efforts to give them everything that a boy and girl needed to be a success and a credit to their parents. Her heart warmed with the thrill of being young and alive in the Glasgow of the nineteen fifties and that same heart told her it could only get better. She had just to give the house a quick dunt with a duster. Then she would visit the steamie and get rid of the grime of the old year and have everything spotless to start the New Year. She had seen her mother and all the other married women do this since she was a wee girl and now she could take her place along side them.

Magrit was sweeping out the old year and cursed under her breath at every grain of dirt that did not surrender itself to her but obstinately stuck to the floor. To Magrit the dust seemed like a living thing that tried to take refuge in a corner which was difficult to get the brush into and so thwart her efforts to dislodge it. But this just made her curse all the more and attack it with a corner of the brush until it was captured and dispensed to the growing mound of grime that seemed to taunt her. She had started in the kitchen, then gone through to the bedroom and finally into the hallway where the combined dust from the two rooms swirled on the floor as they met. She expertly merged the last of the year's debris and swept it towards the front door. As she passed Peter, who was still comatose on the hall floor, she contrived to accidentally hit him on the side of the head with the edge of the brush. She did not apologise. Peter did not need one as he had not felt the blow anyway.

Theresa hurried home through the dark-descending early evening. She was in a huge hurry to get home and read the travel brochure on luxury cruises that she had obtained. There had been nothing suitable locally so she had walked it into the city centre. She had had a brainwave. The one shop that Glasgow boasted, where you could get anything from a pie to a fur coat was Lewis's in Argyle Street. Glaswegians had always known it simply as The Poly, which was short for

Polytechnic, and Theresa just knew that that was the place to get a travel brochure on cruises. Her hunch had proved correct. Not wanting to be shown the door because she was too wee and too poor, she had told the assistant that her rich auntie had asked her to collect a brochure as she was thinking of going on a cruise in the summer. Her ingenuity – or lying, depending on how you viewed it – had paid dividends and now she could not wait to get into the house, close the door of the bedroom she shared with her mother and find out all about the job of her dreams. 'I just hope there's nobody in,' was her only concern as she walked back.

FOURTEEN

Andy McDowell grunted as he lifted the large tin bath full of dirty washing from the floor and on to the trestle table. He removed the number twelve that signified not unexpectedly that it was twelfth in line for a service wash. It had been handed in on behalf of the doctor's wife Jeannette McInnes, with the instruction that it had to be washed and ready to be collected that night. It was Andy's responsibility to see that that would be done. It seemed to Andy that he had too many responsibilities. He was responsible for opening the doors of the steamie if he was on the early shift and he was responsible for closing the doors if he was on the late shift. He was also responsible for making sure the boilers that dished out hot water to the eighty-five wash stalls and the hot air that permeated the venting behind the stalls and allowed the clothes to be dried as they hung over the rails – or 'horses' as the women called them – were always in top working order. He had to order the coal that made this possible. He also took it upon himself to keep up the spirits of the women as they rubbed and scrubbed with a constant supply of banter and be available to listen to and advise on their various complaints as well. He felt sometimes that the title of Washhouse Mechanic did not adequately cover his talents.

Although numbers ten and eleven were, strictly speaking, next in line to be handed out and old Mary Culfeathers was due for one of them, Andy noticed that the load inside the doctor's bath was not so full as the others that were left, so he decided that he would give this one to old Mary. This bit of beneficence on his part made him feel that, despite being underpaid and not appreciated, he was still what was referred to by the populace as a 'real gem'.

Lifting number twelve to just above knee height, he walked among the stalls, his wellies slapping noisily on the wet floor. As he walked, he could imagine the women all admiring the ease with which his muscular arms carried the wash load – a bit like Clark Gable carrying Vivienne Leigh out from the burning ruins of Tara in *Gone with the Wind*. Actually, it was getting very heavy and the handles on the tin bath were cutting into the creases in his fingers. The rim at the bottom of the bath was digging into his thighs and they were hurting as well but he would not, for love nor money, have let any of the women see that he was struggling. He started to whistle nonchalantly in the hope that he would appear even stronger. Of course, nobody took a blind bit of notice of him.

The handles of the bath were really starting to dig into his fingers and he was very glad to see Mrs Culfeathers resting outside of stall fifty-seven. She saw Andy approach and gave him a wave. Andy's face was starting to turn a dark puce colour when he finally drew level. Mrs Culfeathers gave him a worried glance. 'Are you all right wi' that Andy? There must be an awful weight in it, son.'

Andy was forty-four and loved it when anybody called him son. 'Ach, nae bother, Mrs Culfeathers,' he said, lowering the bath on to the slotted wash top while the blood drained slowly from his face back into his body. He tried to uncurl the fingers of his hands but they were stuck like claws – only the feeling of pins and needles consoled him with the reassurance that they would eventually return to normal.

'This'll be your last one the day, eh?' He gave the bundle of washing a pat. 'It's the doctor's – McInnes's. Do you go to him?'

Mary surveyed the bundle with a practised eye. 'Some nice stuff they've got, eh? Be nicer when it's clean, right enough.'

She directed Andy's eye to another tin bath, containing a far bigger bundle than the doctor's did, nestling on the floor. 'I'm finished wi' that lot, Andy. Will you take it away for me, son?' He stole a quick look at his fingers and decided, as they were not yet uncurled from the last load, he may as well grasp the nettle.

As he bent down, Mary drew the back of her hand across her forehead. 'It's awful hot in here isn't it, Andy?' Andy nodded as he took a firm hold on the wash tub. 'Aye! It's the heat that does it,' he said wittily.

Mary nodded, bowing to Andy's superior intellect. 'Is that whit it is? I knew it would be somethin'.'

Doreen Hood swung into view pushing an ancient pram on to which her washing was loaded just as Andy, bent double with the tub, turned from Mrs Culfeathers stall. At first she didn't notice him as she was studying her ticket. She looked up and saw that her stall fifty-nine was just two along from Mary Culfeathers. She noticed Andy staggering with the load. 'That looks heavy Andy. Wait till I get mine emptied and I'll let you have this pram,' she offered.

Andy would rather have stuck pins in his eyes than be seen pushing a pram. 'Naw, you're aw' right Doreen,' he gasped, 'It's nae bother.' His puce-coloured face said differently.

'No' be long till the bells, Andy,' she called after him, hoping it would offer some consolation. As she turned back she saw that Mary Culfeathers was unloading her recent bundle. 'Hello, Mrs Culfeathers – workin' away, I see,' she said pleasantly, raising her voice in the way you do to people who are of a certain age – even when they're not deaf.

'Nothin' else for it, eh Greta?' Mary nodded in agreement, separating the linen sheets from the blankets.

'My name's Doreen, Mrs Culfeathers – Doreen Hood – my mother was called Greta.'

Mary looked up from dissecting the bed linen. 'I'm sorry, Doreen, hen – I tend tae forget things these days. I didnae mean to offend you.' She felt foolish. She seemed to feel that more and more these days too but she didn't mention that to Doreen.

'No offence taken Mrs Culfeathers,' Doreen smiled, setting about unloading her own stuff. 'I'm the same. Magrit – over here!' she hailed Magrit who was searching the pockets of her coat and making exasperated noises.

'I've lost the bloody ticket noo.' Her mood had not picked up since banging Peter's head with the sweeping brush.

'You were in front of me,' Doreen said helpfully. 'Just go into number fifty-eight.'

Magrit grunted tersely at Doreen and moved into stall fifty-eight. She undid her coat and placed it on a hook at the back of the stall, away from where any wet things would dampen it. As she began sorting out the various articles to be washed, she was still muttering to herself, 'Wait till you see, I'll just get started and some wee nyaff'll come in and say, "Excuse me, is that your stall?" Well,' she muttered on, her face tightening with just the sheer annoyance of being Magrit McGuire, 'they'll get a moothful from me. I'm just in the mood, so I am,' she seethed, turning on the hot tap and throwing a half dozen pairs of sweaty socks into the bottom of the large gun-metal-coloured sink.

The wash stall that Magrit seethed in was typical of the washing set-up at that time. They were about seven feet long by five feet deep and consisted of a large rustproof black alloy sink to the right of the stall that held the majority of the coloured clothes to be washed. Behind this was a set-in boiler that the women put their whites into and this contained constant boiling water. On the opposite side was another slightly smaller sink made from delft or a similar material. This was usually used to steep blankets in as they were unusually dense when wet and, therefore, much too heavy to be washed by hand. In this particular steamie, the clothes were dried out by means of putting them through a mangle and then draping them over wooden rods that were encased in a cage-like contraption, called a horse or donkey, that slid in and out of the washhouse wall. Once inside the wall, there was a continuous draught of very hot air piped along the hollow space that received the horse and allowed the clothes drying time. When the horse or donkey was pulled out to allow access to the clothes, steam would escape adding to the condensation in the atmosphere.

Soap was of the solid bar type. The women used it to attack stains as if they were hitting them with a brick. They then rubbed the clothes up and down a washing board. There was also a very effective gel that was sometimes added. The whole added up to an efficient not to mention extremely hygienic way to wash.

All of this was not uppermost in Magrit's thoughts as she continued to plan her attack on the week's grime that had affixed itself to the family wash. She had just stuffed the last blanket into the steeping sink and turned on the tap when she heard a voice over her shoulder, 'Magrit? Is that your stall?'

There was a slight but definitely ominous pause. 'How?' Magrit answered without turning round.

'You left your ticket at the desk,' the voice continued.

Magrit's attitude softened slightly. 'Oh,' she replied, turning round to see that it was Dolly Johnson who was standing in front of her.

Dolly had on a dark blue bobbled cotton coat that seemed to have no waist. Her hair was encased in a yellow flower patterned scarf done up like a turban. Beneath the coat was a grey wool and mixed cotton frock and beneath that was Dolly's bowly legs, wrapped in thick nylon stockings that were held up by a sixpenny coin implanted at the top of each stocking and then twisted round till it was tight and held in place by a miracle of gravity and luck just above the knees. Beneath her legs, her feet were contained in shiny suede bootees that managed to cover her feet but not her ankles, which tended to swell up and escape gratefully over the edges of her footwear. She was smiling.

'Is that what happened?' Magrit said, acknowledging Dolly's explanation and holding her hand out for the ticket.

Dolly continued by studying her own ticket before informing Magrit that, 'According to this, I'm in fifty-eight and you're in number sixty.'

Magrit could feel her attitude un-softening again. 'Are you wantin' me tae shift, Dolly?' her voice was taut. She was about to teach Dolly why it was taut.

'I thought maybe you wanted number sixty?' smiled Dolly totally unaware of the tension she had caused.

'How? Is there somethin' special aboot number sixty?' Magrit asked, her voice now a heady mix of sarcasm and impatience.

Dolly glanced at number sixty, then shook her head, 'I don't think so, Magrit, but, if you want it, I don't mind lettin' you have it.'

Dolly missed the irony of Magrit's reply, 'I might let you have it. Right now.'

'OK, Magrit,' Dolly said, turning to number sixty, 'Save you starting all over again, eh?'

As Dolly turned away, she called over to Doreen, 'Hullo,

Doreen. Aye, Mrs Culfeathers's workin' away eh?' Her voice contained a note that was permanently optimistic yet also embodied great realism. This, combined with what was often described as her cheery wee face, made it very hard to dislike Dolly Johnson.

Both Doreen and Mrs Culfeathers looked up from their tasks and replied, 'Aye, Dolly.'

Dolly, realising sadly that this was going to be the extent of their conversation, entered number sixty and, like the others, hung her coat up at the back of the stall. She perched on a stool that was provided so the customers could have a sit-down and removed her bootees and put on a pair of her husband's old boots along with the rubber apron that was almost standard. She went through the normal procedure and began the wash. However, enduring periods of time that did not involve conversation was not a part of Dolly's personality. After barely a few minutes, she called out to Magrit, 'Magrit, did you know Cissie Gilchrist?'

'Aye,' Magrit replied unenthusiastically, 'she used to be pals wi' my mother.'

'Well,' Dolly announced momentously, 'Her man's died.'

'Has he?' Magrit's voice signalled total disinterest.

'Aye, he passed away a couple of nights ago,' Dolly carried on relentlessly, waiting for Magrit to carry on as well. Her wait proved fruitless as Magrit poured all of the day's annoyances into battering one of Peter's shirts with a bar of carbolic.

Dolly turned her attention to Doreen. 'Doreen, did you know Cissie Gilchrist?'

Doreen answered without interrupting her work, 'I don't think so.'

Dolly watched her sinks filling up as she continued, 'Aye, you do. Stays oot in Garngad noo but came fae here originally.

She'd be ages wi' me or your granny. Well – her man's died.'

'Has he?' Doreen replied politely but uninterested.

Again Dolly waited in vain for a response. She got one but not from Doreen. She heard Mrs Culfeathers' voice call out to her, 'Dolly.'

She looked out of the stall to see Mrs Culfeathers beckoning to her, to come over to her stall. Dolly turned off the faucets in case the water spilled over and crossed to Mary Culfeathers.

For some reason best known to herself, Mary Culfeathers did not want any of the others to hear what she was about to say to Dolly. In an apologetic and low voice that was just above a whisper she said, 'I couldnae help overhearing you Dolly! You say the lassie Gilchrist's man's died?'

'Aye – very sudden, Mrs Culfeathers,' said Dolly, adopting Mary's tone without knowing it. They were now two experts on the subject of contemporaries who had left this life of toil.

'She'll miss him,' said Mary knowingly.

'That's true,' said Dolly in agreement. Then adding as proof, if proof were needed, 'You never miss the water till the well runs dry – eh?'

Mary nodded indulgently at Dolly's flash of insight. 'That's true, Dolly. They were a happy couple – she thought the world o' him.' Her head bobbed up and down slightly in a mannerism that showed she was feeling the sorrow that Cissie Gilchrist was going through.

Dolly's head nodded in agreement with this. 'Aye,' she sighed.

Mary sighed again in concordance with Dolly's sentiments, 'Aye.'

They shared a silence in respect of his loss to the world.

'Of course, he wasnae liked himself, though,' Mary said, demonstrating that realism should never be sacrificed for sentimentality.

'Naw – he was a wee shite. How's Mr Culfeathers? Will youse be celebratin' thenight?'

Mary shook her head, 'Naw, Dolly, we never bother wi' Hogmanay noo – with the family away, it's no' the same.'

'You're welcome tae come up to us, you know,' Dolly said sincerely.

'That's awful nice o' you, Dolly,' Mary said, but her tone indicated she wouldn't.

'It's no' formal nor nothin' – just a terr wi' the neighbours. It'll be a wee break for you,' Dolly persisted.

Mary smiled at Dolly. 'By the time I finish here, well . . . I'll be ready for my bed. To tell you the truth, Dolly, I'm frightened to leave Harry too long by himself. It's his chest, you know.' Her shoulders shrugged in resignation.

'Is it bad then?' Dolly asked in sympathy.

'It's no' good, Dolly. And, Dolly . . .' she said, her voice going back to its conspiratorial tone of a moment ago, 'Noo, it's maybe my imagination . . . but . . . I think . . . I think he's beginnin' tae wander . . . in his head, you know? No' all the time, of course – just noo and again. Sometimes I think he thinks he's livin' in the past.'

Dolly gave Mary's arm what she hoped was a reassuring pat. 'It's just as well that you're there tae see he's awright.'

Mary's expression signalled she was not too sure of Dolly's assessment of the situation. 'How are the boys gettin' on? Are they still doon in London?' she said, changing the subject hurriedly.

'Oh, they're fine, Dolly – we got Christmas cards fae both o' them.'

FIFTEEN

Theresa was alone in the bedroom. She stood in front of the wardrobe mirror with a plate in her hand, which she was holding shoulder high. She walked back and forth disappearing from the mirror frame and then reappearing. Finally she stopped and smiled at the mirror. 'I'm sorry, were you wanting a stewardess? . . . Yes, I am the head stewardess – just leave everything to me.' She turned her back to the mirror and walked a few steps away before turning round and again addressing an imaginary passenger sitting at an imaginary table on an imaginary transatlantic liner, 'Youse were requiring something to drink? Leave it to me, I'll send someone who does drinks to attend to youse. May I ask, do youse take butter or margarine on your pieces? Well, thank you – it's all part of the service,' she responded to an imaginary compliment. 'It's nae bother . . . My name? It's Ther . . .' She stopped before completing the sentence. She had always considered her first name too common. Her second name was alright as there was already a Hollywood actress called Dorothy McGuire but she definitely did not like the name Theresa – there were another four in her class at school for a start.

Theresa saw her new career as the perfect opportunity to ditch her first name in favour of something more glamorous. What would go with McGuire? She pondered excitedly. In a flash of inspiration the answer came to her. She had been reading in a film magazine about the hit movie based on one of the most dangerous and seductively beautiful women of all time – Salome – that would be her new name. She addressed the imaginary passenger, 'My name is Salome – Salome McGuire.'

As Salome McGuire turned to sort out drinks for the imaginary passenger, she started to sing Frankie Laine's hit song 'Jezebel'. Her voice had automatically lowered Marlene-Deitrich style to suit her new persona. Her ears rang with the make-believe passengers' imaginary applause and she envisioned herself being spotted by a movie producer. Unfortunately, all that really happened was the sound of her wee brother Frankie banging on her door and shouting, 'Gonnae shut up? Ma da says you're burstin' his heid.'

SIXTEEN

Inevitably there was a queue for the wringer. It was always a hold up and the women had continually asked for more wringers to be installed. What was the point of building nearly a hundred stalls and only putting in two wringers to service all of the stalls? The common answer to the question was that a man must have designed it – a woman would never have made that stupid a mistake. One of the women in waiting said to another, 'Did you see in the papers that Cissie Gilchrist's man has died?'

The other one answered, 'Naw, but I was talking tae Sadie Hendry and she said that Dolly Johnson had told her aboot it.'

The first one nodded sagely. 'That's right. It was in the evenin' edition – "Passed away leaving a grieving wife," it said.'

A third woman, tall and thin with a worldly-wise air about her, interjected, 'Nae money?'

'Naw, just a grievin' wife,' came the doleful reply.

'Selfish wee bugger,' was the reaction to this by the tall one. She furthered her reasoning on this theme with the explanation that, 'It's awkward dyin' at this time o' the year as well – for the family and that, you know?'

'You mean wi' everybody celebratin'?'

'It's no' so much that, it's just that they've got tae lie a long time – wi' the holidays 'n' that. He could lie for a week before he got buried,' she informed the throng that was now in on the discussion.

'In the hoose?' said one, incredulously.

'Could be,' she said, pleased that she was now the centre of information. 'I think Catholics let them lie in the hoose – before they take them tae the chapel.'

'Is that a fact?' said a non-Catholic.

'I think so. Hing on a minute – Anne,' she called out to a passing Catholic.

'When one o' youse die, do they stay in the hoose till they're buried?'

'Aye – sometimes,' clarified the Catholic.

'For a week though?'

'Oh, God, naw! No' for a week,' she further clarified as she carried on to her stall.

'They'll probably cremate him if there's naebody opened – or he'd smell,' explained a small woman with greying hair.

There was general agreement on this point, till one voice asked, 'What if the crematoriums are all shut for the holidays?'

This caused further mystification as to the outcome. 'What did I say aboot him bein' a selfish wee bugger?' explained the tall one in self-exoneration.

Dolly had been at the sink for a good ten minutes and she decided that was more than enough time not to have been talking. She turned to Magrit who was engrossed in scrubbing, rubbing and pounding. For Magrit, it was a release of tension, taking her feelings out on the washing. Her concentration was interrupted by the sound of Dolly enquiring from her stall, 'Are you goin' first-footin' thenight, Magrit?'

'We were supposed to be,' said Magrit. 'But he's lyin' up in the hoose – drunk already – oot the game.' She picked up the soap and began battering Peter's overalls with it. 'Sick a' over the carpet – his breath's like a burst drain – you could strip paint wi' it.'

Not wanting to come between husband and wife Dolly said in a compensatory way, 'Aye, he likes a drink, your Peter.' Then she changed on to safer ground, 'Did you have a good Christmas? – Oh, here, I never wished you a merry Christmas.' Wiping her hands on her apron, she reached over the top of the stall and gave her hand to Magrit. 'Merry Christmas, Magrit.' As she smiled, her cheeks, which were like a painter's palette of thin purple veins interspersed with red and white patches of marbled skin, bunched up on each side of her upturned nose and forced her eyes to screw up until they were mere dots. Below this, an eager smile topped off a personality that was put on this earth with the sole purpose of getting on with people. Magrit's personality was not quite as developed in that way, so she just nodded, shook Dolly's hand and said, 'Merry Christmas, Dolly.'

This brief exchange was never going to satisfy Dolly's need for social involvement so she called out to Doreen in the next stall to Magrit, 'Merry Christmas, Doreen.'

Doreen looked up from her washing and called back at Dolly, 'Merry Christmas, Dolly – Merry Christmas, Magrit.'

'Merry Christmas, Doreen,' Magrit grunted back as Dolly's voice leapfrogged over her and Doreen till it reached Mary Culfeathers.

'Merry Christmas, Mrs Culfeathers,' she shouted out, waving to Mary Culfeathers, who looked up without knowing for certain who had wished her a merry Christmas.

Not wishing to appear rude, Mary took a chance and waved back, 'Merry Christmas, Dolly – Merry Christmas, Greta,' she said to Doreen. Then lowering her voice she asked, 'Will you wish Magrit a Merry Christmas for me, hen? I don't want to disturb her.'

Doreen nodded as she said, 'My name's Doreen, Mrs Culfeathers.'

Mary put up a hand to signify that she understood, but she didn't really.

'Magrit,' Doreen called out, 'Mrs Culfeathers is wishin' you a Merry Christmas.'

Magrit's patience was running on almost empty but she held it in check long enough to shout out, 'Merry Christmas, Mrs Culfeathers.'

Mary smiled back and said to Doreen, 'Thanks, hen – Merry Christmas.'

'Merry Christmas,' Doreen replied as Dolly appeared outside her stall.

'Did I wish you a merry Christmas, Doreen?'

Laying down a bottle of bleach that she had been dishing out to the whites in the boiler, Doreen turned to where Dolly was standing, one hand on her hip while the other scratched her head in a gesture of forgetfulness.

'Aye, I think so, Dolly.'

Dolly chewed at her bottom lip. 'I'm no' sure if I did, you know. Ach, I'll wish you it again, just in case. Merry Christmas, Doreen.'

As Doreen replied in kind, a low groan escaped from Magrit's stall.

Dolly did not pick up on it. 'Did you get nice presents, hen?'

Doreen stopped what she was doing and turned her attention to Dolly. 'Oh, aye. My ma and my da gave me a lovely table lamp and John gave me a dress and money tae get my hair done.' She undid the top of the turban she was wearing to protect her hair from the damp, just long enough so Dolly could see it.

As she was putting it back under its protective cover Dolly

asked admiringly, 'Where did you get it done? It looks beautiful – it really does.'

Doreen preened openly. 'Francini's up in Sauchiehall Street,' she said and subconsciously pursed her lips in a gesture of acknowledgement that said she knew it looked beautiful. 'It was three pounds,' she announced, grandly.

Dolly gasped. 'Was it? Three pounds,' she repeated incredulously. 'They've made a lovely job o' it, though,' she reasoned. 'Is that a bubble cut?' Dolly continued.

'Aye.' Doreen was glowing with the knowledge that she was the height of fashion.

'Oor wee Angela wants one o' them – she's too young for it, though.'

'Is that your granddaughter?' Doreen enquired as she checked to make sure that her hairdo was properly protected.

'Aye.' It was Dolly's turn for a bit of preening and glowing. 'She's too young for it, though,' she continued, warming up to her favourite subject. 'She's only twelve. She's champin' at the bit – cannae wait to be a teenager. You should see her in the hoose all dressed up wi' her mother's lipstick and make-up on. She thinks she's a right wee glamour girl – it's a bloody shame. Oor Helen clatters her if she catches her an' all.'

'That right?' said Doreen, who was now caught up in Dolly's enthusiasm.

'Nae wonder, but – she ladles it on somethin' terrible. She's got the lipstick all over her face, she uses it for rouge, on her cheeks – yon way? And she tries tae put shadin' roon her eyes like the big lassies – you know? Her faither says she looks like an apache.'

Magrit's voice cut through them – she had come to the conclusion if you can't beat them join them. 'Does she wear her mother's shoes? I used to do that.'

Dolly shook her head. 'Naw, she doesnae do that – her feet are too big.'

Magrit stopped her exertions. 'What size are her feet?'

'She's a size seven,' was Dolly's emphatic response. 'Oor Helen's only a four and a half.'

'That's big for a lassie o' twelve, right enough.' Doreen tried not too sound too critical but it was hard.

Dolly nodded in acceptance of the fact that her granddaughter had enormous feet. 'She's sweatin' blood in case they get bigger – her faither torments the life oot her as well. 'Cause you know how she's awful like him?'

Doreen did not, so she said so.

'Oh, she's his double – thon thick wiry black hair.'

Magrit and Doreen said, 'Aw – shame,' not only in sympathy but also in unison.

'She's got his blue eyes, she's even got his nose and, of course, he keeps tellin' her that she takes efter him, of course – he takes a size eleven.'

A gasp of compassion flew from the lips of her audience.

'He says he's gonnae leave her his sand shoes when he dies and that he's put her name doon tae join the polis when she leaves the school. And then he says she hasnae to hang up her stockin' at Christmas as it wasnae fair to the rest o' the weans.'

Doreen turned to Magrit, 'That's a shame, isn't it?'

Dolly carried on before Magrit could reply, 'She says to me the last time I was up in their hoose that aw the lassies in her class were always measurin' their busts, she says, "I'm no' worried aboot my bust, Gran – it's my feet I keep measurin'!".'

Magrit joined the conversation proper by advising that, 'Oor Theresa's aye measurin' her bust – she's doin' exercises for it. Ah caught her over a week ago staunin' in front o' the wardrobe mirror wi' her hands oot in front and clasped together. She was pressin' the palms into each other and recitin' wi' her eyes shut, kinna rhythmic like,

> I MUST
> I MUST
> I MUST INCREASE MY BUST.
> A BIGGER SIZE
> IS THE PRIZE
> FOR DOIN' THIS BLOODY EXERCISE.

I thought I was gonnae wet myself,' she laughed for the first time that day.

Doreen and Dolly were laughing as well. Mary Culfeathers stopped what she was doing, and unknown to the others, had a wee listen to what was going on. 'Wait till I tell youse though,' Magrit carried on, 'she comes in from the room, aboot ten minutes later, and she makes her and I a cup o' tea – there was just the two o' us in the hoose, Peter was oot workin' and the boys were still oot playin'. So she's drinkin' her tea and I says to her, all innocent like, "Here, is your chest no' getting bigger?" "Is it?" she says, tryin' tae appear as if she's no' botherin'. I says to her, "We'll maybe need tae think aboot gettin' you a bra soon." She jumps right oot the chair and she shouts, "Can I get one for my Christmas, Ma?"'

Dolly said softly, ' Aw, the wee soul.'

'Did you get her one Magrit?' Doreen asked, mirroring Dolly's sentiments.

'Aye. On Christmas morning, I took her aside and gave it to her privately. She was nearly greetin' she was that happy. She says tae me, "That's the best Christmas present I've ever had."' Magrit turned away slightly, as she gave a bit of slack to an uncharacteristic soft side of her character. 'I was near greetin' myself.'

'We used tae use bandages when I was a lassie,' Mary informed the company. 'Just tied roond aboot tae support you,' she said, miming the procedure. 'It was great. You felt that secure.'

Magrit surveyed her own mammoth mammaries. 'I think I'd need a bloody hammock tae support these.'

'Aye, you're big that way Magrit,' concurred Dolly.

'Peter says it was the first two things he noticed aboot me – the thing is I had my back to him at the time,' she said ruefully.

Mary turned away. No one had acknowledged her bit of information so she felt a bit foolish at having tried to join in the conversation. 'What does anybody care what we were wearing when I was a lassie,' she thought to herself as she went back to sanitising the doctor's washing.

SEVENTEEN

Harry Culfeathers sat at the kitchen table, still in his pyjamas. His breathing although heavy and laboured was relatively under control. He lifted his favourite cup and had a sip of tea from it – or he would have done except that there was no tea in it. He shook his head in a gesture of resignation as he placed the cup back down on to the table. Squinting through his spectacles at the mantel clock and then at the wag-on-the-wall, he shook his head again as he realised that Mary would not be back for hours yet. This meant that he would have to make his own tea. He started to weigh up the pros and cons of going down this avenue. First he would have to remember where she kept the tea. He paused while he wracked his memory cells – the solution did not leap immediately into his head. What did leap into his brain was that he did not know where the sugar was kept so that meant there was the sugar to find as well. He couldn't take tea without sugar – that much he did know. There was something else that would be needed for the tea but he couldn't think what that was either. 'You're gettin' worse,' he thought aloud.

He propped his elbow on the table and rested his head on the palm of his hand. His eyes alighted on the Christmas cards for the umpteenth time that day. He stared at them – something about them bothered him. It was all distraction Harry thought.

His whole life was getting too complicated – simple things were becoming an impossible chore. He remembered when he ran a business and brought up a family at the same time and thought nothing of it. Now? He couldn't remember the last time he had been out of the house. Although he had never been one to blaspheme, he swore inwardly. 'Christ.' He couldn't even make himself a cup of tea. The frustration of it all began to well up inside him.

He rose up from his chair and roared at the walls of the kitchen. The effort made him stagger but an inbuilt core of determination kept him on his feet. Winning that small battle gave him a bit of dignity back so he roared at the walls again and this time he didn't stagger. Self-confidence started to ebb back into his being. The ramparts of frustration that he felt could have engulfed him and thrown him into a pit of bewilderment eased back. Shaking his fist at the walls he shouted again, 'You'll no' beat me. I'll beat you. How do you like that then, ya bastards?' There was no reply from the kitchen walls – or the world at large.

Harry felt new energy pour into him. He had always responded to a challenge and usually won. It was good to win again. He knew he had got some of his old fizz and pizzazz back and, for the first time in a long time, he felt good, he was master in his own home once more.

'I'm goin' tae make myself a cup o' tea and nothin' is gonnae stop me.' His jaw set firmly as his gaze swept round the kitchen. He saw a note propped up against an empty milk bottle on the table. Sitting down he took hold of the note and read it. It was in Mary's handwriting. Harry's self-esteem got another wee bolster from his ability to still recognise that. It said, 'We've run out of milk. I'll bring back a pint on my way from the steamie. Mary.'

Harry listened to his breathing as he read the note. It was

long and loud and intrusive, not like his breathing at all. 'I sound like an old man,' he thought to himself. A vision of a black tin box with gold Chinese flowers painted on it flashed into his consciousness. 'That's where we keep the tea,' he cried out to the kitchen. His fists punched at the air. 'Beat you, ya swine, you.'

Life was good again as he surveyed the kitchen. He still had it in him to win a battle and that was important to him. He also felt a bit drained with the effort that had been required of him to triumph. He'd earned a rest so, steadying himself with the aid of the tabletop, he sat down.

Once more his gaze settled on the Christmas cards from the boys. There was something about them that puzzled him but, for the life of him, he didn't know what it was. His new-found confidence would not give up so he concentrated on the cards to try and win this battle of wits also.

As he studied them, another flash hit his brain and his scrutiny shifted to the note left by Mary. Uneasiness entered him and took the place of the feeling of confidence that had been prevalent only a second or two ago. Leaning across the table, he picked up the note and read it again. Laying it down beside the Christmas cards, he compared the handwriting. The silence of the walls seemed to mock him as they scrutinised his bent shoulders and his chest that heaved and strained under the pyjama jacket.

'Christ – I hate bein' old,' he thought in tacit despair. On the kitchen wall hung a clay plate that had been given to them by the boys as a Christmas present many years ago when they were all younger. It was sky blue with a motto picked out in relief white lettering:

To the world's best Mum and Dad

I thank the Lord who dwells above;
He gave me a mum and dad to love;
He created the sky and the beautiful sea,
But the best thing of all he gave to me.

And though I may fail in what I endeavour,
I'll never fail to love you forever.
I'll always be happy;
I'll never be sad;
For I'll always have you for a mum and dad.

EIGHTEEN

The sound of deep snoring rang round the lobby of Magrit's house. It emanated from Peter who was still comatose on the carpet where, earlier on, he had been sick. There was a damp ring round Peter's inert jaw from the stain that was left where Magrit had cleaned it up so it would not smell the house out. He snored the snore of a just man, a man who did not have a care in the world, a man whose conscience was clear, a man who was pissed out of his skull. The living room door opened cautiously and Tim eased his way out from behind it and into the lobby. His tread was soft as he tiptoed towards his father. Tim surveyed the carcass on the floor and smiled as he knelt down beside Peter. He put his hand softly on his father's shoulder and gave him a gentle shake.

'Da – are you all right?' he said in a voice that was not much above a whisper. There was no reaction, either vocal or physical, apart from the continuous snoring.

'Da – will I make you a cup o' tea?'

Tim prodded his father a bit harder but still to no avail. He placed both arms under his father's inert form and with a great deal of effort managed to turn him over on to his back. Peter's face contorted with the movement and he groaned inwardly. Tim looked at his father with genuine concern and tenderly slapped his face. There was no reaction at all – even the snoring failed to stop. He studied his father intently, noticing how his chest rose and fell evenly indicating he was deep in dreamland. He reached down and, with a touch as light as a feather, stroked his brow soothingly with the back of his right hand. While his right hand continued to administer a touch of tenderness, his left hand, equally feather-like, began to rifle through the pockets of his father's trousers. As he continued to search, he was interrupted by his dad's voice, 'Tim, son.'

Tim froze mid-search. His left hand totally still where it rested in his father's pocket.

'You're too late – your mother beat you to it.'

NINETEEN

Dolly had stepped outside of her stall for a break – she had been hard at it for a quarter of an hour or so. The reason she felt in need of a break was not because she was tired but because she was just the type of woman who needed to talk – or, as her husband put it, she was a right gab. Smokers were addicted to nicotine – Dolly was addicted to blethering. She looked around for someone who was in a similar state of need as herself.

Magrit's whole body language gave out a definite 'Leave me alone – I'm busy' attitude. Doreen was likewise getting tore in to her washing. Mary Culfeathers was trying, not too successfully, to load wet articles on to a pram in order to wheel them off to the wringer. This was in order to remove ninety-odd percent of the water from the washing, thus making it dry enough for the dryers to finish the process and ensure a clean dry bundle ready for ironing. Mary Culfeathers was trying to get as many wet articles as possible on to the pram so she would maybe only have to make the one trip to the wringer. Dolly saw an opportunity to not only have a blether but do someone a good turn as well. She lost no time in setting off for Mary's stall.

'Mrs Culfeathers, do you want a hand doon tae the wringer wi' them?'

Mary looked up as Dolly advanced, her bow legs accentuating

the width of her leather apron and inducing a slapping sound with each stride as she approached. Mary thought it sounded like a round of applause. 'Are you no' too busy, Dolly?' she said, hoping that Dolly would say no.

'No,' said Dolly, obligingly, 'I've got blankets lying steeping – they can lie there till I get back.' She started to load the washing from Mary's stall on to the pram. As she did so, she seized the opportunity to take stock of what she was loading. Her eyes alighted on a pale pink bedspread that was a cut above the ordinary. She held a corner of it up for a closer inspection. As far as bedspreads went, this one was a definite ten-out-of-tenner. Dolly gave a small whistle of appreciation. 'That's a beautiful bedspread that, isn't it, Mrs Culfeathers?' she said to Mary.

Mary nodded in a continuous way. One nod would have done but lately she had inexplicably taken to nodding continuously when asked a question – even if it was her asking herself the question, which was another thing she had been doing lately. Mary was unaware of this phenomenon but she had observed Harry doing it and wished he wouldn't.

'It's the doctor's wife's,' she nodded, with a touch of reverence in her voice.

'Is it?' Dolly said slowly and quietly as if sharing a secret that few were privy to. She turned to Magrit. 'Magrit,' she called out, 'have you seen this? Beautiful, isn't it?'

Magrit sighed impatiently but turned from what she was doing to see what Dolly was on about. 'Aye, it is,' she was forced to admit.

Doreen's inquisitiveness got the better of her and she had a look as well. 'That is beautiful,' she nodded but only the once in her case.

'It's the doctor's wife's,' Dolly informed the bedspread appreciation society.

'Wee McInness?' Magrit asked Mary Culfeathers.

Mary nodded her head, unaware that she had never stopped nodding it. 'They've got a lovely hoose, Magrit.' Her voice was respectful – as Mary felt it should be when speaking of anyone who kept their house in a manner that could inspire such a remark. 'Lovely stuff, isn't it? Wait till you see this tablecloth.' She rummaged around in the wash till she found it. Removing the objet d'art that was the doctor's wife's tablecloth, she shook it in the air to remove as many creases from it as possible then draped it across her arms and displayed it to the gaze of Magrit & co. 'That's Irish linen, that – the embroidery is all hand-done.'

Dolly gasped in admiration. 'I'n't that lovely, Doreen? What does the writin' say, Mrs Culfeathers?'

Mary smoothed the cloth to reveal the motto writ in an old-fashioned lettering of earthy brown embroidery:

YESTERDAY IS HISTORY.
TOMORROW IS A MYSTERY.
BUT TODAY IS A GIFT.
THAT IS WHY IT IS CALLED THE PRESENT.

'They must have got it as a present,' Mary explained.

'I'd be feart to put that oan the table in case I spilt somethin' on it,' Doreen said, thus bestowing the importance she felt the tablecloth deserved.

'If that was mine, it would never get oot the drawer,' Dolly concurred.

'He's bloody useless him,' Magrit said, referring to the doctor and restoring a sense of sanity to the conversation. 'No matter what you go tae him with, he tells you it's your nerves.'

'I think he's creepy,' Doreen said, adding her own version

of embroidery – not on the tablecloth, but on Magrit's opinion of Doctor McInness. 'I hate goin' to him. They're nice curtains, them – I'd like a pair like that in my big room.' She was now rifling through the wash as if she was at the January sale counter at C&A's in Sauchiehall Street.

'They're a lovely colour, aren't they, Greta?' said Mrs Culfeathers.

'My name's Doreen, Mrs Culfeathers,' said Doreen automatically.

Dolly interrupted by saying quizzically, 'I don't go tae him. Is he no' homeopathic?'

'I think he's homeo somethin' – I don't know aboot pathic,' Doreen volunteered.

'More like homeopathetic,' Magrit said venomously. 'He gave me tablets the last time I went – for my leg, you know. I said, "You gave me these before and they never did any good." He says, "These are different ones." So I went back to the hoose and checked – they were the same bloody tablets.'

'Did you go back to him?' Doreen asked.

'Aye, of course I did. I showed him the two bottles and I says, "You tell me this and tell me nae mer – are they or are they no' the same tablets?" You know what he says?' Magrit didn't wait for their answer. 'He says, "These last ones are a different strength, Megrit." I says to him, "Well, they look exactly the same to me." and he just gave me one o' they stupid wee smirks o' his – you know that way as if to say you're no' right in the head.'

The women nodded in concurrence.

'So I says to him,' Magrit carried on, ' "Well, I'm no' wantin' them 'cause, as far as I'm concerned, they're the same and they're no' helpin' me."'

'Did he give you somethin' else, Magrit?' Mary Culfeathers asked, her voice almost quivering with concern.

'Bloody right he did. He says, "Well, you're obviously not happy, Megrit." and he writes oot another prescription for some other tablets. "We'll try you on these and see if they're any better. Come back and let me know how you get on with them."' Magrit was now reliving the moment, her face red with anger.

'He's a plausible wee swine,' she spat out, 'but I let him have it, so I did. I says, "You listen here to me," I says. "Do you think I'm a bloody guinea pig? Am I a bloody test case or somethin'?" Excuse my language Mrs Culfeathers.'

She nodded in deference to Mary Culfeathers, who was already nodding back anyway. 'It's all right, Magrit.'

Magrit continued, '"'Cause, if I am," I says, "I want to be tested by somebody competent. *I* could do what you're doin' – handin' oot pills and sayin', 'Try that and, if they don't work, we'll try somethin' else.' Any stupid bugger could do that."' Magrit was now transposed in her anger. 'An' then he says to me as if it was my fault, "Well, maybe you should think about registering with another doctor."' She paused while the injustice of the remark settled into the psyche of her confidants. 'I says, "Listen you, I'm here wi' a sore leg, I cannae go traipsin' two mile tae the next doctor,"' she shouted.

'Is that Bell? Is that Doctor Bell?' Doreen asked the assembly.

'Aye – that's who I'm with. He's smashin' – it's hard tae get on his books, though,' Dolly advised Doreen.

'Is his wife no' a doctor as well?' Doreen asked, not realising that, by altering the course of the discussion, Magrit was seething at being stopped in full vitriolic flow.

Mary Culfeathers was more sensitive to Magrit's urgent need to vilify Doctor McInness. 'What happened then, Magrit?' she enquired sympathetically.

'He gave me an appointment tae see the top man in the

Western Infirmary,' she announced triumphantly. Then added emphatically, 'He should have done that long ago.'

'What did he say was up wi' your leg, Magrit?' asked Doreen.

Magrit shook her head in resignation before replying, 'He says it's my nerves.'

'Is it sore?' Dolly enquired.

'Of course it's bloody sore,' Magrit answered vexed with Dolly's pointless question.

Dolly shook her head in a gesture that said she was annoyed that Magrit thought her question was pointless. 'Naw, I mean is it sore just noo?'

'Naw, it comes and goes. It's thrombosis. That's what it is,' Magrit stated, clear in the knowledge that she knew better what her malady was than any medical expert.

'Thrombosis? Is that no' a clot?' asked Doreen before re-entering her stall.

'Aye,' Magrit verified as she too headed back to the drudge. 'And so's that bloody doctor.'

Mrs Culfeathers announced that she would go and see if there was a ringer free.

'I'll gie you a hand doon wi' these to the wringer, Mrs Culfeathers,' Dolly volunteered, because she could see that the load was large and would need someone to push the pram and another one to steady the wash and make sure it didn't fall off.

'You're a saint, Dolly,' said Mary, beatifying Dolly without any official qualification. Saint Dolly Johnson, patron saint of the steamies, dismissed the honour with a wave of her arm and started on about the price of fish.

TWENTY

Theresa studied herself in the wardrobe mirror for the umpteenth time. The problem was trying to look older – well, old enough to be considered as a viable candidate for a position as a stewardess. She retreated a couple of yards back from the mirror, pouted her lips and pulled her hair down over the left side of her face in the style made popular by Veronica Lake. She studied this effect with her right eye and was pleased with what she saw. Apart from the fact that her hair was mouse brown, while Veronica Lake's was blonde, and apart from the fact that she had on her flair skirt and blouse, white ankle socks and lace-up black shoes, whereas Veronica Lake had a slinky black low-cut shimmering evening dress and silk stockings with stiletto-heeled black satin dress shoes, there really wasn't that much difference.

Undoing the top four buttons on her school blouse, she pulled the left side down over her shoulder. Turning side-on she lifted her shoulder and smouldered at her reflection. She licked her lips to make them shine a bit, drooped her eyelids, then vamped her way towards the mirror. Stopping at the mirror she looked it up and down and announced in as husky a voice as she could manage, 'I was wondering if youse were starting any stewardesses? My age? I am nineteen – and a half.'

Theresa's considered opinion was that she could pull that

one off – if only her breasts were bigger. Taking off her blouse, she cupped her hands in front of her and began her daily bigger bust campaign.

Outside her door Tim and Frankie were taking it in turns to look through the keyhole. Peter snored on.

TWENTY-ONE

Magrit had knocked off for a breather and lit up a fag. Even that had annoyed her because the matches were damp with the humid atmosphere of the steamie and she had had to waste three before one finally succumbed to her threats to 'Throw the whole bloody lot o' youse at that drier door'.

Doreen didn't smoke but she was in need of a break too. Adjusting her turban-like headscarf to ensure that her new hairdo remained protected from the sodden atmosphere, she joined Magrit. She planked herself down on a stool provided by the management for the comfort of patrons at the side of all the stalls.

'Have you been to the pictures this week, Magrit?'

Magrit exhaled her Senior Service. Cigarettes were the only luxury she had so she bought good ones. She had tried Player's, Capstan and a few others but her mother had always maintained that Senior Service was the only dignified cigarette for a woman. In her considered opinion, 'Other fags only made you look cheap'. Magrit usually followed her mother's advice. The only time she had gone against it was when she married Peter. That was a lesson that she never forgot.

'We went to the Rex aboot two weeks ago. It was . . . what was it called . . .? Eh, I've seen it before . . . Fred MacMurray and . . . ?'

'*Double Indemnity*?' volunteered Doreen.

'That was it,' Magrit confirmed, stretching her legs out and crossing her ankles.

'I saw that. It was great, wasn't it?'

'Aye, he's good – I like her as well.'

'Barbara Stanwyck?' Doreen volunteered again.

'That's right. They're good togither – as a pair, you know?'

Doreen nodded in agreement. Then stated, 'I like Doris Day as well.'

'Oh, aye,' Magrit enthused. 'Marvellous singer. I've got a cousin in Riddrie can sing like her,' Magrit said as she sucked in another lungful of tobacco for females who did not want to look cheap.

'Can she?' Doreen's eyes widened at the thought. 'Lucky thing,' she said, enviously.

'No' really,' replied Magrit. 'She's got a face like an elephant's airse.'

'That's a shame,' said Doreen genuinely. 'Have you ever seen Tony Curtis?'

Magrit shook her head, 'Naw – I've heard o' him, though.'

'Oh! He . . . is . . . beautiful,' Doreen gasped. 'And he's got a fantastic haircut and beautiful eyes and a dead low voice.'

Magrit studied Doreen. Her enthusiasm stirred memories of being that age. She was sure she must have been like that at one time too, but too much had happened and now numbness had taken precedence in her heart.

Andy strolled between the stalls. He had finished in the basement checking the pressure levels for the furnace-fuelled main boiler that serviced the entire washhouse and, now that that was out the way, his next duty was to inspect the steamie stalls and make sure everything was in order. Andy could usually manage all this without ever taking his hands out of his overall pockets. As he strolled along, he whistled the Nat

King Cole hit 'Because You're Mine'. A woman with the complexion of an alcoholic beetroot winked and smiled at him with a mouth that had not contained teeth for many a year. Andy smiled back and subconsciously changed to whistling the Roy Rogers' hit 'A Four-Legged Friend'.

Doreen was still enthusing about Tony Curtis. 'He wears smashing suits as well but it's his eyes – they go right through you. John and I went to see a picture he was in. It was the first time I'd seen him. I'm no' kiddin' you, Magrit, I was actually droolin' . . . my insides were all goin' . . . see when the lights went up, I was dead embarrassed. John says to me, "Are you all right? You're all flushed. What's the matter?"'

'What did you say?' Magrit asked, with the glint of a smile playing round the corners of her eyes.

'I just told him it was women's troubles. Well, so it was – in a way,' laughed Doreen. Magrit, caught up in Doreen's vitality, joined in.

Dolly's voice mingled with their chortling, 'Am I missing something?' She had made sure that Mary Culfeathers was safely in line for the next shot at the wringer and was now about to tackle the blankets that had been steeping in the low sink provided for this purpose.

'Have you ever seen Tony Curtis, Dolly?' asked Magrit.

'Naw. Does he come from roond here?'

Magrit shook her head as Doreen went into another fit of merriment. 'He's an actor. Doreen says he's a right fine boy.'

Dolly dismissed the question as the current crop of romantic leading men held no interest for her. 'I've no' been to the pictures for years. We used tae go before we were married. My hero was George Raft – he was a marvellous dancer.'

'I thought he was a gangster?' Doreen said, her face registering puzzlement.

121

'Aye, he was. But he was a marvellous dancer too. The tango was his speciality – it was mine as well. I was good at it when I was younger.' Dolly's eyes were alight, full of happy memories. 'I was never away frae the dancin'. We used tae got to the Playhouse, the Albert and the Barrowland. That's where I met Boab.'

'John and I met there,' said Doreen.

'So did Peter and me,' Magrit pronounced darkly. 'It's got a lot tae answer for, that place.' Then she added, 'I liked the quickstep and the foxtrot.'

'Of course, they don't dance noo, Magrit,' Dolly declared. She shook her head at the bizarre behaviour of the younger generation. 'It's that jitterbuggers they dae just noo. Naw there was nothin' tae beat the tango. My partner was always Big Agnes Gillespie,' she said proudly.

'Did you no' dance wi' men?' Doreen asked, puzzled again.

'Aye – what I meant was Big Agnes and I always palled each other to the dancin'.'

'To get a lumber,' said Doreen, using the Glasgow slang word for an escort of the opposite sex.

'We never bothered wi' that. We went for the dancin' – no' for a click,' Dolly stated emphatically, using an even older Glasgow slang word for the same escort. 'There was plenty o' time for a' that nonsense later on. Andy McGhee always got me up for the tango.' She paused while the memories flooded back before adding wistfully, 'He used to say I was good 'cause I had the bowly legs.'

'You should have warmed his jaw for him,' Magrit snapped.

'Naw,' Dolly said impatiently. 'He meant they came in handy when I leaned back.'

Magrit looked at Doreen for enlightenment. There was none so she looked back at Dolly. 'How do you mean?'

'Well, it meant, when we were doin' the lean-back, he could

get his legs in between mine faster than usual,' was Dolly's reasoned reply.

'No fool, Andy McGhee, eh?' was Magrit's summation of Andy McGhee's ability to seize the moment.

Dolly reasoned the lassies didn't know that, during the tango, for dramatic effect, there was a bit where the female leaned right back, held by the male's arms. The ultimate objective for the female was to lean as far back as she could and, if possible, touch the dance floor with the back of her head. In order to make this happen the male would prop her up with his leg so they could hold the position while their heads darted left and right in a staccato movement. Dolly also reasoned it was quicker to show them. 'C'mere and I'll show you what I mean, Doreen.'

Doreen recoiled. 'I don't know how to do a tango,' was her only defence.

Dolly was not in the mood for negative responses. It was a character trait that she'd had all her life. 'Come on,' she urged. 'You'll enjoy it.'

Doreen backed further into her stall as if being attacked by a rabid animal. Dolly grabbed her arm and began to pull her out. Doreen was starting to panic.

Magrit was getting fed up with it all, but didn't want to leave Doreen to fend off Dolly by herself so she tapped Dolly on the back and said, 'I've got a rough idea how to do it. Show us what you mean.'

Dolly beckoned Magrit eagerly towards her, her eyes aglow with the excitement of dancing the tango.

It has to be acknowledged that it did not take a lot to get Dolly excited but a chance to dance would do it every time. The fact she was in a steamie dressed in a rubber apron and an old pair of boots and her partner was not George Raft but a woman in wellies mattered not a jot. She assumed the stance for the dance and began the lesson.

'Right, Magrit, gie's your hands.'

Magrit joined Dolly with her left hand clasping Dolly's right, both held aloft, while their other hands held their respective waists – or, in Dolly's case, what used to be her waist.

Dolly's face was now a study of concentration as she nodded silently to Magrit to confirm that her partner was ready to commence. Magrit nodded back. Dolly counted, 'One, two, three,' and began to 'da-dum' the tango.

'Da dum dum dum dum – da da da dum dum – da dum dum dum dum – da da da dum dum,' she sang while gliding over the Palais de Steamie.

Despite herself, Magrit was enjoying the moment. This was Dolly's natural gift, lifting you out of yourself and finding that you were joining in with her enthusiasm. If the fates had so decreed that she be born into another perhaps more affluent stratum of society, she could easily have been a successful socialite, holding the best parties in town, for people who liked that sort of thing.

'Right, Magrit,' she said in between the da-dum-dums. 'Brace yourself. When I nod tae you, we'll dae the lean back.'

Magrit nodded that she was ready whenever Dolly was. They danced in unison across to where Doreen was watching in rapt attention. They came to a dramatic halt directly in front of her and Dolly called out, 'OK, Magrit, I'm gonnae lean back. Hold me tight and stick your leg in between mine.'

'Overheard in a back close at midnight,' thought Magrit, in a flash of temporary distraction, before bracing herself to hold Dolly's not inconsiderable bulk as she bent backwards from the waist and tried to relive her youth by touching the floor with her hair.

In reality, her head did not get within two feet of the floor.

However, reality, unlike enthusiasm, was not uppermost in Dolly's mind. She was convinced that her head was a mere inch or two above the floor as she hung with her head upside down and looked at Doreen with a smile that was telling her a round of applause would not be inappropriate.

Doreen did not disappoint. 'That was rare, Dolly – you as well, Magrit. Youse were brilliant,' she enthused as she put her hands together.

'You're a great partner, Magrit,' complimented Dolly graciously. 'I can still pick up a hankie off the floor wi' my teeth,' Dolly informed Doreen, once she had straightened up and extricated herself from Magrit's grip of steel.

'Can you? I'd love to see that,' Doreen said, with a mischievous look at Magrit.

'C'mon, Magrit, we'll show her,' said Dolly, now totally carried away with the success of the moment.

Magrit stood with her hands on her hips. 'I'm supposed to be doin' a washin' here. My name's Magrit McGuire no' Cyd Charisse.'

'Ach, tae hell. It'll soon be Hogmanay – c'mon,' was Dolly's totally illogical reason for Magrit to abandon her washing chores in favour of dancing the night away.

Magrit shook her head in resignation. 'A' right, ye daft wee bugger.'

'I'll get a hankie oot the washin',' said Dolly hurrying into her stall.

Doreen and Magrit exchanged looks of 'what the hell', before Dolly called out, 'I cannae find a hankie – this'll have to dae.' She emerged from the stall brandishing one of her husband's undervests.

'Zat no' a semmit?' Doreen asked incredulously.

'Aye,' Dolly agreed as she swept past Doreen to the centre of the washhouse floor. 'But he's hardly worn it. This is actually easier than a hankie,' she explained, plumping up the semmit so that it rose in a peak that would be easier for her to reach. 'But it'll give ye an idea.'

She stood up from the semmit, which now resembled Mount Everest after a particularly heavy avalanche, and placed herself again in front of Magrit.

Magrit stared at her unbelievingly before bowing to the inevitable. 'I must be aff my head. Come on then.'

Dolly counted up to three and away they went once more. As they danced the prelude to the picking up of the hankie/semmit, Andy turned the corner that led to where Mrs Culfeathers' stall began the row of women that da-dum'd instead of washed. He stood watching them – unlike Mary Culfeathers, who was so wrapped up in getting the doctor's washing dried in the wringer to the high standards that befitted his station in the community that she was totally unaware of what was going on further up the washhouse.

As they approached the vital moment of picking up the vest between her teeth Dolly got herself mentally attuned. 'Are you ready, Magrit?'

Magrit nodded back in assent and prepared to take Dolly's weight once more.

'Right.' She leaned backwards as before. This time, however, by introducing the vest, she had unwittingly made her task a lot harder as the only way to prove that she could still reach it was, in fact, to rise with the vest between her teeth. She leaned back as far as she could but was some way short of attaining her goal.

'Let me doon a bit further, Magrit,' she instructed.

'I'm as far as I can go,' Magrit threw back at her, her jaws clenched with the effort. 'My back's near broke in two tryin' tae hold on to you.'

Dolly could see defeat looming. In desperation, she reached

down with a hand, snatched the vest from the floor and stuffed it into her mouth. 'Tarraa,' she mumbled in an attempt at a fanfare as her arms flew apart – a gesture that proved just too much even for Magrit's powerful grip. Dolly tumbled from her grasp and crumpled in a heap on the floor.

Andy walked over to the dancers

'Not *the* Fred Astaire and Ginger Rogers,' he said sarcastically as Dolly picked herself up and Magrit rubbed her back.

'She should have done it wi' a hankie,' Doreen elucidated.

'From whit I saw, she should have done it wi' a Yankee. You know there's no drunks allowed in here,' he informed them wittily.

'How did you swing it then?' countered Magrit, with no conscious attempt to top him but doing so anyway.

'Whit the hell are youse doin?' was his not unreasonable retort.

'We were showin' Doreen the tango,' Dolly explained. 'Can you dae it Andy?'

'Aye, but I never knew you had to eat a semmit during it. When did you two discover youse were attracted to each other and where have you got all the drink stashed?' he continued, doing a mock search of their stalls, hoping the women would find his antics amusing and, despite their reactions, somehow convinced that they did.

Mrs Culfeathers appeared with a worried look on her face at the side of the stall that Andy was doing the mock search in.

'Andy, son,' she said apologetically, 'There's something wrong wi' the wringer. It's no' goin' right, son.'

'Andy smiled indulgently at her. 'I'll away and sort it oot. Do you know where they're getting all the drink from Mrs Culfeathers?'

'What drink's that, son?' Mary replied, mystified.

'Pay no heed to him, Mrs Culfeathers,' advised Magrit.

'Did you know Magrit and Dolly are havin' a wee affair, Mrs Culfeathers?' Andy asked, mischievously.

Mary nodded. 'Aye, Dolly asked me up to it but I'm too tired. I'm just gonnae have a quiet night in the hoose,' she replied.

Andy stared at her, disbelievingly. 'I think I'll come back and start again,' was the only solution he could come up with.

TWENTY-TWO

The family album lay opened on Harry Culfeathers' lap. It was an expensive one that had been given to them as a present from both their parents to remind them, when their first-born had arrived, that family values were precious. Leather-bound, it was very extensive with thick vellum pages that contained photographs – some so old they were in tin plate. The first pages were devoted to severe men and women who stared out from images frozen in a technology that was new to them. Dignified and unsmiling, the men in their Sunday-best suits, complete with walking sticks and pocket watches, posed beside women in dark, heavy and forbidding dresses. From the past, they stared suspiciously as they emerged to us in a future they had no knowledge of. Perhaps they were right to be suspicious.

These gave way to the next generation, then to Harry and Mary's wedding and finally to the boys as babies, then toddlers and schoolboys. Of course, eventually, the boys' weddings were recorded in film also. They were bright and relaxed, in marked contrast to their ancestors. They were smiling confidently as they mingled with aunts and uncles and best men and bridesmaids. The last pages were given to the children of the two boys. The boys posed, as proud of their children as Harry and Mary had been of them.

Harry and Mary's grandchildren, they were the only ones in the past ninety years of the album that they had never met.

They were, at the present time, the only ones that Harry and Mary wanted to meet.

Harry had been wading through their past, as he often did lately, and had fallen asleep, as he also often did lately. He awoke slowly, his eyes red and hot with the recent strain of reading the informative notes that were written under the photographs in the album. He took off his glasses and placed them on the table beside his favourite chair. He rubbed at his eyes hoping this act would relieve him of the burning sensation in them. It never did.

He felt a bit chilly as well. Glancing at the fire, he saw that it had faded in the hearth and needed tending. He rose with difficulty, noticing that, as always, this simple act was now accompanied by groans of effort from him.

'You're soundin' like an old man,' he admonished himself, as he reached for the poker to give the fire a rummle up. Searching for some suitable small lumps of coal, he placed these on the now glowing embers. The consequence of doing this, however, caused the fire to smoke and it set Harry into a fit of coughing. Breathing heavily, he sought refuge in his chair and, grasping it by the arm, he lowered himself down to safety. Picking up the album, he opened it and tried to take up from where he had left off. The pictures were hazily unfamiliar and indistinct – they seemed to drift away from his gaze. His brain chased after them. 'Come back,' he whispered. Harry was confused and frightened. He began to panic that he was not in control. An unspoken fear that he was losing his mind caused the panic to well up inside him and this made his breathing even harsher, as the gulps of air he was now snatching at bounced around inside his lungs. He stared wildly away from the album at the kitchen walls that were also as if enfolded in a hazy muddle of what should have been familiar surroundings. He thought he was about to plunge into the strangely comforting dark pool of insanity when a thought drove through the mire and entered his consciousness. Raising his hand he stretched out his middle finger; closing the surrounding digits he lifted it till it was directly in front of his face. Then he brought it in towards his face until he could feel his clenched fist touch the damp patch that was recently omnipresent on the tip of his nose. Lowering the finger he placed it gently on the bottom part of his nose and then slid his finger up towards the bridge on which rested his spectacles. His fingers registered that his nose was a spectacle-free area. 'Nae wonder everything's blurred,' Harry sighed in relief.

As the wave of panic subsided and his breathing returned to its normal uneasy state, Harry decided that a cup of tea would be the thing to settle him. Putting on his spectacles, he lifted the kettle from the top of the cooker and crossed to the sink and turned on the tap. As the kettle filled up, he gazed round for his matches. 'I've lost the bloody matches noo,' he complained to himself.

He became aware that the kettle was now full and brimming over. 'Tae hell wi' it,' he swore, as he turned off the tap and emptied some of the water back out the kettle.

Once more he sought out the box of Swan Vestas matches kept for lighting the gas rung – nowhere to be seen. 'She'll have hidden them,' was his solution to that mystery.

After placing the kettle on the gas rung, he crossed to the mantelpiece and treated himself to a fag. He needed a light of course but could not find the matches. This problem, however, was easily solved. Harry tore a strip of paper and folded it into a taper. Tentatively he knelt down on one knee in front of the fire and lit the taper. He removed the taper and offered it to his cigarette. Without removing the cigarette from his mouth, Harry lit it and then, raising himself up, he crossed to the cooker. Turning on the gas, he took a deep satisfying draw from his cigarette. The inevitable coughing fit followed but Harry deemed it was worth it for the satisfaction and calm that settled over him.

He placed the kettle on the gas ring and applied the taper to it. He could not understand why it would not light. He could hear the gas escaping – it was loud and he could smell it too. 'What the hell's the matter wi' this noo?' he cursed. Again he applied the taper to the ring under the kettle but, unfortunately, it was the wrong ring that Harry was trying to light.

He became more aware of the sound of escaping gas – he could smell it and he could hear it. It reminded him of another time, a time that would never be fully erased from his memory. It was buried deep inside him but there were occasions when it rose to the surface uninvited and unwelcome and he relived it. The sound of the gas became louder in his ears as it mingled with the noise of guns and bombs that were all around him and his comrades. None of them knew if their bodies would be whole or intact or even if they would be alive in the next thirty seconds. Twenty-four hours a day, day after terrifying day, they lived with that horrific reality.

When they were first thrown into the conflict that made a lottery of their lives, this knowledge terrified each and every one of them. They did not admit it to their mates, of course, and hid it beneath a thin veneer of jokes and false confidence, but the fear was there, stark and inescapable. It was there every night when they huddled in the trenches surrounded by cold and wet. The smell of dust that had turned to mud would mingle with the acrid gun smoke and the stench of human excrement, and their young minds would try to drive it from their brains and allow them to sink into some kind of sleep before the next onslaught. It was still there, haunting them, when the scream of shells bursting overhead forced them to wake up. Eventually, if they survived, they adapted somehow to living with the fact that death could erase them from everything they held dear as easily as they might swat a fly.

Harry heard a disembodied voice call across the battlefield, 'Gas! Gas!' He tried to fathom out what was happening as he stared intently at the still-alight taper hovering over the ring.

Explosions were erupting all round him. His head began to ache with the pounding from the German guns. He stared once more at the taper that seemed to be flaring up.

'Gas! Gas!' came the warning again but Harry didn't know what to do about it. The hiss of the escaping gas was now indistinguishable from the hiss of bullets flying past him. The taper's flame hovered over the ring, its glow reflecting on Harry's face, now fixed in a state of confused anxiety. Unbelievably, a smile started to play over his mouth as he relived those long-gone days of danger. The gas continued to escape, Harry looked at the lit taper hovering over the wrong ring as the noise of war became deafening in his ears. His face broke into a broad smile as he said, 'Ehh?' and then he saw the flames erupt in a perfect circle and spurt upwards towards him as if someone had struck a dozen matches all at the same time.

He lifted the kettle and placed it on the correct gas ring, blew out the taper and shook his head in resignation for what must have been the twentieth time that day. 'Cannae even light the bloody gas noo,' he said, lost in melancholy. 'Where did she put that put that album?'

Irritation was fast replacing his melancholic air. 'I wish she would leave things alone.' This was, of course, unfair but it probably helped Harry to feel his age was not to blame for all the tribulations that visited him. Like everyone when they get older, deep inside himself, Harry felt he was still a youngster. It was only this feeling that made his present life bearable.

Something, some inner sense, told him that this deep-seated

and illogical sentiment was vital. It allowed him to keep his independence and his dignity. He was not about to give that up easily.

TWENTY-THREE

John Hood turned up his jacket collar to give him some protection against the chill in the night air. He could have worn a coat but he had never liked coats. It probably stemmed from when he was wee and his mother used to bumffle him up tight in a scratchy double-breasted tweed coat that finished just above his knees. This blanket with buttons did not allow him any movement, and when it was raining, the water would drop off the bottom of it on to his legs and result in him developing a red weald scurf mark that burned at his legs. All this had to be endured so he wouldn't catch a chill that had been the death of his mother's father's brother.

Doreen had offered to buy him one for his Christmas but he had declined and had got a tie and two pairs of socks instead. One day, they would have children and Doreen would protect them in a manner that would elicit John's mother's approval.

He turned into Henderson's licensed grocer.

Theresa studied her tiny breasts for any appreciable evidence that her exercises were paying off. She had adopted the technique of placing a tape measure round each microscopic mammary and registering their size. She was delighted to note that they had gone up by one of the marks that denoted a tenth of an inch. This signalled definite proof that her exercises were paying off. With a song in her heart and a spring in her step, she put the tape back in the drawer she had got it from and set to with renewed vigour on her exercise. She knew her only passport to wealth and excitement and a successful career as a stewardess was to increase her present cup size A to an F cup like Rita Hayworth and, of course, grow legs like Betty Grable.

On the other side of the bedroom door, Tim and Frankie were playing pontoons using their father's inert body as a table. They had become bored waiting for Theresa after she had stopped her first bout of exercising and were now passing time with an old pack of cards till something else took their fancy. At the sound of Theresa's muffled 'I must. I must.', they abandoned the matchsticks they had been using instead of money and raced to the keyhole for another glimpse of the forbidden fruit that was their sister's bare breasts. What attracted them to this mode of behaviour was not the thrill of seeing Theresa's boobs but the fact that they were not supposed to do it. This taboo, therefore, made it compulsory viewing for them.

The sound of their muted giggling, mixed with a million other jumbled thoughts and dreams, clanged together inside the constant throb that was Peter's head as it lay, seemingly detached from its body, on the hall carpet. An all-pervasive smell of disinfectant, that Magrit had used to counteract the smell of alcoholic vomit after she had cleaned the carpet, made Peter think that he may have been in a hospital. His head ached with a dull pounding that was nigh on unbearable.

He tried raising his head a little from the carpet to alleviate it from the rhythmic pulsing. A wave of nausea instantly engulfed him and caused his head to sink back down to the comfort of the damp smelly threadbare wool and nylon mixture in some kind of oriental motif that was trying futilely to service his head's need of comfort and normality.

A groan escaped from his lips – a groan that made Tim and Frankie cease chortling as their heads spun round to check if they had been rumbled. On seeing that this was not the case, they went back to keeking through the keyhole.

The ache that was now the sole sensation inside Peter's head threatened to burst through and spill on to the floor. Another groan broke free from him as he tried to raise his head. This had the effect of relieving the pain that surged back and forth through his clogged-up cranium. Unfortunately, it also had the consequence of returning the swell of nausea that broke over him like surf pounding on a beach. Torn between unrelenting pain or unmerciful nausea, he lay like this for what seemed an eternity as he promised himself over and over, 'Never again. Never again.'

Harry had found the album and was smiling wistfully at it as he surveyed it on the kitchen table. 'Happy days,' he thought wryly, as his eyes focused through the lenses of his National Health specs on a photograph of him and some of his old army pals. They had been snapped just before they had gone on active duty and were all smiling the smile of confident heroes who were about to embark on a great adventure. None of them had ever been outside the British Isles – most of them had never been outside Scotland. This was their chance to see the world and they were going to enjoy every moment of it. Everyone said it would be over in six months, then they could come back and have a host of stories and tales to tell of their exploits and deeds of gallantry. It was going to be great fun.

> The best-laid schemes o' mice an' men
> Gang aft a-gley.

The well-known lines from Burns caused Harry's sardonic smile to broaden. Memories that he had thought forgotten came back with a clarity he had not enjoyed for a long time.

Peter's head registered another form of pounding. It was not quite so dull and insistent as before but it was there nevertheless. He felt his body start to rock from side to side. This did not help the nausea and he cried out in protest. His lips were incapable of forming actual words but he did his best to protect what was left of his automatic response to self-preservation.

Tim's squeaky wee voice found its way inside him and he heard it say, 'Da? Mister Hood's here tae see you. He says it's important.'

Peter tried to focus on John and rise up from the supine position that had served him so well for the past couple of hours to greet him. He failed miserably. The best he could manage was a thumbs-up sign as he sank back down on to the imitation Axminster.

'You OK?' John asked tentatively.

'No' bad,' Peter replied. His voice tailed off at the end of the sentence because of the effort the answer required from him.

TWENTY-FOUR

Dolly was sitting on the stool in front of her stall. She had removed her boots and socks and was intently surveying her left foot, which was perched on top of her right knee. In vain, she tried to get a look at the sole of her foot but this was proving impossible due to her waist being three times the size it used to be. 'Doreen,' she called out, 'gonnae come here a minute?'

As Doreen appeared at the side of Dolly's stall, Dolly held her leg out and up so that the sole of the foot was facing towards Doreen for inspection. 'Is that a wee corn I'm gettin' there, Doreen, or is it just a bit o' hard skin?' she asked, her face creased in earnest consideration.

'I think it's just hard skin, Dolly,' was Doreen's diagnosis.

'Thank God for that. My mother had awful bad feet and I'm feart I get them as well 'cause I take after her, you know. Gonnae give us a hand into the step-in sink?'

Doreen nodded and offered her shoulder, which Dolly steadied herself against while she stepped up about a foot and a half into the low sink that contained blankets steeping in warm soapy water.

'Is that you OK, Dolly?' Doreen enquired before she retreated back into her own stall and, indeed, into the blankets that were lying in her sink also waiting to be washed.

Dolly thanked Doreen and proceeded with driving the dirt

from the blankets. The way the women tackled this arduous and heavy job was to trample on the blankets much in the same as winegrowers did with grapes. It was an extremely effective way to drive any dirt that may have accumulated on them. This was an age when most men worked with their hands on building sites or in shipyards or factories and there was no disgrace in bedclothes or, indeed, any washing being soiled – the only disgrace would have lain in not doing anything about it. Then you would have become what was known as 'the talk of the steamie'. This was not a term that suggested you were the envy of your peers or anyone else really and was to be avoided at all costs.

As Dolly trampled all the offending microbes from her blankets, she watched the water seep through her toes and noted, 'This'll save me washing my feet thenight.' There was no reply from any of the others so Dolly carried on, 'It fairly gets the dirt oot o' them.'

'What? Your feet?' Magrit threw back.

'Naw, the blankets.'

'It's amazin' where the dirt comes from,' Doreen joined in, as she too surveyed the murky water that was gathering slowly round her feet. 'I can understand sheets gettin' dirty but no' blankets.'

'It comes off the men,' Dolly said, informatively.

'Right enough,' agreed Magrit. 'He's mingin' when he gets in the hoose. If he's been workin wi' the boilermakers, he's covered in rust.'

'Aye. John's the same,' Doreen affirmed. 'But he always has a good wash in the kitchen sink, though and he comes up here to the baths and has one twice a week.'

'Peter's a bit like that – except he has one twice a year,' Magrit said scathingly as she too climbed into the step-in sink and commenced to tread the pile beneath her feet. 'See my two boys? They will not wash themselves. It's a fight to the death every night. You want to see their shirt collars – you could plant tatties in them.'

'Men are all clatty in their persons, though,' was Dolly's verdict, arrived at after a lifetime's experience.

Doreen was almost daydreaming as she tramped absent-mindedly through this part of the wash cycle. 'What I would like eventually is a hoose wi' a bath inside it,' she said, wistfully.

Magrit considered this piece of fantasy for a moment before replying firmly, 'Naw, I like the sprays better. I never have a bath in here. I always go to the sprays.'

Dolly decided that she should share her ablutionary habits with the others and voted in favour of having a bath.

Magrit stated that, as far as she was concerned, you were simply lying in your own dirt in a bath.

Dolly countered that by protesting that it was your own dirt you were lying in and nobody else's.

This piece of logic stopped the discussion for a moment, before Magrit took up the cudgel and again stated that she preferred the sprays.

Doreen furthered the discussion by announcing, 'See, in America, they've all got them in their hooses – except they call them showers and no' sprays.'

'Is that no' just in the Hollywood pictures that they have them?' Dolly asked in politeness to Doreen's fanciful statement – although she was convinced in her own mind that it was, indeed, only in the pictures.

'Naw,' Doreen explained, 'aw the hooses have got sprays – and washin' machines as well.' Doreen was now in full flow and continued with the lesson on Mr and Mrs America's average home, 'And they've all got refrigerators and telephones and . . . and televisions as well,' she concluded.

Dolly shook her head in wonderment. She had never

suspected that this was the case but Doreen had said it with such conviction that she felt the lassie must be right. Indeed, she remembered something that would be of interest to her two pals. 'Here,' she called out, thus attracting their attention for what she was about to announce. 'My sister Jenny's daughter's husband's bought one o' them.'

Doreen was immediately all ears. 'What? A television? . . . Have you ever seen it?' She was so excited that she stopped tramping.

'Naw, but Jenny's seen it. She says it's great,' Dolly said.

'I know all the big hooses in Dalmeny Crescent have them. You can see the big things stickin' oot the chimney pots,' Magrit said sagely while the rust-coloured water lapped between her toes.

Dolly added ominously that they cost a fortune and Doreen threw up the argument that you would actually save money because you would never have to go out. Dolly agreed this was, indeed, the case and said that her sister Jenny's daughter and her husband never went anywhere now. Indeed she said that they used to visit her sister quite a lot but, lately, they hadn't gone near her. It got so that Jenny had taken to going round there more and more but she eventually gave up because nobody talked to anybody while it was on.

'That wouldnae suit you, Dolly, eh?' Magrit said, looking over into Doreen's stall and winking to Doreen.

Dolly agreed without moment's hesitation. 'Ye're right there – I like tae hear people talkin'. My Boab says it's a wonder my lips are no' frayed at the edges. I'd be as well talkin' to myself as tryin' to haud a conversation wi' him, though,' she grumbled, as she started to drain down the dirty water from the step-in sink.

'What kind o' things do they see on the television, Dolly?' Doreen persisted.

'I couldn't tell you, hen,' Dolly answered, as she turned on the tap that let clean water pour over the blankets to give them a rinse out.

'That's my dream,' Doreen stated firmly. 'A hoose in the country wi' a television, a bath and a phone – and a garden as well,' she added.

'You're no' wantin' much,' was Magrit's response.

'I'll get it eventually, Magrit. I've put my name doon for a hoose in Drumchapel,' Doreen said resolutely, referring to the vast sprawl of greenbelt that had been allocated for corporation housing to relieve the overspill from the destruction of old housing stock that was about to devastate the city.

Dolly looked up from her chores and said, offhandedly, 'Drumchapel? She'll no' be talkin' to us, eh, Magrit?'

'Between being out in the garden, watching the television and having baths, she'll not have the chance to talk to anybody,' Magrit replied in a posh voice which, considering her background, she did very well.

Doreen smiled at Magrit's send up and decided she would join in, with an even more posh voice. 'Of course, you would always be able to PHONE for an appointment.' A large grin spread over her face at topping Magrit's jibe. Glaswegians, whether men or women, have always found the lure of a verbal joust irresistible. Magrit was in the mood for one and so, it seemed, was Doreen.

'Aye, right enough,' Magrit answered, before picking up the scrubbing brush, dialling a mock phone number and then holding it up to her ear. 'DRRING-DRRING, DRRING-DRRING. She's no' in, Dolly. Of course, she might be oot in the gairden. I'll keep trying.'

Dolly didn't reply as she was still busy unloading blankets from the sink.

Doreen was not to be outdone, however. Picking up her

own scrubbing brush, she answered Magrit's scrubbing brush with the mother of all affected voices, 'Hellooo – Drumchapel 3776. To whom am I speaking?' She grinned inanely at Magrit, well pleased with herself.

Not to be outdone Magrit carried on with the charade. 'This is Magrit McGuire here. I was wondering if perhaps I could have a word with Mrs Doreen Hood who resides at The Willows, Drumchapel,' Magrit smiled back to Doreen, with a top-that-if-you-can expression.

Doreen smirked wickedly. 'This is her maid. I believe Mrs Hood is in conference with the workmen who are putting in the new TERRAZZO MARBLE flooring in the BIG room.'

'Well,' Magrit smirked back, 'I don't want to disturb her while she is servicing the workmen. If you could just say that one of her old friends from the Carnegie Street steamie called, I'd most grateful.'

Before she could replace the receiver/scrubbing brush, Doreen fired back, 'Oh, just a moment, I think you are in luck. Mrs hood has just entered through the FRENCH WINDOWS. I'll see if she's free.'

'Thank you – you're very kind,' Magrit responded with a curled lip.

Doreen pushed open an imaginary door at the front of her stall and stepped out on to the steamie floor. Nodding graciously to no one in general and Magrit in particular, she said, 'This is Doreen Hood of 73 The Willows Drumchapel speaking to you PERSONALLY.'

From over Magrit's shoulder in the Johnson stall, Dolly's voice said, 'Is it her? We were lucky we got her in, Magrit.'

Magrit turned to smile knowingly at Dolly but was surprised to see that Dolly was still busily working away and not even looking their way.

'Helloooo, is there anyone there?' Doreen cooed.

Magrit turned her attention back to Doreen and answered, 'This is Magrit McGuire – we used to be friendly – in the old days – I don't suppose you'll remember me, though?' Her lips were smiling but her voice was acidic.

Doreen replied with a beaming grin, 'That's right – I've forgot all about you.'

Dolly's voice again cut in, 'Ask her if she minds o' me. She'll remember me.' She was wiping her brow and sighed with relief that the blanket situation was put to bed – so to speak.

Both Magrit and Doreen looked at Dolly quizzically and both thought, 'Surely not.'

Doreen carried on regardless, 'Eh! Do you have an appointment?'

Magrit answered with mock humility, 'I'm very sorry, I'm afraid I don't.'

At this, Dolly appeared by Magrit's side in the stall and, wiping her hands on her backside, she said, in a manner that was bereft of any nonsense, 'Gie it to me. Let me speak to her.'

Magrit's mouth, much to her surprise, fell open.

Doreen saw there was sport to be had and asked, 'Is there someone there with you Mrs McGuire?'

Magrit lifted the brush to her ear and could not fail to notice that Dolly was on her tiptoes trying to listen in to the conversation by placing her ear next to the brush. 'Yesss, there is, indeed – another old chum of yours – a Mrs Dolly Johnson?'

Both Magrit and Doreen saw that Dolly was listening intently. 'Dolly Johnson?' Doreen said, tentatively, as if searching her memory banks. 'Dolly Johnson . . . Now, just a moment, does she have bowly legs?'

Magrit started to laugh openly before she heard Dolly say emphatically, 'See, I told you she would remember me. Give us the phone.'

It appeared that Dolly's love of talking had just passed the line of demarcation. 'There isnae a phone,' Magrit said, incredulously.

Dolly eyes shone with intensity, as she said impatiently, 'I know that – I know that – but,' she continued, 'give us it anyway.'

To say that Magrit and Doreen were astonished would be almost accurate – incredulous would do more justice to their astonishment.

'Hello, Doreen, hen,' Dolly spoke into the scrubbing brush to Doreen with the air of someone she hadn't spoken to in years. 'Are you up to your eyes in it, hen?'

Doreen was still in shock but came to as Magrit's elbow dug into her ribs and egged her on to see how far Dolly could be swept along by the moment. Doreen took a deep breath and then joined Dolly in her flight of fancy. 'Oh! Goodness me, yes – what with the workmen being in and everything.'

'Aye – they'll cause an awful stoor,' Dolly nodded in sympathy with Doreen's plight.

'Well, it's been one of those days, Mrs Johnson.'

'Oh, naw, has it, hen?' Dolly said with warm compassion.

Doreen glanced again at Magrit who signalled her to go for it. 'You see, John and I are going to the opera tonight and I went and dropped my tiara on the bathroom carpet and, of course, the pile on that carpet is so thick that it took me ages to find it.'

Dolly had now rested her behind on the sink to make herself comfortable, obviously she was up for a right old chinwag. 'Is that right, hen?' she replied earnestly to Doreen's assertion of the trials and tribulations of a typical Drumchapel dweller.

Magrit was eating a wet sock to stifle her laughter.

'Oh, yes, Mrs Johnson,' Doreen prattled on. 'And, of course, this terrazzo marble just arrived from Italy this afternoon and, when the workmen were carrying it in, they nearly broke the TELEVISION SET.

'Oh, naw,' Dolly gasped.

'But, fortunately, the DISPLAY CABINET got in the way – and they only just missed the RADIOGRAM too.'

'That was lucky, hen, eh?' Dolly said into the brush.

'Anyway I've just sat them all down in the DINING ROOM and told the maid to bring something in from the REFRIGERATOR. I just hope the noise from the WASHING MACHINE in the kitchen doesn't disturb them too much.'

'Well, let's hope no', hen, eh?' Dolly concurred respectfully, before carrying on with, 'Do you no' mind o' Magrit McGuire, Doreen? Her maiden name's Docherty but she got mairried on tae Annie McGuire's boy, Peter. They stayed up the fish pen.'

'I don't think so,' Doreen squeaked as she tried not to dissolve.

'You must know Annie McGuire,' Dolly persisted. 'Her uncle used to work in the fish shop at the corner o' Balshagray Lane.'

Doreen tried to speak but all that came out was a thin squawk, shaking her head she signalled to Magrit that she could not keep going.

Dolly stared at the phone. 'Hello? Hello?' Are you still there, Doreen?' She asked the scrubbing brush.

Magrit took up the cudgel as Doreen collapsed. 'Hello. Is that Dolly Johnson?' she said severely.

Dolly stared at the brush. 'Is that you, Magrit?' she asked, incredulously.

'Yes. I would just like to say that if you don't get aff that phone, you'll never get your washing done thenight.' Doreen and Magrit laughed like drains.

The spell was broken. Anyone else would have felt very foolish at being so silly but not Dolly Johnson. She had enjoyed herself immensely and, to her, that was all that mattered. For a wee while, she had been taken out of herself by her own innocence and enthusiasm and it would have taken a cruel disposition to blame her for that. Holding her hand up to her cheek in a gesture that showed disbelief, Dolly enthused to Doreen and Magrit, as they slid cheerfully back into their stalls, 'I got right carried away there. I actually thought I was phonin'. I enjoyed that . . . Oh! I'd like one o' them in the hoose.'

She hurried down to Mary Culfeathers' stall where Mary was unaware of what had gone on because of her exertions at the sink. She looked up as Dolly hailed her with a voice that still registered high excitement, 'Mrs Culfeathers – Mrs Culfeathers, did you hear me phonin' there?' Dolly asked, pointing to her stall – proud of her prowess with the new-fangled technology she had just mastered.

'Naw, I was busy, hen,' Mary answered, a bit taken aback. 'I never knew they had a phone in here,' she thought as Dolly made her way back to her own washing.

Andy was whistling Frankie Laine's hit 'The Girl in the Woods' when he informed everyone that a wringer, that had been out of order, was now back on-board. The women all shouted OK so he turned to give the remainder of the steamie washers the good news.

Before he left, Mary Culfeathers ushered him over to her. Andy thought she had maybe not heard him due to her advanced age so he repeated it as he drew opposite her stall, 'That's the wringer fixed noo, Mrs Culfeathers.'

'Thanks, son,' she said, before adding, 'Andy, where's the phone in here?' She gestured to her stall with her head.

'Phone? In here?' Andy replied, justifiably puzzled.

'Dolly Johnson's got one in her stall. Is there no one in here?' Her head beckoned again towards her stall.

Andy was unsure where to go with this. He shook his head. 'Not that I know of,' was the best he could do.

'Ach, it doesn't matter. There's nobody would be phonin' me anyway,' she said, retreating back into her stall.

Not for the first time, Andy left mystified as to what was going on.

TWENTY-FIVE

John surveyed Peter as he sat at the table. The contents of the paper bag he had brought with him from the licensed grocer were about to run out on them and Peter's eyes were beginning to regain their old sparkle as the hair of the dog did its magic. Peter looked up from the quarter-full McEwan's screw top which, apart from the one John was drinking, was all that was left of the half dozen John had brought in with him and pointed a shaky finger at John. His voice was still just a croak but twice as good as it had been a half hour ago when John had first knocked on the door. 'That's the second time you've saved my bacon theday. Eh – I'm really sorry that you've had to come a' the way up here for the money you lent me. Fact is I cannae pay you back – I never picked up my wages – sorry.' He sheepishly drained the last bit from the bottle and spread his arms out in the universal gesture that said there was nothing else he could do.

John waited a second or two, then reached into his pocket and threw a brown envelope on to the table. It hit the table top with a dull thud. Peter stared at the packet uncomprehendingly. John coughed and then held up three fingers. 'Third time,' he said, as he took a swig from his own bottle. Peter's eyes finally focused on the name at the top of the wage packet.

Theresa was in the bedroom, studying herself in the wardrobe mirror. She made a small adjustment to the strap of the new bra she had got for her Christmas. Putting it on made her feel that, at last, she was growing up for real. She was so glad that her mother had given it to her privately. The last thing she needed was Tim and Frankie sending her up. She turned her back to the mirror to see how she looked from the rear. 'Mmmm,' she thought, 'not bad.'

She could cheerfully have strangled the pair of them. If only they could be like the brothers that were in films, they would not be so annoying.

Maybe, she thought, as she surveyed her reflection from the side, it was a sign of her own maturity that was making them so unbearable. She quickly rejected this, as they had, as far as she could remember, always been unbearable.

She turned around and stared at the other side of herself and couldn't help notice that she did not look as buxom as she hoped. 'A wee bit of paddin' might do the trick?' she reasoned – but what to use? She hurried over to the chest of drawers. One by one she opened up the drawers of the dresser that her mother kept their clothes in. They were empty. She had taken everything to be washed – well, everything like socks, knickers, etc. that would have done as padding. There were jumpers and some blouses but they were all too big. There must be something that she could use to give her an idea of how she would look once her bust exercises had attained the effect that she strove for. Breast-wise, Jane Russell was her ideal. She and Rena had gone to see the hit Hollywood movie *The Paleface*, which starred Bob Hope and Jane Russell. Hope was as always hilarious and had the audience rolling around in their seats but, as far as Theresa was concerned, Jane Russell was the best in the picture. She was voluptuous, witty and strong-willed and her lips always glistened and shone. When she smiled her top lip curled up at the corner, giving her a smile that was wickedly seductive and making her irresistibly attractive. That was the ideal Theresa strove for.

Her eyes raked the room for some kind of padding that she could use. It seemed she was out of luck, then she spied the copy of yesterday's newspaper her mother had been reading lying by the side of the bed. Picking it up she separated the pages and began scrunching them up and shaping them into what could pass as Jane Russell's breasts.

Peter was smiling the smile of a hanged man who had just been reprieved. He had been feeling steadily better since the McEwan's had sloshed round his digestive system. 'Now, I'm no' takin' no for an answer,' he rasped. 'You and me are goin' oot and you are not goin' to put your hand in your pocket a' night – that's settled, OK?'

'I need to get back for Doreen comin' in from the steamie, Peter,' John said, 'but, up till then, I am willing for you tae ply me wi' free drink, if you've got your heart set on it.'

'That's us, then. I'll throw a jacket on and we'll head off.' Peter clapped his hands and rubbed them together to signify that a deal had been struck.

Tim and Frankie were engrossed in a game of snap with a packet of cards that had long ago lost at least half a dozen of its cardboard characters.

This condition normally would have rendered the pack useless but the shortage only added to Tim and Frankie's enjoyment – it meant they could argue the toss that whoever won had done so unfairly and any excuse for the brothers to argue and cause what their parents called a ruction was always all right with them.

Frankie was just about to call out SNAP on a jam-stained

eight of clubs with his own dog-eared eight of diamonds when the door opened to the kitchen and Theresa was revealed framed in the doorway. Her lip was curled up in what she hoped was a provocative smile but was actually more like a nerve ending that caused her mouth to look a bit deformed. However, it was her chest that made the two boys' eyes stand out like saucers on stalks. Under the greying-white school blouse that she wore, her breasts were three times their normal size and also looked a bit deformed. This was due to the strange bumps and indentations that the scrunched-up *Daily Record* had been subjected to in the trial run that was Theresa's first go at the art of exuding femininity. She mistook the boys' open mouths for unbridled male admiration and vamped her way over to the table where her father sat also staring at her. He knew something was wrong with her but couldn't figure out what it was.

Turning her new-found allure fully on John Hood, she leant on the table and made sure that her arms were pressing tight to the side of her chest. This would double up on the effect of the sport section that was crumpled up inside her bra. She ignored the sound of paper rustling and, through half-shut eyelids, asked with the lower register of her voice, 'Would youse perhaps care for a cup of tea, Mr Hood?' Theresa was revelling in the attention she was getting.

The moment was spoiled a bit, however, by Tim shouting, 'What's happened to your tits, Theresa?'

The moment was then rent asunder by the two lads collapsing in peals of laughter as they rolled around the floor holding on to their sides and pointing at Theresa's maladjusted mammaries.

Peter and John looked on in mystification as Theresa screamed at her two brothers, 'Shut it . . . just . . . shut it . . . I hate you . . . I hate everybody in this hoose.' Her screams of

153

frustration rang round the kitchen and were still reverberating in the ears of the bewildered John and Peter as they watched her run out and slam the door.

Eventually it dawned on Peter why his daughter reacted as she did. He rose from the table and crossed over to his two boys. Their eyes looked up at him from the floor expecting retribution. He grabbed both of them by the back of their shirt collars and hauled them to their feet and gave each of them a clip around the ears. 'Don't you ever . . . any of youse . . . ever again . . . call your sister's breasts "tits". OK? . . . Is that understood?'

The boys feigned regret and snuffled their apology as they wiped imaginary tears from their eyes, then smiled secretly at each other because they had discovered a brand new way to bring misery to their sister's life.

TWENTY-SIX

Harry stared fixedly at himself in the full-size swivel mirror that had been a decorative fixture in their bedroom when it was first bought. Encased in an oval walnut frame, it rested on a brass fulcrum that allowed it to turn all the way round. Mary had been wanting one for years so Harry had splashed out and made it a birthday gift from him to her. He remembered the delight she had shown when Pickfords had delivered it. She had, of course, admonished him and said he shouldn't have spent all that money on her but he knew that she was not all that annoyed by the way she was hugging him. He very seldom went into this room these days – it was too cold. However, this time Harry didn't feel the cold due largely to him having his First World War uniform on. When he had been demobbed, he had managed to hold on to it – 'Just as a keepsake' – and placed it underneath his other clothes in his private drawer at the bottom of the wardrobe. It had lain there for the last thirty-odd years but, tonight, something inside Harry's brain urged him to put it on again.

Standing there, surveying himself, he was like one of the characters in a cowboy movie. The upright guy who has lain away his guns but now has to strap them on one last time to ensure that good will triumph over evil.

Harry was young again. The voices and the sounds of battle were again ringing in his ear. Mortar shells exploded and men yelled as they fell all round him. Smoke swirled and officers bellowed commands. As they were running up the beachhead, the whistle of mortar shells screeched through the night air and briefly clothed, in an eerie grey and white stark light, tragic scenes of death and destruction as they exploded, sending sand spuming all over. Again, the panic-stricken cry of, 'GAS! GAS!' assailed his ears.

'PUT YOUR MASKS ON! MASKS ON!' was the frenzied clarion call. Harry was oblivious to the danger. Something had forewarned him all this would happen and he was prepared for it. His face was devoid of all emotion as he saluted his reflection. 'Aye, Sir. My mask is on.' And it was.

TWENTY-SEVEN

Dolly had been hard at it for quite a while – long enough for her to feel in need of a break and a chat. This was not a feeling Dolly ever ignored. She never knew what she was going to talk about when the notion took her – she just knew, if she opened her mouth, nature would supply a topic. Wiping her hands on her skirt, she left the stall and crossed into Doreen's. Sure enough, in the few seconds it had taken her to accomplish this, a subject had metamorphosed in her brain and was ready to be put up for discussion. This one was a peach. 'Did you hear Maureen McCandlish is getting married?' Dolly threw the statement in front of Doreen.

Doreen's jaw sagged and her whole body seized to a halt as she turned to face Dolly with an expression of total disbelief. 'You're kiddin' – Maureen McCandlish? Getting mairried?' Her voice had risen in such shock that it carried over into Magrit's stall.

This information made even Magrit stop. She laid down one of Frankie's shirts that had stubbornly been holding on to small barnacles of snot, encrusted under the arms, and joined in the latest news from *Pathé News and Gazette*'s correspondent in Glasgow – Dolly Johnson. 'Who the hell is she getting mairried to?' Magrit asked, echoing Doreen's enquiry.

'I think it's some fellah from Springburn. Anyway, that's what I was told,' she stated, shaking her head in a way that suggested there might be more to this than she had been led to believe.

'Who told you?' Doreen pressed.

'Isobel McNee in the fish shop,' Dolly said firmly, naming one of the best sources for gossip in the neighborhood as verification.

Magrit shook her head in wonderment. 'Christ – he'll no' have his troubles tae seek, him.'

There was a brief moment while they all silently agreed with this, then Doreen added, 'It'll no' be a white weddin', that.'

Dolly nodded assent to this and then said, 'Naw! They're a bad lot, them.'

'It's well seen she had to go oot the district to find somebody that didnae know her,' Doreen opined, folding her arms and leaning against the side of her stall. 'Has she no' had a wean already?' She threw this open for discussion.

Magrit was not one to let the side down by not discussing it and then some. 'Aye. She was away for a long time aboot two years ago. Supposed to be workin' in England – but she was havin' the wean. You could see it before she went. She was goin' aboot sayin' she'd have to go on a diet and stop eatin' sweeties.' Magrit made a face that suggested a high degree of scepticism. 'Must think we came up the Clyde on a biscuit.'

The others snorted their approval of Magrit's summation, then gasped as she added, 'She was seen up at Blythswood Square.'

Blythswood Square, as everyone from Glasgow knew, was a notorious part of the city where the ladies of the night plied their trade.

This news was so delicious that Dolly and Doreen, in their excitement, spluttered 'She was not, was she?' at the same time as their senses thrilled at what they were about to hear.

Magrit sensed the floor was now hers and pulled a cigarette out from her pack. As she lit it, she informed them, 'Bella McNaughton saw her.' Magrit allowed herself a smirk. 'Of course, you know what Bella's like.' Her face showed that Bella was a firm favourite in the district and was noted for not being averse to a bit of fun and nonsense.

Doreen and Dolly were acquainted with Bella. 'Aye,' they chorused.

'She's a hell of a woman, Bella,' Dolly added, her voice laced with affection.

'Bella says she seen her standin' aboot one o' the corners,' Magrit continued. 'Of course, Bella watched her for aboot ten minutes – to see what would happen.'

Doreen's face was aglow with the prospect of new scandal. 'Did somebody pick her up?'

Magrit nodded. 'Bella says this fellah walked up to her and they were talkin' away – you know . . .' Her voice was heavy with inference.

'That's terrible,' Doreen said to Dolly, full of moral indignation.

Dolly sighed righteously. 'So it is, hen.'

Magrit interrupted them, trying to get on with the story, 'Aye, right enough, but wait till you hear. Apparently he kept shakin' his head. She must have been askin' for too much money.'

'She's nae oil paintin', right enough,' Dolly reasoned.

'She's got a face like a coo's airse,' Magrit agreed.

'Whit happened?' said Doreen, impatient to get to the meat of the story.

'Eventually, this fellah walked away. So the bold Bella saunters up to her and says, "Hello, Maureen, it's a lovely night, isn't it? You oot for a wee walk?"'

The women gasped in pleasure at Bella's audacity.

'Bella says her face went pure purple. She says to Bella, "I'm just waitin' here for my boyfriend. He's a wee bit late, so he is." You know thon voice of hers as well. It's like a bull fartin' through a fog horn.' Magrit's description was cruel but accurate. 'Anyway, she's dyin' to get Bella oot the way but, of course, Bella does not want to play that game. She keeps talkin' to her. "And what does your boyfriend work at?" "How long have you been going out together?"'

'She's pure evil, Bella, once she gets started,' Doreen enthused.

Magrit nodded her agreement on that score, then continued, 'By this time Maureen's gettin' agitated and she says, "I think I'll just go home. He'll probably turn up at my mother's." Just at that this wee coolie comes daunerin' up to them – from one o' the boats, you know?'

'Oh, Christ,' Dolly blasphemed loudly in astonishment.

'Naw,' Doreen echoed her astonishment.

'Aye,' Magrit confirmed. 'And he says to Maureen, "You come jig-jig on boat?" and Bella said the Maureen wan says indignantly, "I'm afraid I'm not like that." The wee coolie says to her, "Same price as last night – only, this time, you not be so rough."'

'Agghhh,' Dolly cried with delight. 'What did Bella say?'

'Oh! Bella got aff her mark. But she met her again in the butcher's, aboot a week later, and she says to her, "Aye, Maureen – you still goin' oot wi' that wee guy wi' the baggy troosers?"'

Doreen glanced at Magrit and Dolly, unconsciously secure in the knowledge she was part of their lives and not the McCandlishes'. 'She's a bugger, Bella. I'd heard Maureen was hawkin' herself but I didnae know it was true. That's horrible, isn't it? She's filthy dirty as well.'

'They're all mingin,' Dolly agreed. 'The sanitary's never away from them.'

'The faither works beside Peter,' Magrit volunteered. 'You know what they call him? The carbolic kid. When he dies they'll no' bury him, they'll plant him.'

TWENTY-EIGHT

Peter turned round from where he had been giving his face and upper body a wash in the sink. He dried himself off with a damp towel and addressed John who was inhaling on a Player's cigarette.

'We'll go oot and get a right drink noo,' Peter announced grandly. He was getting back more and more into the party mode as the beer worked its magic on his system.

'I don't want to get blootered before the bells, Peter,' John said cautiously.

'I know how you feel, John,' Peter lied. He called over to Tim and Frankie. 'Away and tell Theresa to make us a cup o' tea.' He winked at John. 'We'll have a cup o' tea first – that'll put a lining on our stomachs. That way we'll no' get blootered too quick – and, mind, the night's on me. I owe you big time and Peter McGuire is not a man that only takes – he gives back to those who deserve it and you've been a good pal to me so you definitely deserve it.'

John was starting to realise that Peter was beginning to talk a lot of crap and that a cup of tea lining his stomach was never going to be an adequate defence for ensuring sobriety.

Frankie came back in from the lobby. 'She's no' in, Da,' he said in his squeaky voice. 'She left this lying on the bed.' He placed a note on the table. It was a page ripped out of a school jotter.

Peter crossed over to it still trying to dry himself on the wet towel. He picked it up and read aloud as he scanned it. It was in a hastily scribbled form and said:

I cannae stand it here any longer. I'm away. Tell my ma I'm sorry to leave without seeing her.
Theresa.
PS
I love you all. I just can't stand you.
Sorry.

Tim and Frankie sniggered to each other but they stopped this when Peter grabbed them both by the necks and growled, 'Right, ya wee bastards, see if anything happens to her, I'm gonnae knock the pair o' you good lookin' – so you better hope I find her before your ma gets back.'

Tim saw before Frankie did that the look in his father's eyes and the firmness of his grip at the back of their necks meant he was not issuing an idle threat.

'Do you want us to help you look for her, Da?' he asked, trying to avoid further retribution that might be heading his way.

'Naw – one missin' is bad enough. Stay here in case she comes back.'

Like Tim, John could see that all thoughts of further drinking or any kind of revels had vanished from Peter's demeanour. It was probably the first time that he had ever witnessed Peter genuinely worried about anything.

'She cannae be that far. Come on,' John said, rising from his chair and pulling on the jacket that he had hung over the back of it.

The sound of the front door slamming shut signalled to the brothers that they were alone in the house. Frankie sat in

163

silence, lost in his own thoughts.

'She's just wantin' attention,' was his considered opinion on Theresa's sudden departure.

Tim deliberated on his brother's pronouncement. 'So?' was his considered opinion.

TWENTY-NINE

Doreen was still trying to come to terms with the McCandlishes' mode of living. 'Her brother was at school wi' me. I always felt sorry for him. He'd to sit by himself 'cause he'd beasts in his head. He'd had his head shaved and that blue stuff dabbed a' over it but he was no' a bad-lookin' boy – you know, if he'd been turned oot right?'

Magrit nodded agreement. 'You're talkin' aboot Davie McCandlish?'

'Oh, aye,' Doreen hastily consented, remembering that there was another male McCandlish – one who was never going to make it as a matinee idol. 'No' the other one.'

'Naw, naw, no' – the oldest wan – no' Humphrey! You'd think somebody had sat on his face while it was still warm,' Magrit agreed, a bit harshly perhaps.

'Aye, him and Maureen take after one another,' Dolly decreed, adding her own ruling to that of her companion's final, if unflattering, judgement.

Fixing on their eyes with a slow burn that made the blood freeze in their veins, Magrit asked the others, 'Have you ever been in the hoose?'

Doreen's eyes responded to Magrit's like a rabbit trapped in the headlights of a car. 'Naw,' she croaked.

Dolly replied with an indignant shake of her head, 'Not me. I wouldnae go in there.' For Dolly to leave a sentence that short meant only one thing – she wanted more information, information that could be stored and regurgitated at some future moment in time, and she was willing to pay what was, for her, the high price of not speaking for a wee while to achieve this end.

Magrit took her cue and then held the pause as expertly as any seasoned actress before continuing with her account. 'I had to go in to it once. I cannae remember whit for but, dear God, you want to see it. I mean none o' us have got much money,' she paused dramatically, 'but there is no excuse for that place. You can always afford a bar o' soap, eh?'

Dolly gasped with horrified relish. ''Zit as bad as that, Magrit?' she muttered, grimly.

Magrit nodded somberly, 'You wipe your feet when you go oot o' that place. Noo I'll say it myself, my hoose is no' palace . . .'

'Naw,' Dolly agreed readily, without thinking the full implication of her statement through. Fortunately Magrit did not pick up on it either. 'But,' she continued, 'how any woman that calls herself a woman could let things get intae that state . . .? They've got a cat – supposed to be a pet but I think it's tae keep the rats to a minimum.'

'Oh, don't,' Dolly shivered. 'I'm hell of a feart o' thae things.'

Magrit held up a hand to signal that this was a perfectly valid fear and then carried on, 'Well, this cat had . . .' her eyes rolled in disgust . . . 'shit on the floor . . . and she had just left it lyin' there.' Her face rankled in distaste. 'I can *not* tell you what the smell was like – I was just aboot boakin' my guts up.'

Doreen's face confirmed that she was in a similar state just listening.

'Then,' Magrit continued resolutely, 'then she asked me if I'd like a CUP OF TEA.'

166

The other two gagged at the thought and held their hands up to their mouths.

Magrit cupped her hands over her face to compose herself. 'Well, if you'd seen the cups . . . whatever colour they had been originally, I couldn't tell you. My stomach was heavin'. I had tae make an excuse and I left.'

'I've seen that wee cat oot in the street. It's a wee black and white one, isn't it?' Doreen asked.

'That's right,' Magrit replied. 'It's only got the one eye.'

Doreen deliberated on this before adding, 'It's a shame. It never gets fed.'

'It must be hoachin' wi' fleas,' Dolly guessed correctly. They sat in silence and sympathy.

'It's called Lucky,' said Doreen eventually.

'To think a cat's got nine lives . . . and it's stuck wi' this one,' Dolly said, sadly.

'I'll need to get back to this washin' or I'll never finish it thenight,' Magrit said, practically.

They turned and, like high priestesses of purification, went into their respective temples to cleanliness.

THIRTY

Peter and John emerged from the McGuires' close-mouth on to Melton Street and looked around for any sign of Theresa. It was very dark by now and only a pool of phosphorous yellow light from the corner lamp post shed any relief from the gloom. A group of men and one or two boys were huddling under it smoking and laughing and arguing over each other's observations on anything they felt was worth ridiculing or arguing about. It was a form of the Oxford Debating Society – only it was in Glasgow. Mainly they talked about the relative merits of Celtic, Rangers, Partick Thistle and Clyde football clubs. Now and again politics did get mooted but that usually only lasted ten minutes before football took over as the main topic once more.

There was a chance, however, that they might have seen Theresa. Not wanting to be seen to be panicking, Peter and John walked rather than ran towards the group.

'Any o' you seen oor Theresa?' Peter said, as casually as he could.

Big Alec Bailey, known as The Grip because it was thought he was high up in the Masons, nodded. 'Aye, she passed us by aboot twenty minutes ago. She was headin' towards Argyle Street but I don't know where she went then.' He studied Peter and noted that John was with him as well – an unlikely combination. 'Is everything a' right?'

'Aye – nae bother,' Peter lied expertly. 'She's just away wi' the hoose keys – that's all. Better try and catch her up. Have a good New Year, eh?'

John put his thumbs up to signal his good wishes too as they ran towards Argyle Street.

'She'll be OK, Peter,' he tried to console his fretful friend as they ran.

'Aye,' Peter said, not consoled at all. 'If she thinks she was unhappy twenty minutes ago . . .' He left the rest of the sentence unfinished.

Theresa walked hurriedly clutching a small brown stiffened cardboard suitcase. A few blouses some underwear and a pair of shoes were all it would take. Deep in the pocket of her dark blue raincoat a one pound note was wrapped protectively round a ten-shilling note. A half crown, a three-penny bit and five pennies and a halfpenny nestled next to the notes and clunked against her thigh with every fretful step. She had taken the notes from the bit of the carpet that lay under the protection of the carved foot of the wardrobe. It was her mother's plank. Most of the women in her social structure had a secret plank that contained money hidden from the men in their lives. It was kept for dire emergencies or a bit of extra holiday money. They reasoned that was better than bolstering the publicans' or bookies' profits. Of course their men had a similar arrangement that the women also knew nothing about.

Theresa's eyes kept filling up with tears and she said over and over again as she walked, 'I'll pay you back, Ma – I will – honest I will.'

She was headed for the Broomielaw. This was the dockside district of Glasgow that played host to ships from all over the world, a lively bustling heartbeat of a place on which the wealth of the city had been built.

Over the years, the River Clyde had grown from a small stream and gradually it had been dredged and widened till it could accept clippers and cargo ships containing tea, coffee, rum and tobacco from far-flung outposts that Theresa had never even heard of. In the daytime tall cranes that resembled praying mantises loaded and unloaded sacks and crates containing livestock and a hundred other commodities that were suddenly available due to the rationing – from the Second World War that had finished not ten years ago – coming to an end.

Night-time, however, presented a very different scenario. The place took on a forbidding and dangerous mantle. Pools of light from the lamp posts quickly disappeared into shadows that vanished up alleyways and got lost in the dark doorways of shipping offices and derelict wedges of waste ground that were waiting to be rescued and turned into something useful again.

On the quayside, sat the ships, invariably tinted in the colours of whatever shipping line they belonged to, patiently allowing the water to lap against their hulls. It was on one of these that Theresa hoped to stow away to America and become a stewardess. She did not, in her innocence, know that there were no ships bound for the US in the Broomielaw – mostly they were bound for India or China. The Clan Line ships, painted red and black, were headed for the Punjab while the Blue Funnel Line traversed the China Seas.

These were all that were available this old year's eve. Theresa was unaware of this fact when she turned into a dark street that was about three hundred yards long and sloped down to where the Broomielaw and the realisation of all her hopes and aspirations lay.

Hidden eyes followed her as she marched hastily down among the frowning darkness that enfolded her unevenly between the grey gas-lit cobblestones of the permanently puddled pavement.

Peter reached the crossroads where Argyle Street met with two others just before John did. They were both a bit breathless from hurrying. They were also faced with three choices – one way headed east towards the town, the opposite took them westwards and the third to the dockside.

'What way do you think?' John asked.

Peter looked both east and west; his face was a mask of perplexity, when he eventually said, 'She wouldnae have gone that way.' He pointed to the west. 'She doesnae know anybody that lives oot that way.'

John blew slightly from the exertions. 'Are you sure?'

'No' really,' was Peter's unconvincing answer.

'What aboot the toon?'

'She might have gone there. She likes the shops and that.'

'They'll a' be shut by now,' John said. 'Do you want to try doon by the docks?'

'Naw! She'd be too feart tae go doon there at night. We'll head towards the toon and try a' the side streets along the way. She'll know we'll be lookin' for her and be anxious to keep oot o' oor sight.'

John gave him the thumbs up to this suggestion. He thought it unlikely that she would put herself in danger by going off the beaten track but felt Peter needed encouragement not debate.

Theresa stood, huddled up in a darkened doorway at the bottom of the cobbled street watching a ship about two hundred yards away to her left. She had been studying it for about ten minutes because she had seen what she presumed to be two officers climb the gangway. They were carrying luggage and, more to the point, there was a large notice at the bottom of the gangway saying:

DEPARTURE TIME 20.40 hours

Although it did not state where it was going, Theresa just felt that it had to be America. She also reasoned that, if she could stay out of sight till the ship was well out to sea, when she eventually gave herself up as a stowaway they would not turn the ship round just because one lassie was on it. She could then prove her worth by stewardessing for them till they reached America. Once there, she would write to her family and tell them she was all right. She would have to lie about her age of course but felt that, with the help of her bra, she could easily pass for eighteen. She had pinched her mother's lipstick and powder so that would also bolster her claim to being older.

She watched the comings and goings on the ship intently – still unaware that she too was being studied from the shadows. Two bloodshot eyes surveyed her. The owner made no sound except for a slight wheeze from his chest as it rose and fell, releasing stale fumes of alcohol into the chilled night air. Dank wisps of hair blew over the eyes. His gaze remained unaffected and constant.

THIRTY-ONE

Dolly was on her way back from the wringer. As she passed Mary Culfeathers' stall, her ever-alert antennae noticed that Mary was mopping her brow. She stopped for a second, figuring that that was all it would take to check that everything was OK with her.

'Are you gettin' on a' right, Mrs Culfeathers?' she asked.

Mary turned from her exertions and dabbed a bead of sweat from beneath her left eye.

'Aye – thanks, Dolly,' she replied, her voice sounding a bit tired. 'It's awful hot in here, isn't it?'

Dolly, who was blessed with more energy than God, took charge. 'You have a wee seat on the stool there and, while you're havin' a blow, I'll get tore intae this lot – give you a chance to cool doon a bit, eh?'

She smiled easily as Mary Culfeathers nodded her head in acquiescence. 'Thanks, Dolly. I could dae wi' a wee rest. I've seen the day when I could have rattled through twice this and thought nothin' aboot it but . . . I'm getting' too old noo.'

Dolly was already attacking the washing as if it was her sworn enemy. 'Oh, aye, you were always a good worker,' she replied, as she concentrated on the task in hand.

'I always liked to be workin' – I always enjoyed it,' Mary said, more to herself than Dolly. She gave out an involuntary sigh – she did that a lot these days.

It was never in Dolly's character to just do something if she could talk at the same time as she was doing something so she carried on where she had left off with Doreen and Magrit. 'Do you know the McCandlishes, Mrs Culfeathers?'

Mary stopped sighing involuntarily as she mulled over Dolly's question. 'The McCandlishes? From Torphichen Street?'

'Aye. They're at the top end next to the butcher's,' confirmed Dolly at the same time as she strangled a pair of soggy shirts to get rid of the water.

Mary considered the McCandlish question and decided to indulge in what she now did best, remember the past. 'I don't know them tae speak to but I know who you mean, all right. The old granny used tae have a stall at The Jiggy – you know Paddy's Market,' she said, referring to the marketplace down by the Clydeside where second-hand clothes were sold. As well as the Jiggy, it was also known, in local parlance, as The Old C&A. 'She used to sell clothes to the coolies that were off the boats.' She smiled inwardly as she remembered that. 'They always walked in single file tae Paddy's Market and, when they'd bought a' their stuff, they'd wrap it up in an auld blanket and walk a' the way back fae Paddy's Market to the docks – wi' the bundles on their heads. They always used tae walk awful fast, I remember. It was a common sight that . . .' She stopped talking for no reason for a moment, then continued reminiscing, 'She was a hard workin' woman, auld Granny McCandlish.' She stopped again briefly, before continuing, 'They say she left her family a lot o' money.'

Dolly was doing battle with a green cotton dress and a scrubbing board – there was only ever going to be one winner. Although her attention was all on her immediate chore, she said politely, 'Is that right?' so Mary Culfeathers would not think she was ignoring her.

Mary was now thoroughly engrossed in the topic – after

all, it was seldom these days that anyone asked her about anything other than how she was feeling. 'Well, that was the rumour that was goin' aboot – but she always kept to herself.' She stopped again, as though she had run out of things to say – but she hadn't. 'Of course, her man died young and she had to bring up the family on her own – that's a bought hoose, you know,' she stated firmly.

Dolly did not reply but Mary carried on as if she had. 'Oh, aye, she bought that hoose – I know that. Oh, aye, she gave the family a good start – but I think, when she died, they stopped selling things to the coolies.'

Dolly replied without looking up from her washing. 'Well, from whit Magrit was tellin' me, I think they've started again.'

'Is that right, Dolly?' Mary replied innocently, unaware, of course, that Maureen had been bestowing her favours to the male population on a strictly cash basis until she had met the lucky man from Springburn. 'Well, I wish them a' the luck, Dolly. Auld Granny McCandlish would be proud o' them. There's nothing nicer than to see your family all set up and doin' well for themselves. It's just a pity that she's no' here to see it, eh, Dolly?

Dolly decided wisely not to burst the bubble. 'Aye, it's a pity, right enough.'

Mary sat smiling sentimentally. 'But you never know, Dolly,' she continued in her familial reverie, 'even although she's dead, she could still be watchin' over them.'

'She'll certainly be gettin' an eyeful if she is,' Dolly thought to herself as she wrung out the now debris-free green dress and placed it on the pile with the rest of the clean washing.

Mary had just finished what looked outwardly like one of her blank moments but inwardly she was sorting out what to say that would continue to hold Dolly's attention. She was starting to feel her opinions mattered again, instead of just having them politely dismissed as the haverings of an old woman. She felt that, in Dolly, she had found a confidante. Bolstered by this feeling of confidence in her ability to still converse sensibly, she carried on, 'I don't know them noo because I never go to that butcher's. I always go to Galloway's. They've got lovely butcher meat – their mince is marvellous.' She paused again at the thought of the quality of Galloway's mince. 'Marvellous mince,' she said reverently. 'There's hardly any fat on that mince, Dolly. Have you ever tried their mince, Dolly?'

Dolly realised she was now pushed for time if she was going to finish her own washing so she was rattling on. But, again, replied politely to Mary's not exactly riveting conversation, 'It's very good mince.'

Mary nodded in agreement at Dolly's and her own covenant of the delight that was Galloway's mince and then decided to offer proof positive of the unqualified quality of Galloway's mince. 'I've seen me tryin' mince from somewhere else – just for a change,' she explained pointedly and then shook her head in resignation. 'But, no, I always go back to Galloway's mince. I've seen me bringin' in mince from another butcher,' she continued relentlessly, 'and I'll no' say nothin' to Harry but, see when I put it down to him, after the first mouthful, do you know what he says to me, Dolly?'

'Naw.' Dolly was struggling to keep up her feigned interest.

'He says,' Mary continued laboriously, 'and I know he's gonnae say it . . .' She paused dramatically. 'He says, "Where did you get that mince fae?" That's right, Dolly – he can tell it's no' Galloway's mince.' She shook her head in amazement at this testament to her husband's gastronomical expertise and carried on mercilessly again, 'You wouldn't credit that, would you, Dolly?'

Even Dolly, who could talk for Scotland about nothing, was getting fed up with this monologue of monumental monotony. She remained, however, in deference to Mary's age, respectful. 'Naw, that's . . . that's . . . amazin',' she lied.

'Well, that's my hand to God, Dolly,' Mary exclaimed, verifying that, amazing or not, what she was revealing was gospel. She wasn't finished. 'But, the next time, I'll get GALLOWAY'S mince and I'll put it doon to him and, Dolly, this as sure as I'm standin' here,' she said, still sitting on the stool. 'Do you know what he says to me then?'

Dolly was fighting hard not to declare she'd had enough and flee to the comfort of her own stall. 'That's Galloway's mince?' she replied, a tiny note of sarcasm creeping in despite her best efforts.

Mary turned to Dolly and looked askance at this suggestion. She shook her head. 'Naw, Dolly – he doesnae know I get it fae Galloway's – he doesnae know one butcher from another – they're a' just butchers to him.' She shrugged her shoulders in despair. 'You know what men are like. Naw, he doesnae say it's Galloway's mince.' She deliberated on the accuracy of this statement for another moment before adding emphatically, 'That's no' what he says.'

Her eyes gave Dolly a quizzical look that suggested she should have another attempt at Harry's pronouncement. Reluctantly, Dolly stopped scrubbing and tried to answer. 'Well . . . eh . . . does he say . . .' She groped around in her brain for inspiration. 'Does he say, "That's better mince than the last time"?'

Mary studied Dolly. There was a hint of disappointment in her expression as she again shook her head. 'Naw, he doesnae say that either.' Her gaze transferred to the wet floor beneath her feet.

Dolly finally lost the rag. 'Well, what does he say?'

A long exhalation of breath, which was not quite a sigh, escaped from Mary before she answered. 'He says, "Can I have another tattie?"' She went back to studying the puddle of water between her feet.

Dolly had to admit this did capture her attention. She could not imagine why he would want another potato. 'What does he say that for?' she asked.

Mary's expression did not change and she continued to stare at the floor. 'I don't know – but that's what he says. Every time it's Galloway's mince, he asks for another tattie.' She transferred her attention from the floor up to Dolly. 'Do you know why he says that, Dolly?'

'Maybe it's just coincidence?' was the best Dolly could come up with.

'Naw, it's no' coincidence – he's been sayin' that ever since I first bought Galloway's mince.'

'How long ago was that?'

'When they opened that shop. It's over twenty years noo.' Mary was glad this was out in the open. She had lived with it all these years and never told anyone. At first, she had dismissed it as not worth considering but, lately, she had found it was growing in importance and nagging at her. It was the only secret that she and Harry had between them. She could always have asked him, of course, but was afraid Harry would think her silly.

'And he's always said, "Can I have another tattie?"?' Dolly's voice cut in on her deliberations.

Mary nodded and then offered the only explanation that she felt might be feasible. 'Aye – I think Galloway's mince must bring oot the flavour o' the tatties.' She waited for Dolly's approbation that this was indeed the case but Dolly seemed inexplicably to rule it out as a possible solution. She could sense, however, that Dolly too was now wrapped up in her enigma.

Dolly had, by now, abandoned the washing. She had one more trawl through her brain to come up with a reason before admitting defeat – but only temporarily. 'I'm gonnae ask Magrit,' she pronounced. 'Magrit!' Her voice cut into Magrit's ears as she beavered away.

Magrit stopped and turned to see Dolly standing outside her stall.

'Doreen!' Dolly had decided to enlist the help of both in her efforts to get to the bottom of this poser.

Magrit's response was not overly friendly. 'What is it?' she said, impatiently.

Dolly was in one-track-mind mode and did not notice Magrit's impatience. 'Magrit – Doreen,' she began with a heavy indication of solemnity, 'have you ever . . . bought your mince from Galloway's?'

'Aye,' Magrit said.

'Aye,' was Doreen's answer too.

'Right,' Dolly said, addressing Magrit, 'Noo, when you put it doon in front o' Peter, does he ever say anything?'

Magrit could not figure out what the purpose behind this intrusion into her exertions was. 'Does he ever say anything?'

'Aye,' Dolly said, also impatiently, as it seemed a straight-forward enough question.

'I don't know. I never listen tae him. Whit are you on aboot?'

Dolly ignored Magrit for the moment and turned to Doreen. 'Doreen, does John ever say anything to you?'

Doreen thought for a second or two then replied. 'Aye, he does.'

Dolly and Mary Culfeathers looked at each other covertly. 'What does he say?' Dolly pressed her.

'He always asks for sauce. He likes sauce on his mince.' Doreen was totally mystified and exchanged a look with Magrit that expressed her mystification.

Dolly picked up on this and straightaway resolved to let them in on the enigma that was Galloway's mince. 'Well, wait till youse hear this.' She held up her hands to prepare them for what they were about to be privy to. 'Mrs Culfeathers,' she said, her voice slow and laden with the import of what Mary was about to declare, 'tell them what you told me.' She invited Mary to take centre stage.

It had been a long time since any one had paid any real attention to what Mary said and the prospect facing her now was a bit daunting but she felt she owed it to Dolly to explain the situation fully to Magrit and Doreen. She gathered her thoughts and resolved not to get sidetracked from the central core of the story as she was wont to do these days. She began, 'Well, I was tellin' Dolly that I always got my mince oot o' Galloway's because it is lovely mince – there's hardly any fat in their mince, Doreen, you know.' She hoped Doreen would agree with her and thus build her confidence up.

Doreen was, so far, none the wiser, of course. 'Aye,' she replied, mystified. 'It's . . . good mince right enough.'

Mary turned to Magrit hoping she would agree with Doreen. Magrit's face was equally mystified. Mary translated this as disapproval. 'Do you no' like their mince, Magrit?' she enquired tentatively.

'Aye . . . it's all right.' Magrit flashed a hard glance at Dolly.

Dolly realised that Mary needed a bit of prompting to help her over her advancing stage fright. 'Tell them aboot what Mr Culfeathers says aboot it,' she encouraged.

Mary realised that, despite her best efforts, she had strayed a bit from the story and possibly let Dolly down so she redoubled her efforts to concentrate fully on what she had to say. 'Well, I was tellin' Dolly aboot how I always get my mice oot o' Galloway's but sometimes I get it oot o' another butcher's – you know, just for a wee change. And I was sayin' that, when I get it oot another butcher's, Mr Culfeathers can always tell – even though I haven't said what butcher's I got it oot o'. If I put mince doon to him and I havnae got it oot o' Galloway's, he says to me . . . ' she paused so the import of what she was about to tell them would not be diminished, '"Where did you get that mince from?"' Her eyes searched the audience for the befitting amount of awe she felt would be forthcoming from everyone.

Magrit stared at her and then turned to stare at Dolly also. Her face did not register any awe at all. 'Does he?' she uttered flatly. 'Did you hear that, Doreen?' She was registering more impatience than awe, Mrs Culfeathers imagined.

Doreen tried to feign interest but couldn't understand why. 'Aye,' she replied to Magrit, 'that's . . . that's . . . quite interesting.'

Mary was encouraged by Doreen's response. 'That shows you what good mince it is, Doreen,' she said, reinforcing how interesting she had been.

'Oh, it is! It certainly is.' Doreen was losing her way rapidly with this conversation. She turned to where Magrit was beginning to smoulder. 'It is good mince, isn't it, Magrit?'

'Second to none,' Magrit fumed. Her slow fuse beginning to gain momentum.

Dolly sensed it was time to give Mrs Culfeathers a hand with the tale.

'But that's no' the end o' it,' she announced grandly. 'There's more.'

'Is there?' Doreen said, incredulously but also unenthus-iastically.

'You mean even more interesting than that?' Magrit growled openly.

Dolly raised her hands for silence, then said with relish, 'You wait till you hear this.'

Magrit bit her lip and said, with biting sarcasm, 'Well, I don't know how you can top that but do go on.' She swivelled on her heels and fixed Mrs Culfeathers with a cold uncompromising stare that did not radiate encouragement.

Mary did not notice this because she was too preoccupied with the next bit of the saga. She peeped towards Dolly for support and saw Dolly give her a supporting peep back. 'Well, you know I was sayin' that, when I bought the mince from another butcher, Mr Culfeathers . . .'

She was interrupted by Magrit saying grimly, 'We've got that.'

Mary struggled to stay on the through train of thought that would clear up the . . . whatever it was she was trying to clear up.

'Tell them what happens when you get the mince fae Galloway's,' she heard Dolly willing her to succeed.

'Well,' she started again, 'when I don't get it from Galloway's . . . I . . . he says . . . it's no use, Dolly, I've forgot what I was gonnae say. What was it, Dolly? . . . I've lost the thread. You tell it.'

'Are you sure you don't want tae tell it yourself, Mrs Culfeathers?' Dolly asked, concernedly.

Magrit's voice burst on to their ears. 'Dolly, I have got a washin' to finish here. Noo, for God's sake, what are you on aboot?'

Dolly decided it was time to take the bull by the horns.

'Right! I'll make it quick. When she buys her mince oot o' another butcher's, the old man can tell it's no' Galloway's 'cause he always says . . .'

'Where did you get that mince from – we've got that,' Magrit snarled.

'Right – but, if she buys it oot o' Galloway's, what do you think he says?' Dolly asked, laying the trap for Magrit.

'That's Galloway's mince,' Magrit hissed, confident that she was stating the obvious.

'Naw – he doesnae,' Dolly gloated freely.

'Naw, he doesn't say that, Magrit. He doesnae know I get it oot o' Galloway's,' Mary Culfeathers added, hoping to clear things up for Magrit. Not wanting to seem to favour one over the other, she turned to Doreen. 'All butchers are the same to him, Doreen.'

Doreen nodded – she didn't know why. 'Well, he must say . . . ehhm . . . "That's nicer mince than the last lot",' she offered.

'Naw!' Dolly crowed again. 'He doesnae say that either.'

'WELL, WHAT THE HELL DOES HE SAY THEN?' Magrit roared, having finally snapped.

'Tell them, Mrs Culfeathers,' Dolly said, grandly.

'He always says, "Can I have another tattie?"'

The air hung heavy with menace, created solely, it has to be said, by Magrit. 'Well, now – that was worth stoppin' for.' Her face, like her voice, was a study in pent-up hostility.

As she was turning back to re-enter her stall, she heard Doreen say from behind her. 'It's a funny thing to say, right enough. Mebbe it's just coincidence?' She could not believe her ears. Dolly's voice also reached her. 'Naw, that's what I thought. But he's been sayin' it for twenty-odd years.

'That shows you what good mince it is, Doreen,' Mary explained again.

'Aye,' Doreen acknowledged, 'it would seem so.' Then, after a pause for reflection, she dug again into the mysterious case of Mary's mince again. 'But why does he want another tattie? I mean, you'd think he'd ask for more mince.'

'I think the mince brings oot the flavour o' the tatties,' Mary said, advancing her theory again. Frustratingly for her nobody said she was right.

'I don't believe this,' Magrit muttered darkly to herself. 'This is the stupidest conversation I have ever heard.'

183

Doreen was deep in thought, as was Dolly – both trying in vain to find a solution that would answer the dilemma. Mary Culfeathers was grateful they were so concerned but, at the same time, she wished they would just listen to her and accept that Galloway's mince was so good that it made Harry ask for another flavour-filled tattie.

Doreen interrupted her thoughts. 'Mrs Culfeathers,' she said, stroking her chin thoughtfully. 'Do you always get your tatties from the same shop?'

'How do you mean, Doreen, hen?' she responded.

'Well,' said Doreen slowly and very deliberately, thinking her way through what she was trying to wrap her brain around. 'When you buy your mince oot o' Galloway's, d'you get your tatties oot the same fruit shop that you always do?'

Mary could see from Doreen's demeanour that she had to get her answer absolutely accurate. She was determined not to get confused and to help Doreen as best she could. 'Let me think, Doreen,' she began, matching Doreen's slow deliberations. 'Noo, if I buy my mince oot o' somewhere else . . . I just get my tatties oot the nearest fruit shop . . . to wherever I bought the mince.'

She hoped that this would help Doreen and the matter could be put to rest. Her hopes were dashed however when Doreen pressed her further. 'Aye, but when you get your mince oot o' Galloway's?' She emphasised Galloway's and then fixed her with an eye-to-eye contact that forced Mary to concentrate all over again before reiterating, 'When you get your mince oot o' Galloway's, do you always get the tatties from the same fruit shop?'

Mary relaxed – she knew the answer to this one. 'Aye . . . always . . . I aye get them from wee Mr Jackson.'

She saw Doreen's eyes light up with a glow of utter triumph. 'THAT'S IT. That's the answer. It's the tatties from Jackson's that he likes – that's why he asks for another one – it's nothin' to dae wi' the mince.' Her voice was a mixture of relief and self-congratulations as she clapped her hands at her ingenuity.

Dolly joined in and shook her warmly by the hand. 'That's it,' she shouted out. 'You've solved it, Doreen. Dae you hear that, Magrit? Doreen's solved it.' She turned to Mary Culfeathers, her face beaming as if a great weight had suddenly been lifted from her. 'There you are, Mrs Culfeathers, after twenty years the mystery has been revealed – it's no' the mince at all.'

'It's the tatties, Mrs Culfeathers,' Doreen said, happily.

Mary tried to join in their mood. She was not a hundred per cent convinced about Doreen's theory, though she wouldn't have spoiled her moment for anything. 'That's good, hen – well done.' She smiled, then had one more try at furthering her own preference, 'I always thought it was the tatties, myself.'

Magrit's bellow interrupted everything. 'WILL YOUSE SHUT UP ABOOT BLOODY MINCE AND TATTIES – MA EARS ARE BLEEDIN' WI' YOUSE.'

A silence, that only slightly preceded an atmosphere you could cut with a knife, replaced Magrit's shout for sanity. Doreen turned and, inwardly smoldering but wisely silent, went back to her wash.

Dolly and Mary Culfeathers were transfixed and rooted to their spots before Dolly sniffed snootily and made to return to her stall as well. As she turned to leave, she was stopped by Mary touching her on the forearm and saying softly in a muffled secretive voice, 'Dolly.' Dolly leaned in towards Mary to catch what she was whispering. 'I'm goin' to get mince oot o' another butcher's and tatties oot o' Jackson's and see if he asks for another one.'

'That's a good idea,' Dolly whispered back. 'That'll put your mind at rest.'

Mary nodded. 'Aye.' Then she motioned to Dolly that she had something else to impart. 'I'm no' wantin' Magrit to hear me,' she whispered, tugging Dolly further away from Magrit's hearing. 'I still think it's the mince – I'll see you later.' She touched the side of her nose with her finger to signal that they both shared a secret and then moved off to the safety of stall fifty-seven. On her way back to stall sixty, Dolly very purposely gave number fifty-nine an exaggerated wide berth.

THIRTY-TWO

Harry Culfeathers had left the front door of the house ajar as he made his way along the street that led from his close-mouth. It had been a very long time since Harry had last set foot in this street but tonight, dressed in his military uniform and holding his gas mask by the webbed strapping that would secure it to his face if necessary, that did not matter. There was no one around to ask him what he was doing in this garb as everyone was busy either inside their house setting themselves up to celebrate the New Year or in a pub also setting themselves up to celebrate the New Year. This was of no interest to Harry. All that really concerned him was obeying the order to retreat and getting out of the immediate danger that the enemy fire was placing him under.

Peter and John had cut down into Warrick Street. Having called out a few times with no reply, they were now hurrying along an offshoot named Warrick Lane so as not to leave any stone unturned in their search for Theresa. They passed a number of derelict shops. Among the usual flotsam of failed enterprises were a boarded-up turf accountant, a bespoke tailor that could no longer bespeak and the inevitable defunct fruit shop in hand-painted green gloss paint.

Just to the left of it another paint-ragged doorway, that had once held the promise of untold riches to an optimistic hairdresser, now stood disconsolate in its failure to live up to the dreams it had seemed to promise. All that was left of that dream was the remains of a striped pole that had broken off and was now lying forlornly in the gutter like an outsize stick of rock with a pointed cap. Its circumference was only six inches, which maybe explained why it had snapped off.

'Theresa?' Peter shouted down the lane. Sadly, the only voice that he heard was his own echoing back from walls that formed a sounding board of dank doorways waiting to be demolished and a gable end that sealed the lane off.

'She'll no' be doon there,' John said, confidently.

'I know but . . . might as well check it oot,' Peter explained, starting to walk down to the end of the lane. He heard footsteps at the top of the lane and thought it strange because John was just behind him.

'Hey! McGuire!' A familiar harsh, grating voice, like iron chains being dragged along a concrete floor, filled his being with dread.

'Oh fuck,' was his immediate and almost silent response.

His profanity was not silent enough to escape John's notice. 'What is it?' he said as Peter turned round to face the man who had called out his name.

Peter gave John a worried look that just glanced off him. John turned to see a figure outlined in the light of a street lamp walk towards them, the soles of his shoes clacking off the cobbled stones, accompanied by a creaking sound of new leather being worn in. It was almost no exaggeration to say that he just about took up half of the lane. Or maybe it just seemed that way. Finally his shoes finished creaking, as he stopped no more than a few feet in front of Peter. A broad flat face encompassed eyes devoid of any emotion that stared from underneath two jutting simian-like eyebrows. From beneath the shadows that gave him a greyish-black almost monotoned appearance, a squashed nose that looked as if it had been thrown at the face and just sort of stuck there, spread above a mouth that turned down at the corners, even when he was smiling, which he seemed to be doing as he stood facing them. A very powerful frame was constricted by a tight-fitting donkey-brown large pinstripe suit. He ignored John and fixed his shadowy gaze on Peter.

'How is it goin', Peter?' he rasped, with a voice that seemed to sandpaper the eardrums. Although the greeting signalled that the giver was concerned about the welfare of the receiver, somehow this Neanderthal in a suit made it seem that the exact opposite was implied.

'No' bad, Pig – yourself?' Peter's eyes avoided making contact and his voice sounded uncharacteristically nervous as he answered the questioner.

'Oh! Everything's hunky-dory – couldn't be better.' There was a false joviality to the reply which was intended to convey just that. After an intake of breath, he carried on, 'Oh! Wait a minute . . . I tell a lie . . . it could be better.' He stared steadily from beneath his ape-like eyebrows. The small hard black pins that were his pupils glittered with a cold malice.

'Aye! I'm really sorry, Pig,' Peter blurted out, nervously, still not daring to look up.

'What's up?' John said, moving to Peter's side and declaring in a macho way to the man called Pig that there were two of them to one of him.

'You . . . fuckin' wrap it,' Pig growled, without raising his voice or taking his eyes off Peter. 'Who are you talkin' tae?' John moved towards Pig.

'John . . . naw.' Peter's advice to his friend had an urgency that suggested John comply with the command. 'Not a good move – this is Pig Matheson.'

John had never met Pig Matheson as he never had occasion

to have to borrow money but, like everyone in the district, he had heard of him. The tales of Pig's cruelty were legend. He had fought a squad of eight policemen that had been sent to bring him in a Black Maria van to the local cop-shop. He had duffed them all up, bundled them into the van and delivered them back to the police station. He had broken the hand of a rival who had pulled a knife on him simply by crushing it in his fists. It was also said that he would only dance with men as he considered dancing with women to be for cissies. These tales, along with many others, may have grown legs in the telling but the gist of them was that you did not mess with Pig Matheson. John was not a foolhardy man at the best of times and now was not the time to abandon this principle.

'Oh! Sorry, Mr Matheson – I didnae realise it was you.' John stammered.

'That's all right, Sonny Boy – a genuine mistake – I can forgive that,' Pig said, magnanimously but still somehow menacingly. 'What I cannae forgive is people . . . who get a loan of money . . . off their friends . . . at a very reasonable interest rate . . . and don't pay it back.'

'Reasonable? Two hundred per cent? How is that fuckin' reasonable?' Peter sputtered before he could control himself.

A second later, he was already regretting his foolhardiness. Pig's wee eyes flashed danger as he took his hands from his pockets. 'Oh! You are tryin' my patience somethin' fuckin' terrible.' Pig's voice had not risen one bit but Peter could feel his legs begin to jellify. 'Now why don't you put your at-the-moment-unbroken right arm into your pocket and wade in with the spondulix?' He continued to stare unrelentingly into Peter's distressed eyes.

Peter's reply came out as a panicky whisper, 'I . . . havnae got it, Pig . . . I . . .'

'That is an awful pity, Peter. There is something very

likeable aboot you as a person . . . however, as someone who owes me money, I have to try and ignore that side of you as I kick fuckin' lumps oot you – you see my position, I hope.'

He moved back a pace in order to give himself room to start swinging but was temporarily halted in carrying out his trade by John making one last despairing plea on Peter's behalf. 'Look, Mr Matheson – Peter's wee lassie has gone missin' and we're oot lookin for her.' Pig stared at him. 'She's only thirteen – and obviously we're helluva worried – I mean anything could have happened to her.' Pig continued to stare. 'If you could see your way clear to no' breakin' Peter's arm till after we've found her . . . we'd both be very grateful . . .' He looked at Peter. 'Wouldn't we?'

Peter had his eyes shut as he nodded.

Pig's eyes seemed to go blank as he digested what John had told him. After a short and silent deliberation with himself, his eyes refocused and he gazed at them.

'Right – she's only thirteen?'

They both nodded.

'And she's ran away and you cannae find her?'

Again they nodded.

He sniffed, stroked his chin in thought and readdressed them. 'Well – what the fuck has that got to do wi' me?'

He grabbed Peter by the throat and pinioned him against the entrance to what, before the war, had been a fish and chip shop. Now it was acting as an unfortunate link between the past and present in that Peter was about to be battered. Swiftly and expertly, Peter felt his right arm being jammed behind him between his back and the doorway rendering it useless as a force to protect himself with. Pig had his elbow hard against Peter's throat and his left arm in a grip like a vice.

Although Peter was no shrinking violet and could hold his own and a bit more, he felt as if he was a wee boy trying to wrestle with his father. Pig had taken his elbow from Peter's throat but, just by leaning on him, his vast bulk still meant that Peter was struggling in vain to get away. It was with horror that Peter realised why Pig's elbow had slid away from his throat. He felt the top of his left arm start to go numb as Pig's ham-like fist gripped it. Then, as easy as a baby would lift its rattle, Pig straddled the back of Peter's left arm over his leg and Peter realised he was about to have his arm snapped in two.

'Please, Pig . . . don't . . . I'll do anything you want . . . please . . . don't,' he pleaded, his voice pathetic and his sense of his own worth rendered sterile in his desire to escape what was inevitable.

'Too late, Sonny Boy.' Pig's little eyes glinted like black pearls as Peter stared into them. Trapped in their gaze like a moth caught in a lampshade, it flashed inappropriately into his mind that, although the pupils were glinting, there was absolutely no emotion in them. This terrified him even more as he realised that there was no point in trying to appeal to Pig's better nature – there wasn't one.

In blind panic, he looked to see if John would come to his rescue again. What he saw was John running like a man on fire away from them and back up the lane. If he had not been in such a frenzy of fear, he would have understood his pal's reaction but this was not a moment for cold logic. 'BASTARD!' he screamed.

'Who are you callin' a bastard?' Pig snarled.

'NO' YOU PIG – HONEST!' Peter howled again, as Pig began to exert slow pressure.

Pig could have snapped Peter's arm as quickly and as easily as he would have a stalk of rhubarb. But that would have been the amateur thug's approach and Pig was, he liked to think, a consummate professional. He prided himself on being the thugs' thug. The non-payer would tell other transgressors of the pain and terror they had gone through and this, Pig reasoned, would make them redouble their efforts at settling up promptly. The reason for breaking their arms was that the bandaged stookie took about three months to come off and, during this time, it acted like a portable poster, advertising Pig's prowess with poor payers. It was good business practice.

He kept slowly exerting the pressure that would result in a satisfactory snap.

This was the bit that Pig enjoyed. He always liked to look at the face of his victim to see what reaction they showed. Disappointingly, some fainted, others bit their lips or their tongues in fright and some actually cried real tears. Pig preferred the tears to anything else. It made him proud to be him and not his victim and bolstered his sense of manhood.

As he studied Peter, he fancied that he could see tears beginning to well up in his victim. He stuck his large lump of a face right up into Peter's and softly began to speak. 'If you feel like burstin' oot in tears, go ahead – I don't mind. It might make you feel better – go on, cry if you want tae.'

Peter looked into the cruel eyes and felt abject terror take over as he realised that Pig was breathing hard, almost as if he was sexually aroused. 'Pig, please don't,' was the best he could come up with, through the rising tears. Unfortunately, this seemed to arouse Pig even more. He started to moan. 'Oh! Ahh! Ahh! Oh! AHHHHHHH!' Then he actually screamed as he released Peter and staggered back awkwardly. Behind Pig, John was on his knees, bent down behind him and both his hands were up at his mouth in a gesture of extreme consternation. The reason for this became obvious as Pig whirled around still screaming to reveal the barber's pole that John had jammed up his rectum. Pig staggered backwards again, a motion which, unfortunately, caused him to sit back on the pole, which, even more unfortunately if you were Pig, rammed the pole even further up Bovril Boulevard. With a bellow of pure pain he stood upright to gain temporary relief.

Through his tears he saw Peter and John fleeing up the alleyway. Pig tried to take after them but the pole up his arse was not helping. He tried to remove it and then remembered a movie in which his favourite actor John Wayne had an arrow in his shoulder. One of the other actors went to pull it out but Wayne stopped him. 'Leave it,' he drawled. 'If you pull it out, I'll bleed to death.'

What goes around comes around and it was now Pig's turn to panic. If a little arrowhead could make you bleed to death, what chance did he stand with a barber's pole? The only thing he could do to stem the tide of pain and frustration he was feeling for the first time was to yell, at the top of his voice, 'I'll get you, ya bastards.' – that and cry copiously.

Peter turned the corner of the lane and into Warrick Street just ahead of John. 'Thanks,' he babbled breathlessly.

John just nodded his head in shock.

'There's only the one problem,' Peter said, continuing to run.

'What?' John replied.

'He might think that's you and him engaged.'

John did not see the humour in this remark and he could also think of a lot more than just the one problem.

THIRTY-THREE

The atmosphere between stalls fifty-seven to sixty was extremely taut. For twenty minutes, no one had spoken – not even Dolly, which was killing her. But she wanted to make sure that Magrit felt her displeasure and, if that took not talking for an hour or two, then so be it – she could always make up for it later on anyway, she reasoned.

Doreen was similarly displeased with Magrit and, although losing out on small talk was not as much of a strain on her as it was on Dolly, she resented the fact that she had been forced into keeping her mouth closed. Magrit was in between Dolly and Doreen and was only too aware of the tension she had caused by losing the rag and shouting about Mary Culfeathers' mince and tatties.

Mary Culfeathers was also feeling very tense – not about Magrit shouting, she had forgotten that already, but about the slur she felt had been cast on Galloway's mince by the others.

She was working out how to prove them all wrong when Magrit's voice cut through the damp air once more. 'Would youse all listen up for a minute?'

The other two stopped what they were doing and, with frosty faces, turned to Magrit, wearing expressions that said plainly, 'WHAT NOW?'

'I'm sorry I lost the rag – I was totally out of order.' Magrit's face was grim. She was not a natural penitent and apologising did not come easy.

The others feigned ignorance that there was any grievance on their part. 'Och, we never thought nothin' aboot it,' Doreen offered.

'Aye,' Dolly agreed. 'Think nothin' o' it, Magrit – I wasnae botherin',' she fibbed, smiling at Magrit and delighted that she could, at last, get back to battering her gums together.

Magrit nodded her appreciation of their attitudes and then moved out of the stall and crossed over to where Mary Culfeathers was trying to wash garments and, at the same time, plan the revenge of the maltreated mince.

Pausing at the front of the stall, she tapped Mary on the shoulder, which gave her a start. When she turned and saw Magrit the memory of being harangued flooded back and she was visibly not at ease.

Magrit saw how unprotected Mary was and it made her feel very guilty. 'I'm sorry I shouted at you, Mrs Culfeathers.' Magrit was abject in her contrition.

Mary felt at a bit of a loss but she did appreciate Magrit's sincere apology and how much it cost her to do it. 'You don't have tae apologise tae me, Magrit,' she said softly so the others wouldn't hear what she considered private business between her and Magrit.

'Oh, yes I do,' Magrit contradicted sharply, unwittingly making Mary nervous again. 'My mother and father brought me up to respect my elders – if they deserved it,' she qualified. 'And you deserve anybody's respect, Mrs Culfeathers. You're a fine auld woman and I'd no right to shout at you. So I hope you'll accept my apology.'

It would be wrong to say that Mary was not deeply touched – she was – so much that she felt unable to voice her appreciation of Magrit treating her like a human being. These days she felt people thought of her as an old biddy that it was manners to be pleasant to but basically ignore, as they no longer were of relevance to their modern world. She gave Magrit's arm a squeeze that said more than a thousand words could ever express and nodded her acceptance of Magrit's apology.

THIRTY-FOUR

Peter and John finally stopped running after they had put a good half mile between them and the stuck Pig. They cowered in behind a poster on a hoarding that was advertising the fact that Domestos killed ninety-nine per cent of all known germs. Both of them felt an affinity with the germ that had got away as they peered out from behind the hoarding to check they had not been followed.

'Christ, I've done it noo – I'm a marked man,' John moaned as his breath laboured with the exertion of running at full pelt.

'Well you will be if – or should I say WHEN – Pig gets his hands on you,' Peter agreed, fuelling John's already nightmarish vision of the future. 'I'll tell you one thing,' he added, also trying to recover his full breathing capabilities.

'What?' John asked, his face a study in anxiety.

'If I were you I wouldnae get my hair cut for a while . . . A barber's pole?' His question did need answering.

'Well, it was the only thing I could see . . . and I just . . .' John's voice tailed away with the hopelessness of it all. He had no idea how all this had come about. Normally he was known as a guy who would sooner do you a good turn than a bad one. Now he was going to be a marked man in the Glasgow underworld. 'Doreen'll murder me,' he said to no one in particular.

'Naw! Doreen'll nag you. Pig'll murder you,' Peter stated, correcting him on his faulty logic. 'Why did you have to jam it up his arse? Could you no' have hit him ower the head wi' it?' was Peter's next, not unreasonable, question.

'I was gonnae do that . . . but I was afraid I might have hurt him, you know? Gave him a permanent scar on his head, like?' was what John offered instead of a reasonable explanation.

Peter stared at him unbelievingly. 'Eh!! Right enough. Instead o' a permanent limp, you mean.'

'Well, I don't know . . . do I?' John said with a fair degree of irritation in his voice. After a moment's pause, he added, 'He'll probably set his gang on us, eh?' He glanced at Peter for verification.

Peter shook his head and shrugged. 'Maybe no'.' He analysed the situation as his breathing calmed down. 'What's he gonnae tell them? – Get they two – one o' them jammed a barber's pole up my sphincter.' He sniffled in the cold of the night air as he further appraised the situation. 'No' a lot o' credibility there, is there? He'd be known as Pig the Pole – or maybe – The Tripod.' He mused for another moment. 'Naw, I've got it – THE PENCIL SHARPENER.' He started to laugh despite himself and he slapped John on the back. 'A barber's pole – brilliant – I could get tae like you a lot, Johnny Boy.'

Suddenly his laughter stopped and he stared over John's right shoulder with a look of total bewilderment on his face.

John froze, too terrified to look round. His eyes were wide with alarm as he croaked, 'What is it? It's no' Pig, is it?'

John shook his head.

'Naw. I've just seen an auld man wi' a soldier's uniform walk past, carryin' a gas mask,' Peter explained, replacing the puzzled expression for one of sardonic mystification. 'This place is gettin' weirder and weirder,' he concluded, before urging, 'C'mon there's a café along the road. Theresa might be there.'

As they walked towards the café John kept glancing behind them just in case Pig, by some miracle, had decided to chase them. A thought struck him. 'What do they call him Pig for?'

'Well . . . he doesnae look like a horse, does he?' Peter explained.

THIRTY-FIVE

The *Clan Macintosh* had been sailing from Glasgow to India for over ten years. She was a cargo ship of medium tonnage, crewed mainly by dark-hued seamen, from various parts of India, who were overseen by white-hued officers from various parts of the British Isles. Normally, she would have been berthed at the George V Dock in the outlying district of Shieldhall but, due to an excess of ships being loaded and unloaded, she had been diverted to the Broomie-law so she could be on her way back to India before the Glasgow dockers stopped work for the New Year. She had unloaded various cargoes ranging from cotton, tea, leather, etc. and had taken back on board, for export, flour, plastic goods and, most importantly, a very large quantity of spirit in the form of a well-known and popular brand of malt whisky.

The Glasgow dockers had a reputation for extreme cunning in their ability to, shall we say, sample the goods without the owner's permission. They would have argued that, by carrying out this function, they were making sure that no substandard spirit reached far-flung climes and they were, therefore, doing this for the benefit of the export trade – thus being of service to the customs and excise while, at the same time, getting out of their heads with free whisky. It was the duty of the authorities to try to ensure that the dockers did not help out the export business to excess – sometimes they succeeded very often they did not.

Today had not been a good day for the customs officers. Despite their best efforts, the lure of un-sampled alcohol which needed to be unofficially tested, coupled with the fact it was Hogmanay, had swayed the contest in favour of the dockers and resulted in a large police presence to clear the various holds of expert but unofficial tasters. Had the dockers been politicians they would have been described as ministers without portfolios. They were not politicians, however, and so were described on the police charge sheet as looters without a leg to stand on.

The captain had received a stiff reprimand from his superiors and, as is the way in these situations, he had reprimanded the chief petty officer who had reprimanded the petty officers and so on down the line. Consequently, everyone felt glad that the day was over and they were now enjoying some unofficial sampling of their own in the various messes.

Not that they were inebriated – they still had to cast anchor and put to sea, so they would have to be fully functional to carry that out. A small libation to help them unwind was more the atmosphere that prevailed as they sat down for their supper before they embarked on the business of casting anchor and leaving port.

Anyway, the pilot that would be responsible for guiding them out of the river was not due for another hour, so it was the perfect time to relax. This, coupled with the fact that it was New Year's Eve, resulted in nobody being on gangway watch, which was never a problem really as no one had ever wanted to stow away to India anyway.

Of course, Theresa knew none of this. All she was aware of was that a golden opportunity to start her career as a stewardess was beckoning. The creaking of the fore and aft restraining ropes was the only sound that reached her ears. She wrestled with the numerous arguments she was having inside her head. Her overactive brain told her that, on the one hand, she was being extremely foolhardy if she carried out her plan. On the other hand, the same brain told her that if she lacked the courage to carry out the plan then she would have to suffer Tim and Frankie taunting her. They would no doubt tell everyone in the district and she would be held up to ridicule for the rest of her life.

She studied the empty gangway. No one had gone up or down it for at least ten minutes. No one was even on deck. 'If I don't do it now, I never will,' was the thought that kept pinging away at her. She was trapped in a morass of possibilities that were making her head spin with the effort required to make the right move. She regarded the ship for the hundredth time.

Then, without warning, she did not know how or why, but her deliberations suddenly became crystal clear. What did she want more than anything? Answer – glamour and adventure in her life. Did she have the courage? Her mother's steely resolve rose up in her. Answer – yes she did. She regarded the *Clan Macintosh* differently. Before, it had seemed strange and foreboding – now it seemed as a friend that was beckoning her to a new and fascinating life. Her mind was finally made up.

The owner of the bloodshot eyes had made his mind up too.

THIRTY-SIX

Mary Culfeathers wiped the steam off her brow for the umpteenth time and decided that a wee break was in order. She stepped out of the stall and had a look round to see if anyone else was having a break too. She noticed that Magrit and Doreen's stall was empty. As this fact registered, Doreen appeared from round the corner that led to the wringer with a pile of freshly wrung washing in her arms. She passed Mary and gave her a nod before stopping to tip her load into the empty pram that had once been full of dirty duds.

Mary was concerned that Magrit might still be annoyed with her, she thought it best to check just in case. 'Is Magrit a'right, Greta?' she asked Doreen.

'I'm Doreen, Mrs Culfeathers. My mother's Greta – remember?' Doreen answered, perhaps a bit tetchily. 'Magrit's waitin' tae see if she can get a wringer.'

'It's awful busy, right enough, hen,' Mary agreed. She had already forgotten Doreen's name but resolved just to call her by the term that was often used as an endearment by people of her generation.

'It always is this time of the year,' Dolly agreed. Her antennae had picked up that someone was talking and automatically alerted her mouth to join in.

'The week before the Fair Fortnight's the same. You're lucky to get a stall – never mind a wringer,' she continued, referring to the period of the year when Glaswegians traditionally went on holiday.

'It's awful stupid. They should put more wringers in the place,' Doreen replied, showing a grasp of mathematics that had sadly eluded the male planners who had drawn up the designs for the washhouse.

This was a conversation that Mary Culfeathers felt totally at home with. 'It's always been the same, hen. My mother used tae go tae the big one on Glasgow Green and she would take me alang wi' her. I was just a wee lassie, of course, but I can mind o' it well.'

Dolly wracked her brain 'Was that no' the first washhoose that was built?' she asked, making it sound as though the question was a point of information as well.

Mary considered the question for a second before committing herself to a reply. 'I think it was, Dolly – but I might be wrong,' she answered, covering herself just in case. 'It was enormous, I know that. It was open fae seven in the morning till nine at night – every day except a Sunday.' Her face lost its permanently puzzled look and replaced it with one of confidence. 'I can aye mind as a wee lassie goin' wi' my mother and do you know what was lovely? Seein' Glasgow Green wi' all the washin' hangin' from the lines.' She saw the scene clearly in her mind's eye and it brought back happy memories for her. 'Yon was a marvellous sight.'

Doreen, with her expectation of a brave new world free from the chains of drudgery, failed to see why rows and rows of washing could inspire this reaction. 'It doesnae sound all that marvellous to me,' she responded honestly.

'Ah! You should have seen it, hen – especially in the summertime,' Mary answered, secure in her memories. And then, as if to give concrete proof of how good those times had been, she said pointedly, 'Of course we had real summers then

– from May right on till September. It was that hot the tar used tae stick to your feet and the whole o' Glasgow Green was as if it was at the sea. The sheets and mattress covers were like waves as they blew aboot – and there were men's shirts white as snow as far as you could see and lovely coloured silks and woollens, all dancin' in the dryin' wind.' She paused momentarily in her flight of fancy. 'It's funny noo but, at that age, I always thought that they looked kind o' happy. It sounds daft, I know, but it was the men's shirts and women's dresses. You see they a' have arms and, when the wind blew them aboot, they seemed tae be wavin' to each other. It was as if the clothes had a life o' their own. Underneath them the women were a' movin' about, laughin' and jokin' wi' each other. It was awful noisy, of course, but, to me, awful thrilling as well.' She smiled to herself as she remembered her childhood innocence. 'I often think o' them days. We went once a week but you could go and have a wee blether any time you felt like it – anytime except a Sunday – the men played fitba' on the Sunday. It was a great meetin' place. There was never any loneliness in that place.'

Her mind returned to the present with an abruptness that felt unpleasant. Again she felt foolish and that she had maybe spoken out of turn. In her old age, she had become aware that she was gradually getting very unsure of herself. Mary had noticed that as men got older they got grumpier and more positive in their opinions and deluded themselves that they were right, even if they were wrong. She sometimes wished she could be like that but then decided that that sort of thing was best left to Harry. He was better at it she conceded.

Her thoughts on Harry's positive ability to be negative in his delusions of being always right were interrupted by Dolly. 'That's what I like aboot the steamie – you're always busy and there's aye somebody you know to talk to,' she stated in agreement, bringing Mary back once more to the present.

'That's true, Dolly. Mind you, the best of it's gone. But it's smaller noo. And, when you're finished dryin' the clothes, you're out and off home. But back then, you'd always got Glasgow Green to look forward to . . . sort o' round off the day.' She felt the reasoning of her argument begin to dissolve in her head and added before it was gone, 'You know what I mean, Dolly?'

'They're closin' a' the steamies doon,' Doreen announced brightly. 'They say launderettes are gonnae take over.'

'Oor Jenny has one o' them next to her. She doesnae like it,' Dolly said.

'They save you a lot o' work, Dolly,' Doreen argued, with a nod of her head that suggested there was no argument about this fact.

'What are they, Dolly?' Mary asked, trying not to lose out on the gist of the conversation.

'They're awful wee, Mrs Culfeathers,' Dolly responded to her question, with a nod of the head similar to Doreen's. 'There's only aboot ten machines and they only take aboot ten pound o' washin'. Jenny says, when she goes in, she never knows anybody. All she does is sit and stare at the machines. Naebody talks to one an' other except maybe, "Have you got change of a shilling?" or "It's a cold day, isn't it?" kind o' conversations that never seem to go anywhere, Mrs Culfeathers. Everybody's hell o' a polite because they don't know each other.' Her face registered distaste at the thought of this way of living.

'Is that her wi' a daughter that's got a television?' enquired Doreen.

Dolly nodded assent to her enquiry. 'Aye. She's comin' up to oor hoose thenight for a wee terr. She says her daughter's asked her up there but they'll just sit watchin' the television and she'll get bored.'

'I don't see how she could get bored,' Doreen said, with a touch of impatience that her two older companions were unable to see what was glaringly obvious to her. 'I think it would be great to just pop round and watch a television set and have a' your washin' done for you by a machine. I can see your point aboot Glasgow Green, Mrs Culfeathers, but you're just rememberin' it when it was summer. What wis it like in the winter when it was freezin?'

There were times Mary despaired of what she called the younger ones. As nicely as possible, she tried to explain to Doreen that, 'You never hung oot your washin' in the cold weather, hen. It would never dry, you see!'

'That's my point,' Doreen replied, starting to lose control slightly.

'Is it, hen?' Mary replied, trying to be friendly. 'That's nice for you. Harry always says he has a point as well. I've never had one myself but, as the old sayin' goes, "What you've never had you never miss," eh?'

Doreen was not sure if she was being sent up or not. She, of course, wasn't.

Dolly decided to put her oar into the conversation. 'What Mrs Culfeathers means, Doreen, is that, in they days, there were hundreds o' people a' doin the same thing and enjoin' wan and other's company. If it wasnae New Year, we would a' just go hame because the dryin' is a' done for us. But, back then, they could a' keep havin' a blether and a laugh and a joke because they were still in amongst wan and other – no' just inside but ootside while they were waitin' for the clothes tae dry. Isn't that right, Mrs Culfeathers?'

'I don't know, Dolly.' Mary was lost in the intricacies of the argument. 'I'll ask Harry when I get back.'

Dolly couldn't wait that long. 'That is what you mean, Mrs Culfeathers?' she said, thinking she was being helpful.

'Oh, good, Dolly.' Mary smiled, giving her the thumbs up. 'That'll save me havin' tae ask Harry.'

Doreen, although not actually identifying with Mary Culfeathers, was now getting a bit lost herself. 'I'm lost,' she announced, a bit more irritably than the last time she spoke.

Dolly was not and had a remarkable grip on the discussion. She usually did. 'Mrs Culfeathers is tryin' to say that she's noticed that people are no' as tight wi' wan and other as they used to be. It's what I was sayin' aboot the launderette things. Naebody speaks to wan and other and,' she added in emphasis, 'when you have a machine in your hoose and a television as well – well, you'll no' need to go to the steamie or the pictures. There'll be nae point to goin' oot at all – we'll a' just sit in the hoose starin' at wee boxes.'

There was a pause while Doreen digested what Dolly said what Mary Culfeathers had said differently, during which Mary Culfeathers said affirmatively, 'I think that is what I meant, Dolly – thanks.'

'Nae bother, Mrs Culfeathers,' Dolly acknowledged.

Doreen adjusted her argument and came from a different angle all together. 'That'll just give us a lot more leisure time.'

Dolly and Mary looked at each other for help. 'What's that when it's at hame? What's leisure time?' Dolly asked, genuinely puzzled.

Doreen tried to explain what she thought was perfectly obvious and did not need an explanation. 'It's spare time. Time to yourself – just time to do what ever you want. You could listen to the wireless or go to the pictures or, if you've a television set, you could watch that instead. It's . . . just . . . time to relax.' Her tone was becoming more exasperated.

Dolly gave a shrug of dissatisfaction. 'Oh, I couldnae be doin' wi that. That's no' . . . what do you call it? . . . leisure time?' Doreen nodded curtly. 'That's just hangin' aboot. That's a' that is.'

'How is it?' Doreen snapped coldly.

'Because you're no' doin' something – you're just watchin' other people doin' something. No, I'm like Mrs Culfeathers – I like to be busy and in amongst people.'

Doreen smacked her hand against her head in exasperation. 'But you can go oot in your leisure time and meet people if you want. In fact, you'd have more time to do that because the machine'll be doin' the work for you. Can you no' see that?'

Dolly realised that Doreen was getting a bit heated up and decided that it wasn't a conversation that was worth creating an atmosphere. 'Aye, I can see what you mean, Doreen,' she said, diplomatically, and then, because she did not like conceding too much, she added, 'I'd still rather be busy and talkin' at the same time but I'll no' be here to see a' that so it'll no' bother me anyway.' Dolly turned and went back into her stall.

'Well, I, for one, am looking forward to it,' Doreen pronounced stiffly to Mary Culfeathers.

Somehow Mary blamed herself for causing this wee bit of friction. 'Och, aye, hen. Everybody's got their own way o' doin' things,' she reasoned before turning away herself.

There was an attitude of the forlorn about her that made Doreen feel a bit guilty.

THIRTY-SEVEN

John and Peter had drawn a blank and Peter was now very worried as they took the stairs two at a time to the top floor and the McGuires' house in the hope that she had come back. Peter searched for his keys, couldn't find them and, in exasperation, thumped on the door.

Inside, Tim and Frankie were reading swaps. These were comics that they had swapped with their pals – thus saving themselves the bother of trying to get money from their parents for more comics. At that moment, Tim was wrapped up in the adventures of Dixon Blake, a detective in the Sherlock Holmes tradition, while Frankie had just finished reading about Limp Along Leslie who was a professional footballer with enormous skill despite having one leg a lot shorter than the other. As if this wasn't impediment enough in his profession, he also had to solve at least one major crime every week before going out or to the pitch, having escaped from usually certain death, and then score the last-minute goal to win the cup for his team. He had just started the next story, an adventure about a blind football manager who used the sound of the ball and the shouts of the players to decide his tactics to ensure his team's various victories, when the sound of the door being thumped by his father impinged on his reading.

'There's the door – you better see who it is,' he said to Tim without lifting his eyes from the comic.

Tim's eyes were glued to Dixon Blake's exploits. 'How should I see who it is? You see who it is!' he murmured in his usual huffy tone.

'It might be Theresa,' Frankie said absently while, at the same time, laconically picking at his nose.

'Well, away and see then,' Tim replied, his voice mingling with the sound of his father pounding impatiently again at the door.

The pounding got louder as Frankie, turning the page, informed his brother, 'If that's my da, you're for it.'

'You'll be for it as well,' Tim casually answered his brother in the same tone of voice as they both pored over their respective comics.

Frankie couldn't be bothered talking any more so he contented himself by shaking his head from side to side as in 'No, I won't.'

Tim responded likewise except up and down as in 'Yes, you will.'

They were both still at it when the sound of a key being inserted in the door, signalling that their father had finally found his lock opener, reached their ears. This galvanised them into action and they threw down their comics and jumped up on to the kitchen sink.

Peter burst into the kitchen to see his two boys sitting on the sink and looking out the window. John followed only a few steps behind as Peter roared at the boys, 'Did you no' hear us at the door?'

'Naw, Da,' Tim said in a small helpless voice as he turned round from staring out the window. 'We've been keepin' watch for Theresa.'

'Did you no' find her, Da?' Frankie added anxiously, a note of concern in his voice that would have done justice to an Oscar winner.

'No, son,' Peter replied, touched by his sons' efforts on behalf of their sister.

He sat down heavily at the table and slumped on a hard wooden chair as his eyes stared unfocused at the opposite wall.

John hovered awkwardly in the kitchen doorway not knowing what to say to ease things for his pal. He and Doreen had no children as yet but, despite that, he could still appreciate what Peter was going through. Even his mind was beginning to envisage all sorts of mishaps that Theresa would be prey to and, though he tried to dismiss them from his thoughts, they still returned like a nagging toothache.

THIRTY-EIGHT

The owner of the bloodshot eyes hugged the filthy carbuncle of a street as he slowly moved among the shadows to where Theresa was hidden. His disturbed mind judged he still had about twenty-odd yards before he would be in touching distance of her. The bitter taste of undigested alcohol rose up in his gullet and burned at his throat causing the blotched purple-stained face to contort in pain. The sour liquid gyrated into foam and rushed from the gullet into his mouth where it sought release by escaping in a hot dribble that slid down the side of his week-old stubble. A tiny cough escaped from him.

Theresa gave a start as she thought she heard something behind her. She turned fearfully to see what it was. Her breathing stopped as she searched the shadows for . . . she didn't know what. Thankfully, there was nothing that seemed untoward. Just as she turned back, her eye caught a fleeting glimpse of something not quite right. Again, she turned towards where her gaze had registered unease and scanned the darkness for movement.

Her worst fear was that there might be rats lurking in the gloom and she had always had not just a fear but almost a phobia about them. The mere thought that a rat might be there watching her was enough to end any thought of turning back. She took one more look at the empty gangway – a look that confirmed it was still empty – and made up her mind to go. She stepped out of the doorway and on to the street, clutching her small suitcase, and made her way to the gangway of the *Clan MacIntosh* that symbolised the gangway to a new and better life.

The owner of the bloodshot eyes rose from his prone position and started to follow her.

Peter slowly turned his gaze from the comfort of the blank undemanding wall towards John. 'I'll need to tell Magrit,' he announced, facing up to the fact that he was at a loss what to do next.

'I think you better,' John said softly, confirming his decision.

THIRTY-NINE

There was no denying the fact that she was feeling guilty. Doreen watched Mary Culfeathers and noticed the air of desolation that seemed, every now and then, to inhabit her frail figure. Dolly was working away. Magrit was still at the wringer. Doreen could not contain the impression that she, by her assertive prediction of a utopian Glasgow, had somehow caused the old woman's unhappiness. She stopped what she was doing and crossed to Mary's stall.

Mary looked up from her tasks at Doreen's appearance beside her. She had been working on automatic pilot – not concentrating on the wash but allowing other unpleasant thoughts to invade her mind. The appearance of Doreen was unexpected and, therefore, worrying. She worried about everything these days.

'Mrs Culfeathers?' Doreen began cautiously. 'I hope you don't think I'm bein' cheeky – I don't mean to be. It's just that you look awful unhappy and you spoke earlier on aboot feelin' lonely.' She stopped and examined her feet awkwardly. 'If it's none o' my business, just tell me to shut up. I just wondered . . . if I could maybe help . . . in some way . . .' she said. Her words stuttered to a halt and she felt as awkward as she had when she started.

'That's awful kind o' you, Doreen,' Mary replied. Faced with Doreen's unexpected kindness, she too felt awkward and, consequently, obliged to offer some explanation for her actions – actions that had apparently upset the lassie. 'I'm no' lonely here, hen, but, when I go back to the hoose . . . well . . . Harry's no' too good these days and . . . maybe I just . . . sometimes it gets . . .' Her voice tailed off as all the fear and uncertainty that getting older entailed invaded and overcame her. Try as she might, the emotions, that had held back for too long, rushed to her eyes for an outlet, spilled out from them and trickled down her cheeks in a silent sob. The silence emphasised her vulnerability.

'Oh! Mrs Culfeathers.' Doreen tried to find words that would comfort the frail old being that trembled in front of her – there weren't any.

Dolly heard Doreen's cry and approached them. Her concern was evident as she asked, 'What's the matter? What's happened?'

'I'm sorry, Dolly.' Mary tried her best not to cry – it was not in her nature to let anyone see her lose control. 'I just feel . . as if I'm finished.'

'Naw, you're no',' Dolly replied firmly, as she put her arms round her. 'There's many a young wan couldnae get through the work you do,' she concluded with, it must be admitted, a great deal of accuracy.

'That's true, Mrs Culfeathers,' Doreen echoed. 'You're smashin' for your age.'

Mary sniffled as she agreed with them, 'I'm healthy enough. It's just, when your family has moved away and you don't see them – it's awful empty.' She took a deep breath to try and regain control. 'I've got three grandweans, Dolly.' The emotional tide began to rise again as she declared, 'I've never seen them – only photos – I've never actually cuddled one o' them, Dolly.'

'Where are they, Mrs Culfeathers? Where are your family?' Doreen enquired gently.

217

'I've nae lassies – just the two boys. They're somewhere in England.'

Doreen was mystified. 'How do you no' go doon and see them?'

Mary's face was a study in helpless perplexity. 'They've never asked me . . . but I'd like to see them . . . I'd like to see my wee grand . . .' She gave up the uneven struggle and the floodgates were allowed their long overdue release. This time there was no silence to her sobbing and the grief that had been allowed to build up over the years was allowed to escape in pulsating gasps.

Dolly cradled Mary's head on her chest and patted her back, as she would have done a child in distress.

Meanwhile Doreen looked on, frustrated in her inability to alleviate Mary's pain. 'That's a bloody shame,' was the best she could come up with.

'They want their buckin' airses kicked,' Dolly said angrily, as she paraphrased the better known swear word. 'Never you mind, Mrs Culfeathers. You've got friends all roond you here. Hasn't she, Doreen?'

'You certainly have, Mrs Culfeathers,' Doreen babbled a bit in her rush to give Mary assurance. From the corner of her eye she saw Magrit as she rounded the aisle that led to their stalls.

Magrit was already cursing under her breath about the lack of wringers when she saw that all was not right with her three cronies. One glance was enough for her to take in the scene and enquire sharply, 'What's the matter?'

'Mrs Culfeathers is just feelin' a bit sad. She's missing her family,' Doreen said diplomatically.

Magrit surveyed the frail wee woman and tried to comfort her. 'It's this bloody time o' the year. That's what it is,' Magrit counselled, following her tried-and-proven method of assigning blame to some outside influence as the cause of any and all upsets. Sometimes it was Glasgow Corporation, sometimes the weather, usually it was Peter. Tonight it was the time of the year.

Her face adopted its usual expression of aggression, which Mary mistook as being directed at her because she was crying. 'I'm sorry, Magrit,' she sniffled laying her hand on Magrit's arm.

Magrit patted her hand and told her that she always cried at this time of the year too. 'So did my mother,' she added poignantly at the thought of her.

'So do I,' said Doreen, her bottom lip just beginning to tremble slightly.

'I just feel . . . I keep rememberin' . . .' Mary could not, for the world, have finished the sentence as the memories of times past, when her life had meaning and purpose, flashed brightly in her brain. The boys were hers to protect, Harry was strong and happy in his role of provider and it all seemed as if it would never end.

Now it had and it seemed to her awful unfair of God to give you all that and then take it away from you and leave you with nothing . . . but memories. Although their lives were different, a bond, that stretched back far into the past and which would also permeate the future, united the three women.

It was this that probably sent Doreen over the edge as she absorbed Mary Culfeathers' sadness. 'I think I'm gonnae cry as well,' she announced, her eyes swelling up and reddening. She put her arm round Mary's shoulder and gave her a squeeze of reassurance.

'Oh! Don't, hen – you'll start me off as well,' Dolly wailed. 'Don't worry, Mrs Culfeathers,' she pleaded.

Mary looked up from wiping her eyes. 'I always worry, Dolly – I cannae help it,' she explained.

'Me as well,' Dolly acceded as the tears bubbled up and overflowed.

'For Christ's sake.' Magrit's oath was not addressed literally to the Son of God – it was more of an admonishment to herself for allowing feelings she tried to deny and had buried as an act of survival to escape and be on full view to the world at large or, in this case, three neighbours. 'I aye feel that stupid when I greet,' she moaned, crying into her apron.

'It does you good,' Dolly advised, still blubbering. 'It gets it oot your system.'

They all grieved as their memories wafted round the chambers of their beings.

Andy's voice interrupted the mood as he hailed Magrit. Peter and John were close on his heels.

'What are you daein' here?' Magrit's gaze had hardened in a moment as her words flashed across to Peter.

Doreen also couldn't figure out why John was with Magrit's man but, before she could ask him, Peter spoke, 'It's Theresa . . . she's ran away . . . we cannae find her.'

Magrit's eyes had the now more familiar look of hardness back in them as she tried to take on board what Peter had said. 'Ran away? What for? . . . What happened? What did youse do?' she accused, the words firing from her like bullets from a Bren gun.

'Nothin,' Peter said, searching in his pockets and withdrawing a crumpled piece of paper. 'She left a note . . . sayin' . . . here it is.' He smoothed the note out and then handed it to her.

FORTY

Theresa stood at the bottom of the gangway. Her heart was racing and she could feel it beating relentlessly at her rib cage. Her eyes strafed the top of the gangway almost hoping that someone would appear to take the onus from her and thus scupper the plan to run away. No one appeared. The decision was still hers and hers alone. Had she the courage to leave her friends and family in order to do something with her life or would she just sink into the mediocrity of her surroundings and become her mother, unhappy and always angry with the drudgery she had settled for? There was only one outcome to this and Theresa recognised that. She began to climb the gangway to her future.

An empty packet of Senior Service cigarettes floated lazily on the oily scum that left blue-grey streaks amidst the silent waters of the River Clyde. The only thing that stopped it from becoming damp and sinking was the oil that formed a protective barrier between it and the water. Something from above splashed into the water beside it and made it bob about before it settled down once more.

Harry stood to attention at the foot of a flight of twenty-two stone stairs that led from the pedestrian pave-way of the Broomielaw down to where the black water of the Clyde lapped at his slippers. He had put on all of his regimental khakis but, due to the ravages of time, his feet could not get into his army boots.

Once more, he aimed a missile made of his spit at the cigarette packet and stared into the waters as his spit narrowly missed a second time causing a small spume of water to rise up where the saliva had disturbed it. Harry saw this and perplexity dug deep into his grasp on reality.

Once more, his brain became prey to flights of fancies. He was on board the packet of Senior Service and shells were exploding all round him sending plumes of spray twenty feet into the night air. Again, he could smell the cordite as his ears were assailed from all angles with the shrill scream of the shells before they hit the water. He knew it was only a matter of time before one missed the water and found him and his companions.

Then his brain seemed to explode with noise and he was thrown against the taffrail as the vessel was all but split in two. He had no idea if his limbs were still attached to his body or even if he was alive or dying. Gradually, when his ears had recovered some of their hearing, he could detect cries of agony that would haunt him for the rest of his life. He also heard another voice, a voice that informed him, 'We're sinking. Jump ship and head for the beach.' Harry fixed his gas mask on and jumped.

FORTY-ONE

Magrit's face was a mask of barely contained fury as she finished reading the note. 'See if anything happens to her . . .' The fact that she did not finish the sentence underlined the threat of what she would do. Her instinctive reaction gave way to uncertainty as she realised the real danger a thirteen-year-old girl could be in, wandering about on her own.

Peter could think of nothing that would ease this and avoided Magrit's eyes. 'We've looked at all the places I thought she might be in . . . but nae luck,' he said, knowing this was of no help to Magrit's increasingly worried state.

Magrit's eyes bounced off her surroundings in a frenzy as she frantically tried to think of something – anything – her daughter had said that might give her a clue to where she could have gone.

The others could only look on helplessly.

Doreen edged closer to John, wanting to ask what his role in all this was but judging that now was not the time for it. John's glance to her confirmed that her judgement was spot on.

Dolly had put aside Mary Culfeathers' troubles as indeed had Mary herself in the light of Magrit's awful plight.

It was, however, Dolly who took charge of the situation. 'Is Theresa no' pals wi' Betty Reilly's daughter Rena?' she enquired.

Magrit – who was now approaching a condition of confused indecision wrapped up in helplessness that was unfamiliar to her – could only nod to Dolly that she was. 'Well, I saw Betty along at the stalls next to the dryers while I was doon that way earlier on and I'm sure that wee Rena was wi' her. Do you want me tae go doon and see if she's still there? Her daughter might have some idea where Theresa would head for.'

'Aye, that would be a start anyway, Dolly,' Mary Culfeathers answered, not realising that, in her wish to help, she had made a decision that was not really hers to make.

'Would you Dolly? Thanks,' Magrit agreed tightly, doing her best not to explode as fear, anger and indecision all fought to be uppermost in her feelings.

'Right. I'll no' be long.' Mary followed Dolly as she felt she would not be of much use where she was.

'John and I tried the café and a few other places but we had nae luck. I've left the boys in the hoose in case she comes back.' Again, Peter could only reiterate his earlier explanation of what he had done so far. Wisely, he left out the bit about Pig Matheson.

'I'm sure she'll come back, Magrit,' Doreen said encouragingly, trying to be positive for her friend's sake. 'Will the boys get word to us if she – or should I say when she? – turns up, Peter?' she asked, trying to continue in the same spirit.

Peter did not answer. He was stuck in a whirlpool of impotence that seemed to go round and round – searching for answers but never coming up with any.

John reacted for his friend, 'Oh, aye, I'm positive one o' them will.'

FORTY-TWO

Pig Matheson had managed to find a phone box that would accommodate him and his newly acquired timber appendage. He had heard of wee boys climbing on backcourt railings, losing their footing, impaling themselves on a rail and being in a similar situation to the one he now found himself in. Any sane human being would have felt distraught and have enormous sympathy at the boys' agony. Pig, in his private world of cruelty, had always found the image conjured up by their plight highly amusing. He had heard that the fire brigade was usually called to free them because they were the experts in that situation. Pig sensed correctly that he could not reveal his plight to any of his cronies as he knew this would leave him up to ridicule in the future – so the fire brigade was his only solution.

As he dialed 999, a terrible thought crossed his mind. The wooden object that was temporarily separating his left buttock from the right one must have been lying around for some time. What if it was infested with woodworms? His rear end, as well as giving him a lot of pain, suddenly started to itch as well.

FORTY-THREE

Dolly called out to Magrit as she rounded the corner with Betty and Rena Reilly in tow. Mary Culfeathers was somewhere behind them.

At the sound of her voice, Magrit and the others turned to face them. 'Dolly's told us that Theresa's left a runaway note, Magrit,' Betty said, before turning to her daughter. 'Rena, tell Magrit what you told us.'

Rena related the saga of her cousin being a stewardess and how Theresa had become excited at the thought of being a stewardess too. She told them how Theresa had set her heart on being on a ship and that she had gone down the town to look at travel brochures on cruising.

'I saw a travel thing in the room when I went in tae look for her,' Peter remembered. 'I never thought anything aboot it.'

'I know it's crazy but did you try doon the docks, Peter?' Dolly asked.

'She wouldnae go there,' Peter said dismissively.

'How would you know?' Magrit snapped at him.

'She's mine as well,' Peter snapped back. Magrit's implied accusation that he was somehow to blame had fired up anger in him.

'Right, youse can fight later but, for noo, let's check the docks,' Dolly said, taking charge of the situation.

She put her coat on and without waiting for the others

226

headed for the front door. Magrit did likewise – at least she was doing something positive rather than just standing about worrying herself to death. Peter and John realised that Dolly had a point and followed too.

Doreen was held up a bit as she explained what was going on to Mary Culfeathers who nodded concernedly, if uncomprehendingly, as she too put her coat on to help with the search.

Georgina McCusker, who worked in the bookie's that Peter frequented to lose the money that he had not spent in the Dry Dock Inn, stopped Doreen as she was heading for the door and said she had heard that Theresa McGuire was missing and asked if it was true. Doreen verified the rumour and also told her that they thought she might have headed for the docks. Georgina's hand flew to her mouth in a gesture that signalled that was very bad news and immediately volunteered to help with the search.

There was really nowhere like a Glasgow steamie for spreading news faster than a snowball in hell could melt. And, before Peter, Magrit, Dolly and the rest were halfway down the street, women were putting their coats on and abandoning their washing to help out one of their own. They poured out of the front entrance and on to the street like an army of turbaned female titans setting out to rescue their princess from the clutches of a foreign foe.

The air rang with instructions and suggestions as to who would do what and where they would do it. Isa McCormack, who had been at the entry desk of the washhouse all afternoon right up till now, watched in dismay as everyone rushed past her and out the front door. She was left in a quandary. Her terms of contract stated that she must never leave the front desk on pain of dismissal. 'Bugger that,' she decided.

Locking up the till, she put on her coat and, closing the office door behind her, rushed down the street after the searchers.

FORTY-FOUR

Andy put his feet down from the table that doubled as a desk in his tiny storeroom and finished off the last cup of tea he would have that year. Rising up from his chair he crossed to the sink and rinsed the tea leaves down the drain. He normally did not do this as it could cause a blockage but it was New Year's Eve and he was in a holiday mood.

He had one more inspection of the washhouse stalls to make and then he could have a real drink. He'd already sank quite a few illicit small snifters of whisky throughout the shift but nothing that would impair his ability to carry out his duties, he would argue. Some of the women had urged him to indulge in a wee goldie as a reward for various obligements that, although outwith his terms of employment, he had nevertheless supplied during the year. It would have been churlish to refuse them – in fact, it would have been very bad manners, he reasoned with himself, and then agreed with himself that his reasoning was very sound.

He also recalled that on more than one occasion he had turned a blind eye to infringements of the washhouse rules in the interest of customer satisfaction. So tonight had been payback time and, as he closed the office door behind him, he was anticipating a few more refreshments from satisfied customers before he closed the place for the night.

He clapped both hands and rubbed them together in a

gesture that signalled he was ready for anything as he turned from the door to survey his kingdom – his palace of purification – and the goddesses of gleam that brought a scintillating sparkle to the weekly washing. Strangely there were none to be seen. 'There must be a hell of a queue at the wringer,' was Andy's explanation for this strange phenomenon. 'I better go doon and see if it's workin' OK,' he resolved.

As he strode down to the wringer, he noticed something else – apart from the fact there was no one in sight, there was also no noise. Turning the corner that led to the wringer section, he pulled up with a start. There was no one there – no one at all.

'Christ. I must have overslept,' he surmised, before looking at his watch. 'It's only twenty-five to nine – where the hell is everybody?'

Quickly, he made his way to the front desk to check with Isa Macormack why there was no one about. Andy gave the rubber swing doors that led out from the wash house to the front desk a kick with his boot and, as they swung open, he strode purposely through them to the window of the front desk.

'Hey, Isa – what's happenin' – there's no' a sign o' anybody in that . . .'

There was also no sign of Isa. This was something Andy could not comprehend. It was a phenomenon outwith anything he had ever experienced. 'I've heard o' abandon ship – but abandon steamie?'

Andy decided he had better alert his employers to the situation straightaway. This was a situation that required immediate action and Andy was the very man to carry that action out – just as soon as he had one wee jolt from a hidden half bottle of Teacher's that he was glad he'd smuggled in at the start of the shift. Checking every stall for some sign of life, he made his way back to the office. 'Kettle on, a cup o' tea, a wee goldie and then I'm on to this.'

FORTY-FIVE

The bloodshot eyes searched in vain along the dock front. They had carefully watched the young woman who had headed for the ship. Then a fit of alcoholic-tobacco-inspired coughing had caused the body they belonged to to collapse in on itself and prevent total seizure. Under this kind of pressure the body – or what was left of it – had closed the eyes in an automatic response to avoid dehydration and maybe even total collapse of the entire nervous system. By the time the eyes had been replenished with watery blood and refocused, the young woman had disappeared.

'Bastard.' The voice that uttered the oath, in a gurgling whisky-mixed-with-cheap-wine-and-tobacco-drenched whisper causing the watery eyes to overflow with the effort, belonged to Richard Hamilton.

Richard had, not too long ago, been a promising feather-weight, much lauded and sought after by many friends and admirers who thought there was money to be made by associating with him.

For a time, there had been. Unfortunately, Richard's talent had not been of sufficient magnitude to escape being frequently battered around the head and body by opponents while, at the same time, having the crap kicked out of his insides by his much more evident talent for bingeing on booze, baccy and blondes. Richard always maintained that he could have handled the booze and the baccy – it was the blondes that did the real damage.

He had acquired the nickname 'Wee Niggles' because, as his lifestyle took its toll, he began to complain of 'wee niggles' that would only go away after he had sank some pain-deadening South African wine. Eventually, the oft-told tale of the Glasgow boxer fulfilled its destiny and Wee Niggles found that all his erstwhile good companions had deserted him and discovered new companions they could feed off.

He now largely lived in his own world – apart from when he was trying to sponge money from passers-by for bevvy. It was in this capacity that he had shown a keen interest in the young lady who had mysteriously disappeared at the foot of the gangway of the ship.

'Bastard,' he cursed again, bemoaning the fact that it was New Year's Eve and he had nothing to deaden the pain that wrenched at his gut due to there being nothing in it. He knew that one drink would sort out the wee niggle in his stomach and now the possible source of providing money for it had 'Fuckin' disappeared'.

All day and into the night, he had heard people wish each other 'a happy New Year when it comes'. Well, it was getting hell of a close and there was nothing happy about it as far as he was concerned. 'NEW YEAR?' he railed at the world. 'HAPPY NEW YEAR? – HAPPY NEW YEAR, MY ARSE.' He searched for someone or something tangible to berate. There was no one. 'YOUSE ARE A SHOWER O' NEW YEAR BASTARDS,' he hurled at the world in general, as he wrapped the three coats he had for protection around him and searched the streets and pavements for any sign of a discarded bottle that might just contain a drop of anything alcoholic.

His words flung randomly into the night reached the ears of Theresa's search party. Well, the ears of Peter and Magrit's squad anyway. They headed for the sound and, in a very few moments, came upon Wee Niggles still shouting and cursing humanity and its gods for the state he was in.

Peter shouted out to him as they approached, 'Hey!'

Wee Niggles swirled round to face them and, seeing a crowd running at him, immediately and instinctively went into the southpaw crouch that had been his trademark. Leading with his right fist, he stabbed at the mob in front of him. His voice crackled and gurgled and sometimes faded altogether as he threw down the gauntlet to them. 'If you want a fight, I'm your man. C'mon a' the gither or one at a time – makes nae odds to me – c'mon, who feels lucky? Who's first for a doin'?'

Despite his dreadful preparations for the contest, there was not a lot wrong with his stance and there was still a natural balance left over from his halcyon days. It was only when he attempted some flash footwork that he let himself down – literally.

Peter bent to pick him up and, as he did so, the smell of Niggles almost put him on his back. 'I'm no' wantin' to fight – listen – have you seen a young lassie, aboot thirteen years old, roon' aboot here?'

'Aye, I did. Who wants tae know?' Niggles bellowed as he strove to regain his equilibrium.

Magrit interrupted Peter before he could answer, 'I do. ya drunken auld bastard – I'm her mother. Where did you see her?' Magrit's tone, as always, was not one of diplomacy and the harshness in her manner served to bring Niggles out of his alcoholic fog.

'She was standin' in that shop front and then she left there . . .'

By the way Magrit spoke to him Niggles was not sure if he was going to be blamed for something in a minute so he tried to guard against this possibility. 'I never touched her by the

232

way,' he avowed. 'She left o' her own accordion – nothin' to dae wi' me. OK? Right?' He stared at them defiantly, then softened his response, 'Youse havnae got a shillin' to provide an ex-welterweight champion that fought for his country wi' a bed for the night, have you?' He was lying on all three claims but he was not aware of that – except maybe the shilling for a bed bit. He had not slept in a bed for many a year and any shilling that came his way would be turned into wine quicker than Jesus had managed it at Cana.

'Did you see where she went?' John asked, handing him a shilling.

Niggles bit into the shilling before answering. 'Aye, she went on board a ship. You havnae got another shillin' for a bite to eat?' he ventured, sensing he might have stumbled on to a small vein of possible benefactors.

This possibility was sadly snatched from his hopes when Magrit grabbed him by the lapels and hissed, 'If you don't tell me where that lassie went, I'll hit you that hard you'll land up in bed, in a hospital and you might never get oot o' it again. D'you understand me?'

Niggles understood perfectly. 'I said she went on a ship,' he reiterated.

'What ship are you on aboot?' Magrit was approaching hysteria with the dreadful anxiety that was welling up inside her.

'That yin.' Niggles pointed down towards where the *Clan Macintosh* was berthed. 'I saw her go up the gangplank.'

Turning to where Niggles had pointed, their hearts froze inside them. The reason for this was that they could all see the lights of a ship in the distance that had obviously sailed from where Niggles had indicated.

Magrit began running towards the fast disappearing ship and shouting, 'Come back – for God's sake – my lassie's on board your ship.'

The others joined her in a forlorn attempt at attracting the attention of someone on board the ship but it was quite useless. The lights on board were already starting to fade into the inky gloom of the night sea fog.

'Oh, God, no . . . please no . . .' Magrit started to sob and sank to her knees.

As Peter realised the awful implication of his wee lassie's action, he screamed after the ship, 'Come back, ya bastards – that's my wee lassie you've got – come back.'

Of course, no one could hear him and his voice echoed back from the far bank, in a cruel mockery of his distress.

Doreen looked at John for some kind of a lead that might alleviate the unbelievable grief that was coming from Magrit and Peter.

John shrugged as if to say, 'What can I do?' before he realised that anything would be better than just standing there. 'Peter,' he said softly, moving to his pal's side, hoping he could calm him down a bit. 'C'mon, we'll get back and tell the polis. They'll be able to do somethin'.'

There were tears in Peter's eyes as he faced John. 'She's only thirteen, John.' His fists bunched up and his jaw clenched shut, forcing the words to battle to escape from the terrible thoughts that were going on inside his head. 'See if anything happens to her . . . I'll . . .' he could not finish as emotions he wasn't even aware he had flooded out of him.

'Naw!' John tried his best to sound encouraging. 'She'll be fine. I'm sure o' it. She's a clever lassie, Theresa. The quicker we get the polis on the job the better though, eh?'

A voice permeated their conversation – a voice that did not sound like one of their immediate company. It too had panic ringing in its cadences as it shouted to them, 'Mrs Culfeathers . . . Mrs Culfeathers!'

A red-faced young woman, in her middle thirties, ran

towards them. As she spotted Mary Culfeathers, she redoubled her pace and shouted again, 'Mrs Culfeathers!'

Mary looked at Doreen and asked, 'Is it me she wants, Doreen?'

Doreen was puzzled as well and she nodded, 'I think so, Mrs Culfeathers.'

'What is it, hen?' Mary asked the young woman as she drew level.

'It's your husband, Mrs Culfeathers – he's been dragged oot o' the river.'

Mary eyed the flush-faced young woman with a look that suggested insanity might have run in the family. 'My husband? It cannae be my husband – he's in the hoose, hen.'

'I'm sorry but . . . everybody says it's him. Dolly Johnson said to come and get you – they're along there,' she said, pointing to a throng of women a couple of hundred yards away in the opposite direction from the one the ship had gone.

Mary turned to Doreen. 'What's happenin', Doreen? It cannae be Harry.'

Dolly cradled Harry's head in her arms. Beside it lay the gas mask she had removed. Harry was alive but breathing very heavily. He was also shivering so Dolly had taken her coat off and wrapped it round him. 'You're a' right, Mr Culfeathers,' she assured him as she rubbed his hands with hers in an attempt to put some heat into him. 'We've sent for your wife. She'll be here in a minute.'

Harry looked at her through half-closed eyes. His lips moved but nothing came out of them. His eyes widened and she fancied he seemed to want her to come closer so he could tell her something. Dolly leaned her ear closer to his mouth. 'What is it? What are you trying to say, Mr Culfeathers?'

Harry gripped Dolly's arm and, with a huge effort, strained

235

to make sure that Dolly would hear him. Raising himself up as far as he could, he gasped into her ear. 'Have you got a match – mine'll be a' damp,' he croaked, before collapsing back down as his strength gave way to weakness.

Before Dolly could explain that she had neither fags nor matches, John ushered Mary Culfeathers through the crowd that had gathered around her husband. She could not believe what her eyes were witnessing as she saw him lying in his soaking wet uniform, his head being held off the ground by Dolly Johnson. 'Harry?' she said incredulously.

Harry responded feebly, 'Mary? What are you doin' here?'

'How did you fall into the river?' Mary said, ignoring Harry's question in favour of her own.

Harry was starting to recover enough to say, proudly but still feebly, 'I didnae fall in – I dived in.'

Mary shook her head in disapproval. 'Look at the state your in – you're a' wet.'

'It's the water that does that,' Harry informed her, shivering inside Dolly's coat.

'Whose coat is that? It's no' one o' mine, is it?' There was a definite tone of reprimand starting to creep over Mary's initial one of concern.

'It's mine, Mrs Culfeathers.' Dolly, volunteered.

Mary's face showed visible relief. 'Thanks, Dolly. I'll get it dry-cleaned for you.' With an effort that made her groan slightly, Mary bent down and said, in a confidential voice, 'Dolly, gonnae thank whoever pulled him oot the water? I don't know who it was but they must be soakin' too. Tell them I'll get their stuff dry-cleaned as well.'

John decided to take charge before Harry Culfeathers froze to death instead of drowned. 'We'll get him up the road and dried oot, eh, Mrs Culfeathers?'

Mary decided to enlist John's help as maybe Dolly had

enough on her plate trying to keep Harry from freezing to death. 'John, will you thank whoever pulled Harry oot the river for me before we go. I don't want to appear ungrateful, son. I'd like to show my appreciation for their kind gesture.' She reached into the pocket of her coat and drew out her purse. Then, after some rummling about, brought out a half crown.

John could see that Magrit and Peter were impatient to move off and he wanted to be with them so he shouted out, 'Whoever pulled the old man oot the water, his wife wants you to make yourself known so she can thank you personally.'

'It wasnae me,' a tall thin woman volunteered as she looked round her.

'Me neither,' said a florid-faced wifie who stood behind her.

'He was lyin' there when we got here – sure he was, Rosina,' said Rosa Mucci to her Italian cousin Rosina Nanette.

Rosina confirmed the accuracy of her cousin's statement three times, 'So he was – right enough – that's true.'

'I cannae swim so it definitely wasnae me,' volunteered another from the throng.

'It was me.' A small voice came from the back of the gathering.

John heard Magrit gasp as Theresa made her way through the small crowd to where her mother and father gaped in amazement before rushing to her.

'Oh, God – oh, God.' As she rushed to enfold Theresa in her arms, Magrit couldn't think of anything else to say that expressed the feelings of relief, happiness and euphoria that meant she had her daughter back.

Peter just stood weeping as he surveyed his lassie. Familiarity had conditioned him to really only think of her when he wanted a cup of tea made or a shirt ironed. He would never make that mistake again – though he would continue to expect her to make him a cup of tea and iron a shirt now and then.

'We were worried sick aboot you,' Magrit howled, still clutching Theresa close to her as if she might be snatched away again at any moment.

'I'm sorry.' Theresa was bubbling into her mother's shoulder.

'It's a' right . . . it's a' right,' Magrit consoled. She felt Peter's arms surround both Theresa and her and then was aware that she could hear him crying. She had never known that he was capable of that.

'It's OK, darlin'. Put this jacket round you – it'll help heat you up.' He kissed his daughter on the forehead as he placed his jacket over her shoulders. 'We thought you were on that ship – the one that sailed away ten minutes ago,' he said, the relief that she wasn't evident in his voice.

'I was gonnae go on it,' Theresa gulped through her tears. 'I was halfway up the gangway when I heard a splash that came from doon here. So I ran back doon to see what it was and it was that old man. So I went in and pulled him oot. But I didnae know what to do after that so I just left him lying. I was feart, Mammy.'

'You could have drowned,' Magrit scolded.

'Naw, I'm a good swimmer,' Theresa protested before bursting out laughing. 'See when I was pullin' him oot the water, he kept sayin', "It's a shitey beach."'

John again suggested that Harry and Theresa needed to be dried off and go somewhere they could get some warmth into them. At his prompting, everyone agreed that they had better get back to the steamie and finish off their washing. There was, of course, only going to be one topic of conversation once the women went back inside. This evening would provide endless hours of communal dialogue and discourse or, to give it its real name, gossip for many a day and probably many a year. The tale would, no doubt, grow legs and gather more colour in the retelling – but it's hard to see how. It was, however, definitely going to be the best Hogmanay for many a year.

FORTY-SIX

Andy had made a fresh brew of tea and poured himself a wee sensation in the form of a glass of the amber nectar that is whisky. He was finishing the last of the whisky and putting his third spoonful of sugar into his tea while he waited for someone at the head office emergency section of Glasgow Corporation Baths and Washhouses to pick up the phone.

Angus McPhail eventually answered it. Forty years old and a church elder in his spare time, he was not all that keen on the drunkenness of a traditional Scots Hogmanay. He was a confirmed bachelor whose hobbies were going to work, going to church and going to sleep – in that strict order. With no wife and no children and no friends who were not hell-bent on getting falling-down drunk that evening, he reckoned he would be as well earning a bit of overtime and had volunteered for the shift he was now filling.

He surveyed his office with a sense of achievement. He had worked his way up in the corporation from a young lad to the lofty position he now found himself in as associate assistant to the deputy subordinate head of public health's manager's secretary. It wasn't strictly true to say that it was his office. But it was true that he had been given it for the night.

It was an easy shift he reckoned. Man the phones until the steamies were all locked up and then the rest of the night was his own. He had laid by some ginger wine which he would toast the new year in with and then settle back with a tin of shortbread and a bit of black bun his mother had wrapped up in a Bilsland's bread wrapper. All this, while being paid till midnight, seemed to Angus a great way to spend Hogmanay.

He was in the middle of preparing a draft on how to propel the Church of Scotland into the forefront of Scottish youth culture by involving them in mass accordion lessons when the phone rang. This was something Angus had not bargained for and he was in two minds whether to pick it up or not – after all, if he was being phoned at this time of the night, it almost certainly meant that there was a problem of some kind on the other end of the line and, really, he was not up for getting embroiled in someone else's mishaps at this late hour. The telephone rang again. Its harsh trill seemed to Angus to be admonishing him for failing in his duties. He stared uncertainly as it sounded again, piercing not only his ears but also his conscience. Angus's Protestant work ethic won through and, like the responsible corporation employee that he was, he gritted his teeth, sucked a bit of shortbread that had got trapped in the middle of a top incisor and picked up the telephone. 'Hello,' he answered, not giving too much information away in his greeting.

'Is that the Corporation Emergency Help Section?'

Angus heard a voice that sounded to him as if it had a slight slur perhaps caused by alcohol. 'Aye,' he replied, still keeping the emergency help side of his job on the back boiler.

Andy decided to tell it like it was as he could not think of any other way. 'This is Andy McDowell at Cranston Washhouse, sir. I would like to report that the entire steamie has vanished. Well, wait a minute . . . no' the actual building – just the people inside of the building, you understand . . . No, I have not been drinking to excess . . . Yes, I realise it is

241

Hogmanay and you are snowed in with requests for help but I really think that this is that wee bit out of the ordinary, sir . . . No! I have already said I am not inebriated . . . So your advice is to pray to God for forgiveness and then take a deep breath and go back and check if everyone has still vanished? I'll do that and get back to you. Thanks for your help, sir.'

Angus put down the phone gingerly. He wondered if he was being tested in some way by his superiors – to see if he could handle stress – and decided that, if he was, he had passed with flying colours. Now, about these accordion lessons – should they be compulsory?

Andy let out a puzzled sigh as he turned over in his mind the advice he had been given by the emergency help operator. Pray to God for forgiveness? He couldn't think what he had to be forgiven for – as a washhouse handyman? In other ways, he was no saint – he would be the first to admit it – but what had that got to do with the emergency help section of the corporation? Nevertheless, they were there because they knew what they were doing, he supposed. So, getting down on his knees, Andy prayed for forgiveness for whatever he had done wrong in his capacity as a washhouse mechanic. Then he got up off his knees and went to check on the disappeared damsels.

The scene that greeted him as he left his office and entered the washhouse floor almost took his breath away. There, in front of his very own eyes, were rows upon rows of washerwomen chattering away to each other. He wandered in and out of the various stalls but there was no sign from any of the women that they had mysteriously all vanished.

He was about to go down to the front desk when he heard a peal of laughter coming from the stalls that Magrit McGuire and Dolly Johnson were washing in. He turned the corner that led him past Mrs Culfeathers' stall and his mouth fell open in utter astonishment. There, in Mary Culfeathers' steeping sink, was a naked old man – naked apart from a pair of ex-army underpants, that is. He was being attended to by Doreen Hood and Dolly Johnson, who were pouring buckets of hot water over him. Steam rose from all round him as he sat smiling at Andy.

Doreen saw the old man smiling and turned to Andy.

'A' right, Andy,' she said. Then started to rub soapsuds all over the old fellow.

'Doreen?' Andy said, tentatively.

'Yes,' Doreen answered without stopping in her task.

'Is there . . . an old man in that sink?' Andy felt foolish for asking but, in light of his fancying a whole washhouse of steamie women had vanished and his brush with the emergency help section who advised prayers to the Almighty for forgiveness, this was maybe the final signal that God was telling him to cut back on the bevvy.

'Naw,' Doreen replied. 'Why? . . . Should there be?'

It seemed to Andy as if she then helped Dolly to pour another bucket of water over the old man. The world, as Andy had known it, crumbled as he watched the soapsuds drain down from the old man's head and vanish down the drain.

'Naw – I was just jokin',' he lied. Then, realising that he had indeed transgressed in the washhouse, just as the emergency help section had said, he made his excuses and went back up to his office where he could pray for forgiveness – again.

Doreen was laughing her head off as she watched Andy stagger off in his agony of uncertainty. 'What a laugh, Dolly, eh?' she enthused to Dolly, who was drying off Harry Culfeathers with a freshly laundered clean crisp Glasgow Corporation Public Baths towel. 'I cannae wait tae tell my ma aboot this.'

'Aye,' Dolly agreed as she gave the few hairs left on old

Harry's head a good towelling.

'You'd never get a night like this in a launderette, eh?'

FORTY-SEVEN

An ambulance pulled up at the door of the accident and emergency section of the Western Hospital. The driver and his mate got out the front and went round to the back doors of the ambulance. They opened the doors and very carefully helped a figure with a coat draped over its head to preserve anonymity out of the back doors. As the figure stepped gingerly down on to the roadside, a barber's pole, protruding from the rear end, hit off the road, causing the figure to roar out loud.

As it was led away by a nurse, one of the ambulance men remarked to his pal, 'I'll bet he gives his barber a bigger tip the next time he goes for a haircut.'

THE END

IN NINETEEN SIXTY-THREE, AFTER MASSIVE
PROTESTS FROM THE WOMEN WHO USED THEM,
THE LAST STEAMIE WAS CLOSED DOWN.